DREAM
WITH ME

DREAM WITH ME

Jacqueline Kombe

DREAM WITH ME

iUniverse books may be ordered through booksellers or by contacting:

iUniverse
1663 Liberty Drive
Bloomington, IN 47403
www.iuniverse.com
1-800-Authors (1-800-288-4677)

ISBN: 978-1-5320-5689-5 (sc)
ISBN: 978-1-5320-5690-1 (e)

Library of Congress Control Number: 2018910560

Print information available on the last page.

iUniverse rev. date: 09/06/2018

I dedicate this book to everyone who believes in her or himself that one way or the other they can influence the society. Those whom are ready to take steps ahead no matter the obstacle(s). Those whom can change their loneliness to a meaningful occupation, those whom can transform their breakdown to happiness, those whom can make good use of their sleepless nights and those whom can stand still before the world and smile out their miseries and swallow their depressions – just know, We are Proud of You.

I would like to thank the Almighty God for his love and kindness.

Special thanks to my lovely daughter Kiki-Rehema Mhina for always believing in me and seeing me as your inspiration – I Love You.

My mom & late dad – Thank you for loving me. I am blessed to have you as mine.

My brothers: Henry Kombe, Bernard Kombe & Samwel Kombe – You are my soldiers, Thank you for always keeping up with my mess. I love you all.

My blessed nephew Hallelujah H. Kombe and your loving mother Gladys Kaaya Kombe – my sister in-law. Thank you for being part of my life.

Mwajabu Mtiti – I appreciate you. Mitchel Monahan, Donna Carlson, Reed Samuel and the rest of iUniverse team – thank you so much.

And lastly my best friend, my partner, My Love – Yohane Edward – Thank you for your endless support, you have taught me a lot of things and I'm forever grateful, may God keep blessing you. I Love You.

Monday 4 30am

She woke up before her girl, and before the nana got home, prepared herself and made breakfast and lunch box for her girl. After an hour and a half the neighbors heard the sound of the engine for her antique beetle and possibly the smell from the exhaust, now that was a wake up call for others and her signature presence. She drove off from their tiny condo of two bedrooms and a master room, a living room with an open kitchen and a public toilet, a very squeezed cozy home, dropped her girl to school and headed to work. The girl was always ashamed of her mom's old beetle "Don't be ashamed honey, it's just for now" said as she kissed her girl goodbye.

It took her twenty-ish minutes drive to her office. A multinational consultant firm and she worked at the front desk, only place she got to meet the CEO of the firm without appointment as he got in and out of the office. Three years in the firm, and never heard a chance to sit across or have a minute discussion with Frank Sinclair or Fredrick Sinclair the twin brothers - CEO and CFO of the firm respectively. At least with Freddy, (that's how Frank short named him) once in a while may found himself mingling with the juniors.

"Morning Mr Sinclair" she greeted Frank Sinclair as he walked pass by the reception headed down the hall and got to the stairs on the first floor of his magnificent huge wooden, glass, crystal clear classic designed office. I doubt if Frank actually knew how she looked like but no doubt he may had been familiar with her voice due to constant greetings. She never minds not getting replies from him. She was one peaceful, busy and focused lady. Very beautiful as well, fully committed on her job, worked extra hours to earn for her family of two. She – light skinned, six feet tall, her curly brown hair was long but mostly braided may be she couldn't afford first class hair treats, you could tell from her style of clothing that she was really trying to keep up with everybody but was a survivor nothing like first class or even middle class look-a-like. Her English, you could tell from how she answered calls and attended guests that she was exactly what the firm needed, poor lady the look was probably what made her unrecognized by her boss.

At 4 30pm a school bus dropped the girl to her mom's office so they could leave together. Most of the times she got hold up with work and took thirty to forty five extra minutes to wind up. So this day her girl had to wait for her mom at the front park of her office as she was waiting randomly walking at parking lot, and deep thinking looking in front of her mom's work place, she stood in front of a huge black plated shinning and extremely sumptuous, sublime, spotless car just for seconds she was shocked when the alarm and the lights went on only to find a man standing behind him her mouth and her round brown eyes went wide open,

"Can I help you?" said a man seven feet tall, smart, dark skinned, very good looking.

"You can't!" said the poor girl as she let the man have a way to his car.

"Try me" responded the man with a smile and squinted eyes upon the girl.

"Well let's say I am thinking if we may ever own such a car someday" said the girl to the man.

"Who is we?" asked the man.

"My Mom and I." replied without hesitating.

"And where is your Mom?" (as if he was about to offer her one) he asked.

"Inside working" she answered pointing at the direction of the office building

"What do you think?" he kept asking,

"I don't know" she replied. "Never mind, I should let you go, bye" said as she was leaving.

The man felt touched by the few minutes dialogue he had with the courageous little girl so he jumped into the car started his engine and pulled over to about where the girl was and said to her "it was nice talking to you young lady, think big and believe more." smiled and squinted his eyes and left, she ran back to check on her mom if they could leave and it was a good timing since she was done and just on the door steps letting herself out.

They got into their old beetle and drove home. By 8 pm the nana had left and it looked like there was something for them to eat placed at the kitchen counter. She used to take shower leaving the bathroom door open while talking to her girl laying on bed, afterwards they both jumped into some minutes if not an hour of silence concentrating on their books the girl had some homework to run and her mother took evening classes for a degree in business administration hence the silence.

After couple of minutes they prayed, switched off lights and kept up with their usual girls' chat as they were on bed. "Think big believe more Mom" she said as she cuddled her mother on bed under their cozy old fashion duvet. "Ooh yeah?" "Good talk" said the mother holding her girl tight.

Tuesday

Alarm went off with a praise gospel song, sounded like a wake up call. She did the usual and before time they were both ready to depart.

Nana got home to some households and before she was handed over some tasks, there was a knock on the door, it was Jayda and Jayden all dressed up for school. They were Pamela's twins, lived next-door very close family friends of hers. Most of the time they did round up in taking their children to school so it was hers that day.

"Good morning my love" she greeted the twins as she hugged both of them, very cute identical twins.

"Morning" Jayden replied the sharp one than Jayda.

"Time to go let's get started," sounded ruffled.

They jumped into their old beetle and she shouted to the nana "will call you when I get to the office" that is to task her. And they drove off.

On their way she would sing along and joke with the kids. Kayla and Jayda were best friends of all time. They would share everything from sleepover nights to play dates. Jayden was the little man always felt left out but she filled the blank by indulging with his stories on his new Knack

2 (PS4), Lego Ninjago movie video-games and God knows what.

As they dropped to school Pamela rang her.

"Alright guys here you are, this's your mom I got to answer it, take care love you all" kissed back and slammed the door.

Pam: "Yo girl, what's up?"

Her: "nothing much just dropped them to school" "how did it go?"

Pam: "good girll, wish you were there, Dennis kept asking for you"

Her: "I can imagine he's not going to see me for a while have a paper to submit by end of this week, I am left alone at my department it's just that hectic week of the month" "hey will call you back, love you take care" she hanged up

Pam: "laters"

She got right on time pounded her olden car door and rushed to the office. Walked very quickly onto her black pointed five inches pumps both her hands filled with bags books and other bag. She settled down took a deep breath and started her errands right away.

"Morning Mr Sinclair" She said.

"Morning" Freddy replied as he walked passed by the reception and tried to catch the look.

Freddy was the CFO of the firm, the twin brother actually a minute younger to Frank, he was hairy and had a long ponytail each day tied differently, that day he had his hair noted on the back and as usual his suits were impeccable and he smelled good. At least with him you could catch a reply once he's greeted. A busy day in the firm lots of in & out guests / clients and within a blink of an eye it was lunch time after seeing Shirley at the front desk all dressed up and stunningly beautiful. She admired her for a second and smiled back with a greeting;

Her: "Good afternoon Ms Shirley, what can I do for you?"

"Good afternoon" replied Shirley in her highness tone

Shirley: "Am here for Frank"

Her: "You're welcome, you can go through"

As Shirley was leaving down the hall to head to the stairs a phone rang to Frank's PA

Her: "Ms Shirley is on her way to Mr Sinclair"

Wanitha: "Gotcha, thanks"

Wanitha was probably the oldest employee in the firm but very charming. She had been Frank Sinclair's PA for ages, luckily enough she could still see well, read, speak up and type fast and very experienced in-house company secretary.

We didn't know what happened inside Frank's substantial office but I bet he was pleased to see Ms Shirley. Frank had been dating Ms Shirley for three years and it couldn't get any better seeing them together.

After few minutes, both passed by the front desk off to God knows where.

Two hours later Frank passed by the desk and as usual she never seized to greet him.

Her: "Afternoon Mr Sinclair"

Frank passed rushing inside to meet his deadlines not sure if he heard his name mentioned.

At 4 30pm a tiny girl on her white & blue uniforms stood in front of her desk not to realize there was actually a human being in front of the reception desk.

Her: "hey you, what are you doing here?" "I thought you were going direct home with Jayda, what happened?"

Kayla: "They have music classes to attend and thought I should come wait for them here, I'm tired Mom" just like that when she calls the word Mom her heart was blown away.

Her: "well no worries baby" she hugged and removed the bag off Kayla's back. "Grab a chair let me wind up and will leave soon."

Kayla never stayed put for longer than a minute, she stood and started gazing around reading newspapers from the front table as she waited for her mother.

She called Pam to let her know that Kayla was with her and no need to pick her, as they will head home together.

"Yes, yes, thanks, thank you very much" a voice paved way to the reception and suddenly Kayla stood up intending to greet.

"Hey young lady, you good?" Frank shook Kayla's hand
Kayla: "I'm good thanks"

Frank kept moving towards an exit of the office and Kayla followed him out, both exchanged vibes

"Home time huh?" Kayla posed unexpectedly

"Tell me about it" Frank squinted eyes on her

Kayla: "the best time of my days" smiled as she jumped over the stairs

Frank: "you must be having good time at home huh?" stood on the stairs as his car drove by to pick him up

"You have no idea" replied Kayla as she waved goodbye at Frank.

Frank: "take care of yourself young lady" again squinted his eyes as if it's a disorder.

And the car went off.

A few minutes later Kayla and her mom drove off as well, passed by the bakery to pick a loaf of brown bread and muffins for Kayla's breakfast.

She didn't earn much but tried hard to give the best for her Kayla.

On their way home she refueled her olden beetle as she was leaving the gas station she by passed Dennis. Dennis was a friend to Pamela's boyfriend / baby daddy whom dated her for few months before she called it quits. So Dennis made her pull over to say hi

Her: "honey let me say hi to a friend will be right back" she told Kayla to stay put

Dennis: "hello beautiful" hugged her and headed over to her lips for a kiss only to end up on her cheek.

Her: "Dennis, you good?" she replied getting Dennis' hands off.

Dennis: "I didn't see you at the party, I miss you girl".

Her: "well have been busy lately – work, school parenting as you can see."

Dennis: "I know, anything I can do - don't hesitate" as he caressed her one more time

"Great thanks, be good, bye" She left to her car.

Dennis used to have double dates with his friend George – Pam's baby daddy. They were good buddies so it never occurred to him that She would be less interested with the connection to the relationship they had. She loved her friend Pamela so very much and the twins as much as she loved her Kayla but she couldn't see her relationship with Dennis flourishing at all. Dennis was a lot of party goer, he loved having good time, there had not been a day in his life missing out for drinks after work hours totally not a family type of a man but he was full of love, romance, his sex game was on point but he was just incomplete for her. Of course when it came to wanting to feel good be loved have fun and good sex Dennis was the right man, he could make you forget your problems ever existed. They have done crazy stuff together, slept at his place for more than twice had night outs partying, clubbing you mention all but never took him at her place, never got him meet Kayla because deep down she knew it will all be a history before we already knew.

Well they got back at their tiny cozy apartment finished up their evening preps and had an hour of reading and home works to attend to before they squeezed on a couch with a bowl of popcorn for Kayla's best show. Lights were off, TV was on and they cuddled while watching their show for half an hour before saying a word to each other. Both on different zones of thoughts, she thought on having her paper done by the end of the week, she thought on getting a leave to complete her search plans on the shop she wanted to open, she thought on how much she had spent for that day and how much she was going to spend the next day, she thought if her office loan would mature anytime soon, she thought on how they would end up leaving just the two of them for she had no hope of dating anytime soon, she thought and thought and thought and before she cuts her misery thoughts Kayla whispered "think big and believe more Mom" there again that word Mom really moved her it was like an alarm that kept reminding her of how and what she should be. So she pats her and said out loud "I knew you were going to break the silence, I knew it!" she threw some popcorn over Kayla's head like wanting to play but couldn't get Kayla change her course so they stayed for a little longer after the end of the show was the beginning of bedtime, they switched off the tv, said some prayer and went off to bed.

Wednesday

Just like any other working day an alarm went off for them to start their day. That day the nana came a bit earlier and had made breakfast and prepared lunch box for Kayla it was Pam's round to take the kids to school and before they were even ready a voice from outside was heard Jay twins and their mother Pamela were inside shouting "Kayla! Kayla! Are you ready?" Kayla went over greeted aunty Pam and Pam came all the way to Kayla's mother's room sat on bed as her friend was trying to dress up.

"What's up girl? You look like you haven't heard sex for ages" Pam smiled across the mirror at her friend who was getting dressed.

Her: "oh yeah, what is that food again?" she teased back getting close to Pam to help her zip up her mini black dress.

Pam: "ha ha very funny" as she zipped her dress up. "No but seriously get a life my love"

Her: "gotcha (in Wanitha's voice)"

Pam: "by the way is Wanitha still alive?"

Her: "Pam stop! Why wouldn't she?"

"She should have retired by now and let my madly working ass girl take over" Pam joked

"Hey enough with the words kids are around" She said as they headed out.

The twins ran over and hugged Kayla's mom and all went off with Pam

Pam: "stay close with your phone will ring you soon" shouted at her

Her: "ok! Bye all, take care, love you"

All went off and left the nana free for her errands.

An hour later Pam called but she couldn't respond to the call since she was in a team meeting a quarter passed.

In the team meeting Patrick was chairing and lead through all the agendas one mostly pressing was end of year office party.

In team meetings the CEO, CFO and COO didn't really attend unless they wished to and heads of departments as well although there were representatives from every department attending on their behalf. Patrick was the Administration & Company Secretary who chaired such meetings. So the main agenda was the usual office end of year dinner for the team and stakeholders. Sub agendas were date, venue, invitees, cards, souvenir, and so much more. She was tasked to prepare invited guests' list and their contacts in two days time also circulate groups and responsible tasks to the team before cob that day.

It really was a hectic week for her, two days to submitting her final paper and not even through yet. The firm was also indulging her the most. Good enough she had been through all that before and ready to rumble.

In a normal afternoon she made her call to Pam and told her how tight the week was going forward. Pam always believed in her friend, she had all the encouraging words one could possibly need to keep moving. So they concluded Kayla will have sleepover at Pam's place for the remaining three days of the week. Pam will take the kids to school for the same days as well, so as to unload and make it easier for her to accomplish everything. Thank God they had their back on each other.

4 30pm as usual Kayla popped in her mom's office for them to head home it wasn't the way she planned earlier with Pam but it wasn't much of a big deal since Kayla was not aware of the plans, so she had to talk Kayla through her plan and called Pam to pick Kayla from her office. As Kayla was waiting for aunty Pam, still never stayed at one place, started moving around people's desks and passed others by the corridor greeting everyone on the way, very slowly she got up the stairs to where Wanitha the old lady was stationed. Before Wanitha could ask who she was and what she could do for her a door opened and behold two men were standing on the door one leaving one turned to Kayla

"It's you my friend, your time, come on in" shouted Frank while smiling at Kayla and paved way for her to enter into his massive office.

"Woow!" Kayla was astonished to see how beautiful the office was and the view from outside was breathtaking.

"Can Wanitha bring you something to drink?" As usual Frank smiled and squinted his eyes and asked Kayla who was starring at a splendid crystal whiskey glass jar and glasses. Kayla moved towards another angle, she couldn't stop staring.

"Yes, yes please thank you" said Kayla in hi cups. "I feel like am in a museum or a gallery, I have never been before but I guess they look pretty much like this" she kept talking in pulses while moving from one angle to another looking at every thing without touching.

Frank smiled and went to his grand leathered black office chair. "Well I am impressed if you like what you're seeing young lady" got his mobile and texted for a minute or less.

"Kayla is my name" Kayla turned to Frank and headed to where he was, looking through his eyes and said once more, "it's time for you to call me by my name or at least know my name."

Frank got more interested with Kayla's confidence he called Wanitha "cancel the next two of my appointments please, I may be with Ms Kayla for sometime and get someone to attend her, thanks"

"Very well noted Sir, thanks" replied Wanitha and went to listen to what Kayla would want to be served.

Wanitha: "excuse me young lady would you like something to drink?" asked Kayla who was on the guest lavishing black sit.

"Yes Mam, thanks. I will go fetch some water from the dispenser" replied Kayla as she was leaving to get herself a glass of water. Frank interrupted the conversation "Ms Wanitha here would like to get you the water and let you proceed with our talk, if that's okay with you" raised his eyebrows.

Kayla: "no it's not really necessary let me save you the trouble" she jumped off the sofa passed Wanitha and went out the door leaving both in shock and Wanitha went back to her desk.

A minute later she was back with a disposal glass of water at Wanitha's desk asking if she could get back in Mr Sinclair's office and Wanitha let her through.

Frank: "You back? That was fast!"

Kayla: "I wouldn't let an old lady go through the stairs for my water. That's so disrespectful" she added getting on her seat as she breathed heavily.

Frank was astonished with the braveness of such a minor "wow! So it's about her age? I get you. I like that"

"So tell me young lady. Umm Ms. Kayla who is your mother again?"

Kayla: "don't you know her? she works at the front desk her name is.

(there was a knock the door opened and Kayla stopped talking) It was Fadhil, Frank's driver swapped some car switch and left without saying a word. It looked like Mr Sinclair was aware of what Fadhil was doing and remained focused on Kayla to finish her sentence.

Frank: "okay, so your mom works at the front desk and where is your dad?" asked Frank in a serious note.

Kayla: "I don't know, she continued, my dad is my mom's future husband whom I haven't met yet but it's just a matter of time I am sure I will"

Frank: (momentarily he didn't squint but open-eyed at Kayla as she was expressing her inner self) "okay that's so honest of you, does your mom know all this?" he asked

Kayla: "know what?" she replied instantly

Frank: "the thoughts and feelings you have about your future dad?" he continued

Kayla: "I am not sure but I wouldn't want to tell her now" she responded

Frank: "Why not?"

Kayla: "because it's on the list of her things right now" "I think I know what she's focused on and I don't think my father is on the list".

Frank: "How do you know it's not on the list? Did she tell you?"

Kayla: "she didn't but I see her focusing on my school, her school, her work, and myself like on going projects."

Frank: "but that's what she's supposed to do is there anything missing that she was supposed to include on her focus list?" asked interestingly

Kayla: "like partying, going out with aunty Pam and meeting new friends whom one may end up being her husband just like uncle George and aunty Pam" said freely

Frank: "that's how aunty Pam and uncle George ended up being together?"

Kayla: "I am thinking so, up to now they still go out and party and have fun and Mom is left to take care of us like she has no hobby"

Frank: "how many are you in your family?"

Kayla: "my mom and I"

Frank: "so if she leaves to party and have fun who will be taking care of you?"

Kayla: "will have sleepover at Jays"

Frank: "and who is Jays?"

Kayla: "my closest friends. Jayda and Jayden are twins, they are like my family especially Jayda but Jayden is a boy sometimes he gets bored of us"

(a phone rang and Franks answered the call very briefly "yes please thank you very much")

Frank: "back to our session Ms Kayla where do this twins stay and how close did you say you are to them?"

Kayla: "very close family friends and we stay next to each other, their dad is uncle George and their mom is aunty Pamela"

Frank: "ooooh your mom's best friends' twins are your closest friends, that's good and neighbors as well, I see"

Kayla: "yeah"

Wanitha received a call asking if she happened to see a young schoolgirl laundering around the corridors and she replied that Kayla was having a one-on-one with Mr Sinclair at his office.

The mother was shocked and panicked wondering what Kayla might be saying, quickly she rushed upstairs asked Wanitha to get Kayla off the room for her aunty had come to pick her.

Wanitha didn't sound convinced to cut the discussion Kayla and Frank were having for such a reason. "Let her finish her discussion, the aunty can wait, I must say she's really a smart lady I am impressed" Wanitha continued "imagine I asked her what she would want to drink and replied water and insisted to get it herself, let me save you the trouble" "that's what she said. A good girl you are blessed my dear" Wanitha shouted at her as if Kayla's mother had trouble hearing. "Well thanks Wanitha now please get that girl out of that room I'm beginning to feel she's about to spill the tea. You know what I mean? I can't handle it anymore" she said as she pushes Wanitha to stand up and head to the door and ask Kayla out.

Frank: "I really like you Kayla, you are such a smart, charming and beautiful girl. We should do this more often, same time in my office. I would like to know you better, tomorrow we are going to talk about school and your academics got it?" looking through Kayla's eyes.

Kayla stood up and went over and hugged Frank unexpectedly and Frank had to squat and hug her back and told her to take good care of herself and to always be grateful for everything.

(a door opened and there she was as if she's from a doctor's room, very calm and contented)

Her: "there you are, what have you been doing? Aunty Pam and your friends are waiting for you"

"Mom relax I was chatting with your boss. Why didn't you come and get me? Did they arrive long? "said Kayla looking so excited. She turned to her mother hugged and kissed her goodbye.

Her: "Laters, love you" she said while waiving to everybody in the car.

Pam: "hey Kay you good baby girl?"

Kayla: "am good aunty Pam, I was talking to Mom's boss. He has a huuge office very cool inside"

Pam: "ooh yeah?" "What were you guys talking about?"

Kayla: "nothing much just about myself" heads over to Jayda and starts playing throughout their drive to home.

She got back on her desk and started working on completing her outstanding tasks. Almost everyone left the office except for herself on her earphones listening to her favorite playlist. She had gone halfway her list and started feeling a relief. She paused for a mug of black coffee and kept going. Upstairs was a sound of people murmuring fortunate enough she couldn't hear a sound due to the loud music playing on her ears, she kept working, researching and typing for another forty five minutes and suddenly a huge sound of something had fallen on the floor was heard she stood put her ear phones off and shouted "hello!, hello!, hello! Anyone there?" frightened, she couldn't hear a word so she thought it may have been a mere thought and not actual thing and proceeded with her business and music on.

A few minutes later, she saw shadows of two people approaching her desk from behind. She was scared to death, and could not move an inch. Her heart pumped vigorously. She was not thinking or praying - just faint-heartedly sitting still. She did not know what to do as the shadow approached her desk, but then she heard a chuckle. Totally not robbers' moves, she thought. As the people approached the brightly lit front desk, the shadow disappeared. She saw Ms Shirley and Mr Sinclair looking wasted and happy. They both looked at her and as always she hysterically whispered "goodnight Mr Sinclair" and there was no response but Ms Shirley took trouble and said to him "the front desk lady wished you a goodnight" the response was not heard as they walked out of the building and drove off.

She winded up her work and called Pam to find out how they were doing and left the office.

She got home a bit late than usual, had the house all for herself, Kayla had a sleep over at Pam's.

She undressed, ran a bath on a tub, went to the kitchen opened a bottle of Boschendal 1648 merlot 1972 poured some on a glass and went with it in a bath tub before she could jump in she went to press play her playlist then laid her beautiful naked light skinned flawless body inside warm foam tub. (What a day! the feeling was immeasurable) from a hectic day to almost getting robbed inside your own office only to find the robbers were your boss and his woman – what a day. She thought, sipping some wine rubbing her body with some very affordable lavender bath gel and for thirty minutes of massaging and rubbing her slinky neck, flirtatious boobs all the way to her luscious and alluring thighs down to her shapely legs effortlessly she passed her hand to her gamy ass massages softly plain sailed onto her fruity saucy sultry punani touched every part of intriguing self, feeling her cheap lavender warm foam – it was erotic and she just couldn't stop because the feeling was good, her clitoris was aroused with her warm slippery finger-play, her eyes changed shape, skin turned blue, she lost control of her legs wide spread while she kept rolling her finger gently on her clit inside her punani left hand massaging her raunchy boobs and nubile nipples, she kept going switching hand and swinging swiftly back and forth non stop, feeling her own world skin turning really blue and when she started shaking her left leg she increased the pace of her right hand inside her punani doing faster than before when the right leg fell outta control she couldn't go any further than loosing her breath, her voice, mouth wide opened, her eye balls seen half way, just for seconds there was splash of water onto the tub from her trembling very inviting body, she seemed satisfied put herself together sipped some wine and rinsed her juicy punani and the rest of the body. She got into her pajamas and couldn't wish for more than her bed and slept like a baby that night.

Thursday

(a gospel song rang out loud from the alarm) woke up, did eighty reps of squats & lunges and jumped to shower, she felt brand new that day, singing during her shower after forty minutes she was off to work. That day Kayla was at Pam's and she would come anytime to take her clothes or anything she wanted, both Pam and the nana had the keys to the apartment. She was running out of time to completing her weekly errands and submitting her paper hence had no time to waste. She missed the nana and everyone else because she left earlier than usual. Got to the office earlier than the rest. She had an hour of running errands on her computer before she could proof read her paper for print off.

In between her errands and meetings she got time to make few phone calls one to Pam asking how they were doing and another to the nana.

At half past 12 a black range rover pooled over to the grand glassy French entrance door of the office and a man in his exquisite dark blue suit, glowing black red sole shoes came out of the rover passing through the glass door facing the reception busy on his phone behind his lustrous shades he stood for a minute looking at his watch nodding and replying "yes, sure, that's sounds perfect, thank you very much" he hanged up his phone and kept walking and for a minute she realized it was Mr Sinclair, before she could release her usual greeting he was way gone climbing the stairs to his office.

The office is designed in such a way that Frank, Freddy and other top management are situated on the first floor of the building in a glass office cubicles except for Frank Sinclair's office which was wooden sideways and the front was the glassy part very spacious from within and has a beautiful outside view. PAs for each seniors were placed opposite their offices and the ground floor was filled with glass meeting rooms, cubicle offices for juniors and heads of departments, and a lobby for waiting guests / clients adjacent to the front desk where her desk is located. There was also a back door which led to archive room, a kitchen and snacks corner and washrooms. It was breathtaking and well-designed office; the ceilings were crystal clear, glassy walls and flawless white tiles on the floor.

At exactly 4 30pm the little girl was already at her mother's diameters looking so tired but you could tell very excited being there, she fetched some candies from her mother's desk and started munching.

Her: "hey you, how have you been?" kissed, hugged and pinched Kayla's cheeks as if she had not seen her for ages.

Kayla: "I miss you Mom" hugged her mom and rushed to the candy jar for more candies.

Her: "where are Jays (Jayden & Jayda)?" asked as she typed something on her pc

Kayla: "in school attending class remedial" she said trying to figure out where to start touring

Her: "well settle down miss, get something to read homework may be" said on a serious note working on her pc.

A minute later Kayla managed to reach on the next cubicle greeting everyone she came across with, climbed the stairs and the next thing you know she was at Wanitha's desk.

Kayla: "afternoon maam" sounded very innocent

Wanitha: "afternoon girl, remind me your name please" raised her eyebrows facing down her keybord her glasses half way to her nose. "what can I do for you today?" she asked still on her keyboard.

Kayla: "Kayla, may I see him" she pointed at Frank's door

Wanitha: "do you have an appointment?" smiled and went on typing.

Kayla: "yes maam" with low tone

Wanitha: "what time is your appointment?" kept inquiring while busy on her pc

Kayla: "same time as yesterday" paused raising her eyebrows and making funny faces

A phone buzzed and Wanitha spoke up

Wanitha: "Ms Kayla is here to see you" paused and starring at Kayla

Frank: "Pardon me?"

Wanitha: "Kayla, the young girl you had…."

Before she could finish the sentence

Wanitha: "okay" replied and hanged up the phone. "You can go" said to Kayla

Wanitha was indeed aged and preferred old style of communicating as other PAs wore their ear peace she seemed comfortable with hands on and off the phone.

Frank: "My friend Kayla" said as he rose off his chair towards Kayla and shook her hand, "how are you today?" squinted his eyes and smiled from far his face looked so refreshed seeing Kayla.

Kayla: smiled back at Frank and shook his hand, "I am fine thanks, what's your name?" sounded so pretty, comfortable and innocent moving slowly from one place to the other.

Frank: "my name?" looked shocked as he walked back to his desk

Wanitha: "yes. Your name" responded seriously making herself comfortable on a sofa

Frank: "all this time you didn't know my name?"

Wanitha: "you didn't know mine either until yesterday and almost forgot it today when the lady mentioned it over the phone" she points at the door (meaning Wanitha)

Frank: "hahahahaaaa, I like you" "my names are Frank Sinclair" woke up from his chair to shake her hand. "would you like something to drink?" he asked going towards his luxurious crystal jar of drink poured some on a glass for himself.

Kayla: "I am fine, thanks" and took another candy from her skirt pocket. "do you need some?" raised a bar of candy for Frank to see

Frank: "what's that?" he asked and sipped his drink

Kayla: "KitKat" and bit some of it looking so confident

Frank: "no am good, thanks" "how's school?" as he sat next to her away from his desk like having a close one-on-one and put his glass on the table.

Kayla was swinging her short legs that couldn't touch the floor when she sat.

Kayla: "school is good, I have a presentation next week in front of the whole class" she talked with her hands, eyes and still managed to chew her candy.

Frank: "ooh that's a big task – presentation on what?"

Kayla: "Food" paused

Frank: "what about Food?"

Kayla: "what is food, kind of foods and importance of food" kept talking with her hands

Frank: "oooh so are you ready for it?"

Kayla: "not yet, I have lots of questions to ask and readings to do"

Frank: "you can start by asking me?" paused as he squints his eyes

Kayla: "never mind, I will ask Mom" she said very politely

Frank: "why not? I can help. Don't you think?" raised his voice and sipped his drink

Kayla: "I think I will ask you when I'm half way through, that way you tell me if I'm missing a point or not" confidently she added "Let me start tomorrow with Mom"

Frank: "why tomorrow and not toady?"

Kayla: "she will be free from her work and school paper" she replied

Frank: "oh so your mom also goes to school?"

Kayla: "yes but almost done when she submits her paper" enjoyed her candy bar and swinging her legs

A phone buzzed on his desk he looked over thought for a minute and ignored it.

Frank: "so Kayla, whom do you want to become when you grow up?" he asked like trying to switch on an interesting story

Kayla: "a teacher and a mother"

Frank: "why teacher and mother?"

Kayla: "I want to teach children and also have my own children so that I don't end up lonely"

Frank: "what do you mean end up lonely? What do you want to teach the children?"

Kayla: "if you don't have children your life sucks you have no one to keep you busy or even talk to or laugh with" she continued while chewing her candy bar "I also want to teach about the importance of family and being thankful in life" she stopped

Frank: astonished by her answers and starring at her "Wow" "First let's start with being busy: children are not only the people to keep someone busy, what about work, friends? Can't they keep you busy?"

Kayla: "no, friends and work is outside home, you don't live with inside your home, if you have no children you must feel bored" nodding her head as she emphasized.

Frank: "and what are the importance of family?" concentrated at her

Kayla: "Family is good to our lives: you help one another; you have a constant friend whom is your sister or brother or mother or father; for my self is my mother and what about you?" she threw the question to Frank

Frank: "for my case is my mother and my brother" paused before she interrupted

Kayla: "you live with your mother?" surprised and laughs out

Frank: looking confused "yes I do sometimes and sometimes not, I live with my brother like forever"

Kayla: "how old is your brother? Kept smiling

Frank: "equally older, he's my twin brother" "why were you surprised me living with my mom?"

Kayla: "I thought grown people don't live with their parents any more or even their big sisters or brothers" she replied confidently

Frank: "well, you're right, my mom lives out of the country but when she comes back we have her over our place as a guest for sometime and my twin brother and I are grown ups as you say but we haven't yet got children and wives to live with or at least to part ways"

Kayla: "what's part ways?"

Frank: "separate or live different houses; see my brother and I love each other so very much and we are really close probably as how you and your Mom are, but when one gets married and have a family I think that's when will start living different houses so I guess that's my family at the moment.

A door opened and a man walked in with folders of paper on his hand and a phone on the other

Frank: "Huh! Speaking of the devil" he stood up gesturing the man who just walked in "this is the brother I was talking about" pointing at Freddy whom had been caught with surprise to find Frank at the oval table discussing with a minor God knows what which made him not answer his phones. "Freddy meet Kayla, Kayla – Freddy" exchanged hand directions.

Freddy: "very nice to meet you Ms Kayla" shook her tiny hand and offered a smile from far and starring at her for sometime.

Kayla: "me too, thanks" politely as usual getting back at her seat.

Freddy: "what's up man have been buzzing don't you check your phones? We need to get this thing out today and you're left for review can we go through it right now?" he paused starring at Frank. "by the way this is what we were to discuss yesterday but you cancelled and now looks like you were about to miss it" he added on a serious face.

Frank: "yeah, yeah can you do it without me Freddy? I am having an important session with Ms Kayla here I wouldn't want to cut it but tomorrow if works fine with you get some other time and not the same time cause it's already occupied" pleaded Frank

Freddy looked very surprised and disappointed at the same time he raised his eyebrows and turned to Kayla

Freddy: "Kayla right? Be good" wore a fake smile and left the room, the door shut slowly.

Freddy: "Wanitha, who is that girl in Frank's office"

Wanitha: "which girl? Ooh Kayla, she's Frank recent interest"

Freddy: "since when? What does she want?" looked very concerned

Wanitha: looked serious as well "from the beginning of this week, she comes to greet him and they have some lengthy discussion" should I be concerned?"

Freddy: "not really, just get me her details and whose kid is she anyway?" before she could wait for the answer his phone buzzed and walked away responding to a call. "Freddy Sinclair" and he disappeared.

Inside, Frank and Kayla kept their discussion more and more interesting they talked about each other their likes, dislikes (at least Frank could not be more open than Kayla) their preferences and places they had been around the world (turned out Kayla had not been far than a neighboring Island) where she wished to go someday.

A door opened and Wanitha informed them that Kayla's aunt was down to pick her.

Frank: "I thought you said you were waiting for your mother? Asked Frank

Kayla: "a change of plan from yesterday my aunt picks me up coz I have a sleepover at the twins till tomorrow" she added, "I am giving my Mom some space to finish her stuff, thank you Mr Frank, goodbye"

Frank: "come here you know how we do it" he squatted and opened his arms to hug her with a precious smile and told her to keep being good and to take care of herself.

Kayla let herself out leaving Frank leaned at his desk and wondering how a mini creature can be that much open-minded and interesting. For minutes he calmed himself and called his driver to pullover.

He grabbed his coat, bag, phones and left the office told Wanitha that he's out for the day.

Kayla: "bye Mom", sounded excited and walked away

Her: "hey girl come here" she swung her chair onto Kayla's direction, kissed and told her to be good"

Kayla bumped into Frank at the door as they were both leaving the building towards their cars

Kayla: "goodbye Mr Frank" shouted and waved at Frank not knowing if he was seeing her coz his eyes were behind shades.

Kayla jumped into Pam's car looking ready to transition to another atmosphere she greeted aunty Pam and the twins and they left the premises.

Likewise Frank left a minute later.

Kayla's mom kept reading and reviewing her paper and doing some final touches and sent an email to the team informing them that she would come to the office at past mid day after she submitted her paper.

Pam and the twins got home and went on with their daily schedules: shower, juice and snack and watching TV or playing games and homework falls last before supper and bed. Kayla loved the sleepover either at her place or the twins'. She liked to be kept busy and fun that's all.

Pamela (Pam) was a notarized advocate and worked at a law firm. She rarely went to court most of what she did was paper work and very flexible to an extent of working anywhere and anytime. At times she may end up working at home after dropping the twins and sometimes if the twins were too noisy and she couldn't concentrate she goes to her friend's condo worked on her laptop leaving the kids with Zuhura - her housemaid.

Meanwhile at SincEnterprises Freddy called Wanitha before she left for the day and asked for more details about Kayla. After he found out she was a child of an employee of the firm he was relieved. Fredrick was very protective of his brother and very organized than Frank. He looked like the eldest one although he was not. Frank was the easy one, charming, funny and cool. Both hanged out with almost same friends, while Freddy was more cautious when they went out pretty much like the bodyguard, Frank maintained being the Boss. Their mother, Mrs Zoya Ferdinand Sinclair was colored and her late husband Ferdinand Sinclair, founder of the SincEnterprises was Scottish who lived in US for almost of his life, got married and had beautiful and smart half cast twins Frank and Frederick.

The day ended well for her as she got home right on her usual time, still had the house for herself and all she could think of was submitting her paper and hoping for the best. She didn't do much that night, took her lengthy shower (at least not a bath this time) thinking of tomorrow, and jumped on bed called Pam and spoke with the kids, said grace and began to fetch her sleep.

Friday

The day was shinning and bright through everyone's eyes, you could tell from pedestrians on streets, courier hubs and even in the office they couldn't wait to call it a week,

Friday had always been the best day of the week for her – knowing that she had two days off her desk and more time of sleep and other interesting life cracks. She went to submit her paper at her college and hoped for the best. Even in her college she was less recognized, a shy girl, interacted less and hardly appeared on front rows although her academics seemed to be good and very impressing.

On the other side of her world there was a team meeting scheduled to happen in three hours from then, she managed to return before time and pulled out her updates on her direct tasks for the meeting. Everyone seemed to be in a good mood, the firm worked really hard across the entire year and once they approached to the end of financial year it got more hectic; finance department was overly busy, heads of departments pinned the juniors for annual reports submissions, administration department prepared for prospectus year overall management hence people ran up and down. The meeting had been rescheduled to the last two hours before c.o.b an email popped up her screen reading so, another email from Wanitha with regards to Frank's availability next week that he would be out of the country for regional conference for the whole of next week. Okay she hand down and took a break by making one casual call to her best – Pam.

Her: "hey girl, how you doing?"

Pam: "hey you, better than ever, about to go out for a meeting. Did you managed to meet your deadlines?" as she walked down the hallway off her office building.

Her: "ooh yeah I did, thanks to you"

Pam: "so we are finally going out to night and celebrate" she said with funny face

Her: "do you think that's a good idea?"

Pam: "don't even make me start! You need to ease up a bit, you have been so up to your neck lately girl, you need some life" she went on "I am going to call George to organize something / someplace after work we need this, right? and no but!" switched on her engine

Her: exhale "ok! Whatever you say. I am all yours now" rolled her eyes

Pam: "that's my girl, bye for now talk to you later" and drove off to her meeting

She started thinking on her office loan and went to assistance finance desk to follow up on her request. As she was discussing with Peter a very funny guy, Freddy walked in

Her: "afternoon Mr Sinclair" she said

Peter: "yes Freddy what can I do for you"

Freddy: "hey guys, Pete can I have a word with you?" looked straight to Peter

Her: "I will excuse myself" she walked out of Peter's office and left.

Freddy: pointing at her before saying a word "she…"

Peter: "she's following up on her loan request" said Peter

Freddy: "ooh okay. So was wondering if we could go through the budget prior to the meeting" he went close to Peter's desk wearing a serious face.

Peter: "yes sure" awakened his screen and opened an excel spreadsheet for Freddy and him to review.

It was half past two after midday, she had her lunch and an easy afternoon nothing pressing on her desk and less incoming clients and calls. She called Pam but couldn't reach her. Minutes later a bold man dressed in jeans and shirt passed by her desk only to realize it was Frank Sinclair for once she missed greeting and proceeded with her errands.

Later that day Kayla arrived at her usual time, gave her mom the longest hug ever

Her: "Hey what's all this about? Someone looks happier" she said wiping sweat off Kayla's face

Kayla: "I just feel like weekend has started" smiled and hugged her mom

Her: "ooh yeah? Lucky you, I have some few things before I couldn't agreed more" she added "ooh and by the way is it okay with you if I go out with Pam tonight? You and I will hook up from tomorrow onwards, only if that's okay with you my love?" pleaded politely at Kayla caressing her cheek.

Kayla: "Mom that's cool go have fun you haven't gone out for like ever" she added "you see I told you it felt like a good weekend is about to begin" she bounced off her mother's arms and went for candy bar

Her mom rolled eyes smiled and touched with Kayla's words and went on with her work. Freddy happened to have heard almost every thing they talked. He cleared his throat to draw attention that there was someone around. She stood up at his disposal.

"Hi" Kayla sounded innocent

Freddy: "hey young lady – this' your mom?" pointed at Kayla's mom.

Kayla: "yes" she by passed Freddy and kept following the stairs to her dearest friend's office

Her: "what can I do for you Mr Sinclair?" asked politely

"Nothing really, I couldn't help overhearing your girl, she's quite a thing, imagine she is Frank's biggest fun"

Freddy talked with his eyes and arms "please get back to your stuff" as he was leaving

She felt cool for a second and wondered why she didn't get time to ask Kayla what she had been talking about with Frank Sinclair.

Frank: "here get him to fix it" handing over a pile of folders to Wanitha. "Hey Ms Kayla looking good today is that your Friday look" raised his hand towards Kayla as she approached him

Kayla: "hi maam" said to Wanitha

Wanitha: "hey girl" smiled back at Kayla as she kept sorting her paper folders

Frank: "come on in" he opened the door for Kayla to pass and stood right after it looking at Kayla as she paved her way towards the window behind her desk. "I like your ensemble"

Kayla: "what is that?" bit her candy bar and enjoying her view through the glass window

Frank: "what is?" walked towards Kayla

Kayla: "the word you just mentioned - ensemble" pronounced it incorrectly and turned to look at him

Frank: "I meant your uniform" smiled at Kayla

Kayla: "our sports wear for Fridays" comfortably moved to take her seat

Frank: "sports huh" raised eyebrows "which one is your favorite?" joined her at the oval seat

Kayla: "I don't know, swimming may be" she said hesitating

Frank: "you're not sure?"

Kayla: "I don't really do sport like Jayda and Jayden do, if swimming is sport then mine is swimming"

Frank: "how do Jayda do their sport?"

Kayla: "first Jayda loves relay and jayden loves football"

Kayla: "I don't like either of them except for swimming"

Frank: "so you can swim? What do you like in swimming?" maintained the conversion

Kayla: "yes I can, I enjoy floating on water facing up, it's the best feeling ever" she smiled and kept eating her candy bar

Frank smiled and asked Kayla to pick his buzzing phone from his desk. She quickly got the phone for Frank and went on with their conversation.

Frank: "so where were we?" texted for the last minute and looked at Kayla with a smile

Kayla: "sports – which is your sport?"

Frank: "well I love soccer so very much and boxing" looked at Kayla straight into the eyes

Kayla: "okay" she swung her legs as usual and added "I really like coming here and talking to you"

Frank: "ooh yeah? I enjoy talking to you as well Ms Kayla"

Kayla: she kept talking "you're the only one calling me Ms Kayla" she imitated Frank's voice

Frank wore a big smile at her and squinted "did you just imitate my voice?" both laughed out loud

Kayla: "I think we have some things in common, you have a mother I also have a Mom, you don't have a child I don't have a father yet, you don't have a sister me too, you see…we are almost the same" sounded emotional

Frank: "very true Ms Kayla, very true, but hey we got each other right?" got close to Kayla and held her both hands smiling and squinting directly at her

Kayla: "yes we do"

Frank: "so what you going to do for the weekend?"

Kayla: "the normal things, homework, shopping with Mom, but she said we will go out and have some fun" raised her voice and looked excited

Frank: "ooh yeah? That's nice, well I on the other hand will be in Europe, I have some conference to attend to for four days and will be back next week" looked at Kayla

Kayla: "I am going to miss you" she woke up and hugged him unexpectedly

"Oh will miss you too kiddo, what should I get you from my trip?" Frank asked Kayla

"Anything" Kayla said politely "but let me ask my Mom if it's okay with her"

Frank: "good girl"

Wanitha poped in to remind Frank it's about time for the meeting. Frank had never been in the team meetings but he wanted to hear how far had the team gone with the office event preps.

Frank: "thanks Wanitha" looking at Wanitha as she left the room.

Kayla: "I have to go. Bye" she stood Frank hugged her and told her he was waiting for the feedback from her mother.

She left the office and headed down the stairs to her mother's desk. Frank went back at his desk browsed for some minutes and headed out for the meeting.

Kayla found a bunch of people surrounding her mom's desk discussing on something(s). For a minute, she stood next to them without interrupting letting them finish their talk and sneaked towards her mother and the rest were heading to the boardroom which was also down the hall on their left.

Kayla: "so Mom, Frank wants to bring me a gift from his trip to Europe, is it okay with you?"

Her: "first it's not Frank it's Mr Sinclair and second did you ask for the gift?" saying in a serious tone

Kayla: "no I didn't he just said, I didn't ask for it I swear" tried to reassure her mom

Her: "it's fine" picked her papers for her meeting "you need to stay put when I tell you to do so. I am heading to a meeting aunty Pam will be here for you soon and you and I have a long discussion to do young lady."

"Okay Mom" Kayla hugged her mother "will tell you how it all started" said excitedly.

Frank stood in front of his office facing down looking at Kayla and the front desk lady doing the hugging and talking and that was probably the first time he laid eyes on Kayla's mother. For once he was touched with the chemistry and love the two ladies had each other going and when Kayla looked up she saw Frank looking down at them and she shouted "she said yes!" in a happy and excited tone very loud though that made other people stood for a minute wondering what was going on, Frank gave Kayla a big smile and a thumb up and headed down. "The next thing you know people will not want you in here for you're noisy" said Kayla's mother as she was leaving to the boardroom "sit there young lady and do not move an inch!" on a serious face pointing at a chair she left. "Okay Mom" replied Kayla very politely and went to sit. Frank couldn't help thinking of Kayla's excitement.

In the boardroom Frank came in last and they began once he got in, Patrick was chairing the meeting and Frank sat aside him listening closely looking at each and every one of his team. She was on the other corner of the room his eyes managed to reach her and for the second time he paid close look at her as she was listening to Patrick looking on her writing pad and getting back at Patrick until for a second both their eyes met and she quickly shied away, it was for the first time they were in the same room together and for the first time he paid a tremendous amount of time looking at her, he starred at her braided hair, her eyebrows were long and dark, her neck couldn't be seen much due to the pull neck dress she had underneath her coat, she didn't realize anything and kept being at her natural best and not the same for Frank who lost track of what was being discussed in the meeting and kept starring at her and got back at Patrick to show he was attentive and he kept paying all the attention to the front desk lady until the meeting was half way to completion. On the other hand the front desk lady kept maintaining her true self and participating in the meeting there was time she left the room to go check whether Kayla was in order and Frank was left with nothing to concentrate on, he bragged his phone and started swapping for a minute, she walked back in and Frank resumed his obsession. She got back to her seat he kept starring at her hair, butts and legs from her back. "She's good only old fashioned" Frank thought silently "let me see what Kayla has got from you Miss" starred at her as she grabbed her seat. Patrick ended his talking and Marian took over all presenting what was ought to happen in the event and further preparations and what to change. Freddy was seriously concentrating on every agenda but wondered why all this time Frank didn't say a word (which is totally unlike of him) and so decided to look at him for a second only to find him busy at one destination of sight. He couldn't tell whom Frank was starring at but he took note of few from the direction of his sight and went on listening at Marian. The meeting was adjourned and everyone dispersed. Frank didn't say a word from the beginning to the end of the meeting not even acknowledging the team for their massive work and most of the staff left thinking he was less impressed even Freddy didn't understand what was on Frank's mind with regards to the meeting. Most of them left the boardroom except Frank, Freddy, Patrick and Marian of course Patrick and Marian couldn't leave until Frank left first just observing protocol. Freddy asked Frank what were his thoughts and Frank cleared his throat and said that it was promising and impressive everyone was relieved to hear that and Frank left the room smiling and ease and the rest followed out.

Walking down the hallway he made a stop at the reception facing outside through the French door and took out his phone and text for a minute wondering his eyes to see if he could see Kayla anywhere around but it occurred to him she had already left. He made a phone call to Shirley while starring at the front desk lady whom was busy talking with people in front of her desk smiling and chatting in her natural self not knowing her boss was starring at her. She collected her stuff, organized her desk and made a phone call to Pam wanting to know what the plan was for that evening.

Meanwhile Freddy climbed the stairs to his office and before he could get in he thought to talk to Frank went over at Wanitha's desk and didn't seem to find any person around he looked down only to see Frank prying at the front desk lady and something triggered his attention something was seriously going on in Frank's mind regarding the lady and the kid. He called Frank over his phone and asked him if he was coming up for a minute chat and Frank headed to the stairs to his office.

"What's up man so you leaving on Sunday? Everything sorted?" asked Freddy

"Yeah I guess so" Frank sat down and looked at Freddy

"I see you're destructed by the front desk lady or may be her kid or may be both?" Freddy looked straight into Frank's eyes

"What makes you say that?" asked Frank on a serious note pretending not to be true and typing nothing on the keyboard or may be his password to awake the pc

"Well first the kid's taking your hours and now the lady is all you have been concentrating on at the meeting" added Freddy, "Am I missing something? Tell me about the kid what do you guys talk about?" Freddy sat down facing his brother.

"Ooh dear brother when will you ease-up?" said Frank in a joking tone "I really like the girl she has touched my heart when we talk I feel so connected, I think it's time for me to have a kid, what do you think?" he paused

"Good! Thanks for sharing are we off for drinks?" asked Freddy as he went out of Frank's office.

"Whatever you say I am done for today" replied Frank but wondered how easy was Freddy on his answer because Freddy had never been easy on any of Frank's matters wanting to know everything and being on top of everything.

All was for good Frank was impressed of Freddy understanding him on his short explanation and Freddy was impressed that he finally realized his brother was on a destructive zone. He went to his office and called Bob the human resource manager of the firm and asked him to pull a file for the front desk lady, Bob already knew what Freddy was requesting so he told him by tomorrow it would be on his desk.

They both took off for drinks to one of the best hotels in town that was not far from their office and met their friends as weekend had just began while Pam and her dearly friend met at their local joint celebrating what was said to be end-of-hectic-week. Kids were already at home with Pam's nana.

Freddy and Frank had a crack down of talk over their drink up about work and other affairs. Freddy tried to ease Frank to make him talk more about Kayla and her mom but before he could get him any further Shirley had arrived and Brenda (Freddy's girlfriend) both worked down town at different offices, but they had been friends for so long due to dating twin brothers. Other guys arrived as time went by and the circle was big such that Paul, Jerry, Michael all their crew were on the spot and that's how their nights began with drinking and talking and laughing with their girlfriends. Their table looked so messy with drinks -bottles after bottles.

On the other side of the world, she started to feel herself after having two glasses of red wine and lots of chats and stories with Pam, George didn't join the club until later on, they ordered some barbeque and kept wining and dining.

"So guess what" She looked at Pam and sipped some wine before she could say more

"What?" Pam looked back at her.

Her: "Kayla has been talking to Frank – my boss since Monday when she comes to my office" she kept talking "at first I thought it's brief and later came to find out it wasn't and haven't got a chance to ask her what they had been talking about" kept talking in slow motion as she sipped her wine in between her talk "so today she came to ask me if it's okay for Frank to bring her a gift from his trip next week? And she claimed not to have asked for it - Frank insisted" she kept going "can you imagine I agreed and she turned back and yelled from down all the way up to where Frank was standing that it's okay I agreed, girrl it was embarrassing everyone stopped for a minute to see what was going on" "imagine with her sharp voice thank goodness Frank was just cool about it, I guess Marian was going to email me or something"

"Is Frank the hairy one or the bold one? I like the hairy one he's cute" said Pam in her deep voice and making faces

"The bold one, you always like them all" she smiled at Pam

George and other guy showed up. This time around was not Dennis. It looked like a double date although it wasn't. They exchanged greetings and intros and made ease to each other enjoying their drinks and music.

On the Sinclair world Frank couldn't stop having flashes of the front desk lady from his mind. So he excused himself from the group and made a phone call to Bob whom was the Human Resources Manager of the firm.

Frank: "hey Bob what's up?" in a manly way

Bob: "nothing much what can I do for you Frank?"

Frank: thought for a second before he could say a word "ooh never mind Bob, I wanted to ask you something but will discuss when we meet" he hanged up the phone then went back to the table

Shirley: "is everything alright honey?" as she kissed and massaged Frank's bold head

"Cool babe" Frank said in a very romantic way

Freddy couldn't help overhearing Shirley and looked at Frank for a second and ignored him.

Their night went on as usual drinking and eating and dancing enjoying their girlfriends and making jokes. Frank wasn't at his best that night so he wanted to leave and go refresh and come back but Shirley insisted on him to stay and leave once they have had enough. Freddy never used to drink as much as Frank so most of the time he looked sober than the rest. As time went on Frank got eased-up with subsequent amount of whiskey and of course Shirley. He was back at his best, made funny jokes, stories laughing out loud dancing with Shirley and later he went to grab his set of cigar and lighted-up at his pleasure now that was epic moment for Frank when he pulled out his cigars to the table just know he was feeling the night.

While she felt she had enough of red wine Pam had just began needing more and feeling good so she didn't want to disappoint her friend by wanting to go home. She kept drinking at a slower pace than the rest but stories were lit and fun at time she broke into being so sweet and started thanking Pam for being there for her throughout her studies and work and everyone felt pity as she was expressing her gratitude to her friend. And they kept enjoying for quite sometime. She made a phone call to Pam's home to find out if the kids were in bed and if everything was okay and so was it. Pam and George were the love birds on air, they couldn't stop touching and caressing each other. It looked like George and Pam had set up the other guy for their dear friend but she seemed less interested with a man that night than her glass of wine, her friends' company and her night-out, that's all she cared at that moment.

Later that day George's friend had to leave. George called his mechanic to take both Pam's and her friend's car back home for he saw the need of driving the ladies back because they were inebriated and so after an hour or so George drove Pam and her friend back home. Pam was beside George and her friend was at the back seat they couldn't stop talking laughing making jokes it was in deed a night for all of them. On their way back she asked Pam to sleep at her place, it was almost in the morning and Pam agreed hence they parked their car next to her condo instead of Pam's.

At 3 30am they reached home made themselves comfortable Pam was never a guest at her friend's place they both shared their places with no limits, so George seemed to be the guest but not Pam. She left Pam and George at the living room and went to shower meanwhile George and Pam were busy kissing and caressing one another they switched on the TV and put the music a bit louder, she finished showering and put her pajamas and went to the living room only to find them making out on the couch she couldn't say a word and left to her bedroom. George and Pam had sex on their friend's couch in the living room and George had to leave and Pam had to go for shower before she could jump on her friend's bed.

The next day was a Saturday, the kids on the next door were up earlier than their mothers, at half past noon Pam and Kayla's mom woke up by the noise from the living room, it was the kids they decided to come to the next house for lunch, she had errands to do such as salon, shopping and going out with Kayla whereas Pam had few on her list such as salon but not shopping since she had been shopping in between the week. So Pam asked if they could go out with one car such that let her friend drive instead because she woke up with a terrible hangover. It was no big deal for Kayla's mom since she woke up without hangover at all. She didn't have much to drink last night and so her body was under control.

The nana had prepared lunch for the kids and also made some kitchen soup for the ladies whom had a long night. After three and a half hours they were all good to go. They jumped into Pam's Volkswagen touareg and left for their errands. They first stopped at a ladies salon for Kayla and her mom to do their hair and nails and meanwhile Pam took the twins to a park waiting for Kayla and her mom to finish their salon treats and after an hour and a half they went to pick Kayla and her mother and went to a supermarket for household shopping. Pam picked her clothes from a dry cleaner store and were all done with their errands and had to go for a nice outdoor restaurant in town were kids could eat have fun and let their moms enjoy their drinks.

During their stay at the restaurant Pam called George to find out if he got home safe this morning and turned out he was still on bed and sounded wasted. Pam brought the subject up about last night sex at her friend's sofa; they seemed to have been familiar with the situation. Kayla and the twins were having fun at the kids' spot swinging jumping sliding and playing some games while waiting for their order.

"So why did u leave?" Pam said in a funny face

"Oh you thought I was going to stay and watch you two fornicating?" She replied in a sarcastic face

"George has no limits" Pam kept adding "I told him you were not going to be comfortable but he couldn't stop and kept going" said as she sipped her drink

Her: "I am just happy that you're happy and I have you when I need you" she told Pam in a sweet smile.

"So how do you find George's friend – Luke?" asked Pam in a serious note

"He's cool." She responded in a serious voice

Pam: "he seemed interested in you"

"Stop it. Don't even go there. I told you guys should stop trying hook me up with different people for the problem is not with people but with me when I am ready to seeing someone I will, meanwhile I am not!" She said with no pause looking straight at Pam's eyes

"Okay ma, we gotcha you" Pam sipped her drink

The orders where ready at the table the kids joined and had a wonderful dinner.

After an hour and a half they had their bill checked and paid and left heading home. This time everyone dispersed to her crib that is Pam and the twins went back to their place and Kayla and her mother went to their own. They put their groceries to the freezer and settled for bedtime. As usual said some prayer and fell asleep.

Sunday morning is for church and the nana takes a rest and never comes to work. So they made themselves ready for church and left and after church they came back home made lunch but Pam and the twins were out with George. So Kayla had quality time with her mother by herself and had a little chat as they were preparing lunch. She told her mother what Frank and her have been chatting for the past week and she seemed to like Frank so very much. Her mother asked Kayla why she had to keep up with the talks everyday "I for once felt like I finally had a dad figure to talk to." Said Kayla. It really cracked her mother's mind and whom for once felt like there was unfinished business with her life that was affecting her daughter, but the mother was glad they had the talking and moved on to another subject which was her next week school presentation about food. She managed to listen on Kayla's idea about food and assisted her on more points and told her to write it all down and giver her for a review.

The Sunday was ease for everyone they settled home prepared for next week and she went through her closet rearranged and planned her next week moves.

On the Sinclair world weekends were filled with nights out, home barbecue parties and beach parties it had always been busy at the Sinclair mansion except for that Sunday that Frank was leaving for his trip to Europe and Freddy wasn't much of a party thrower so the mansion was free from hectics that day.

It was a promising week, all started with the usual errands kids were taken to school by Kayla's mom, Pam left to work as well, both nanas at the two doors kept going with their usual households. In the SincEnterprises plans for end of year office event kept escalating, busy week trying to wind up everything for the party, meetings with suppliers and procurers went on throughout the day. Frank on the other hand left for Europe a day ago. Freddy found a file on his desk with regards to the front desk lady from Bob the HR. He read it thoroughly and found nothing suspicious or query. He decided to use that time when Frank was away to do a clear due diligence on the lady whom was occupying most of his brother's mind. So he phoned one of the top most secret investigators in town and gave him the task. That was the one Freddy used for almost all of his due diligence and surveillance works.

That day she had to go pick the kids from school and take them back home since Pam had been doing so for the past week. Therefore Kayla did not go at her mother's work place. It looked like she was not going to go for the whole of the week if her mother kept picking them from school. She had to drop the kids home and went back to the office.

The week passed by successfully, Kayla had her presentation on food and scored an A, and her mother met all her tasks and in a blink of an eye the week was almost ending.

Freddy hired a private investigator to spy on the front desk lady but the investigator only to discover the lady had pretty much normal life and stayed out of trouble.

One day when she was at home from work about to sit for their favorite TV show they heard a knock on the door, she went to see who it was only to find Freddy standing out, she was shocked to see him outside, she opened the door and let him in. Kayla was already on the couch waiting for her show to start, Freddy had less to say and explained he was in the neighbor hood and decided to say hello. Kayla jumped out of her couch and went to greet Freddy she seemed easy and excited to see him her mother did still not believe on what was happening she offered Freddy something to drink but Freddy was less interested, Kayla begged Freddy to take her mom's best cardamom ginger white tea. Freddy couldn't agree more and was offered the tea. It was indeed the best tea. They both explained to Freddy that they were about to watch their favorite show before they sleep. Freddy felt loved and very welcomed unlike his expectations. He asked Kayla's mom how far had her loan request gone and asked her to follow it up the next day with Peter. And after a while he left knowing that the family was tiny, safe and pretty normal and nothing suspicious. He called his private investigator and told him to suspend the task and send to him his final check for he was satisfied with the results.

She couldn't wait for the next day and decided to ring Pam and told her everything. Pam was a very sensitive person perhaps due to her nature of work so she outlined possible reasons to all that: one had to do with Kayla being very close to Frank so he decided to follow up and know them better, second was perhaps the office loan she was about to receive but that was a weaker reason for the CFO of the firm to do so and third was that she may be about to receive an appraisal and being either of the twins' personal assistant so he wanted to know her better but none the less it was not a coincidence. She assured her friend and both went to sleep.

The following week Pam had rounds to pick and drop kids to school. Kayla's mom went straight to work.

In that said morning a range rover drove right in front of the French door of the office it was Frank in his immaculate looks. He jumped off the car and went for the door straight to the reception desk. She stood and greeted Mr Sinclair as how she always does and for the first time Frank replied with a smile on his face and offered a bag full of candies from his trip and told her that they were for the team. Unlike other days Wanitha gets the goodies from Frank and passes them to the front desk for everyone to have but this time around Frank saved the trouble for Wanitha and dropped them at the front desk by himself and he left to his office.

She felt confused and so happy inside not knowing exactly what was happening immediately sent an email to the team informing them on the arrival of the candies for everyone from Frank Sinclair.

The day went on being as good as everyone would have wished. Later that day Kayla arrived at her mother's just as usual. They exchanged hugs and kisses and went up stairs to meet her friend. She was excited for his return and could not wait to have her gifts and resume their talks. Kayla greeted Ms Wanitha and asked if she could get into Frank's office and she was let in.

Inside Frank's office there was Freddy and one lady whom seemed about to leave. And when Kayla knocked and got in their meeting was adjourned. Kayla was happy to see Frank. She went over hugged him and greeted him and Frank told Kayla to greet the rest of the people in there that is Freddy and Marian. She did as she was asked and Freddy and Marian left the room for Kayla and Frank.

"I am so happy to see you, looks like you have grown an inch" teased Frank.

"I eat a lot" said Kayla with a big smile and lots of excitement.

"You seem excited what's going on or what have I missed?" asked Frank.

"I am excited to see you and I can't wait to have my gifts" right there she said to Frank.

"Oh it's about the presents, there get me that bag" Frank said pointing to where some bags where placed.

And Kayla got him some of the bags and Frank handed a bag having Kayla's swimsuits and swim goggles and another bag for her candies. Kayla was extremely happy "thank you, thank you, thank you" she hugged Frank and kissed him on his left cheek. She started opening up the bags to see more and Frank just stopped for once and starred at the little girl's excitement.

"Why shouldn't you open them at home, I want to know how you have been and how your week was" said Frank.

"Well my week has been good, I got an A for my presentation and teacher asked me to come up with another presentation as fun as it was the food one." Kayla responded hysterically.

"Wow! an A huh! I am proud of you" as he squinted at Kayla

"This time I already know what I am going to present" said Kayla

"What are you going to present?" asked Frank.

"About my new friend" Kayla smiled.

"Who is your new friend?" Frank asked impatiently

Kayla: "You are."

Frank: "me? What about me?"

"Yes you. I want to tell people how we met, how great friends we have become and how I feel about you." said Kayla softly and politely.

"Aw that's so nice, I would like to read it before you present if that's okay with you?" said Frank in a smiling face

"Yes, I will show you." Replied Kayla.

"So what else did I miss?" asked Frank

"Freddy passed by our home last day as we were about to watch our show, mom gave him some tea and after a while he left." Kayla spoke confidently

"Did he?" Frank looked surprised.

"Yes he did, mom was shocked to see him but I wasn't." added Kayla "he has a friend in the neighborhood"

Frank: "Does he?" Frank replied yet restrained and nodded his head.

"Well I have some urgent matter to run to, stay in here get yourself comfortable do your homework may be, let me go attend some matter will be right back" Frank said as he was leaving out of his office.

Frank went to Freddy's office only to find some people and asked them to excuse him.

"What's up?" asked Freddy

"I am told you went to Kayla's home?" Frank seemed upset "what was the matter?"

"I was around the neighborhood and decided to pass by and see what kind of people were they" replied Freddy on a serious face

"And what did you discover – aliens?" he added "when are you gonna stop Freddy? I told you I can handle this" said Frank in a loud voice.

"Up until you cannot, in the meantime I am doing my job" said Freddy in a serious tone.

"Freddy! Just stop please! You wanna do your job? – Make sure the firm doesn't fall bankrupt!" he added "I said I can handle it so back off!" Frank left Freddy's office.

Freddy never bothered and much less never stopped. That was what he was best at - protecting his brother and ensured the firm didn't collapse. Frank went back to his office and found Kayla at her seat looking over her gifts they didn't talk much that day. He had to excuse himself from Kayla and told her that they will continue tomorrow for he had some matters to handle at that moment. Kayla understood, hugged Frank and thanked him for everything and as she was heading towards the door Frank told Kayla to pass his regards to her mother. Kayla looked at Frank smiled and left.

Kayla went over at her mother's desk and showed what Frank had brought for her. The mother asked Kayla if she thanked Mr Sinclair for everything and when it was about time they left for the day.

As days approached to the big day tense grew within the firm every department tried to complete their tasks and aimed at delivering the best hence became the busiest week. However, Kayla managed to get time with Frank everyday for their talk. That day Frank told Kayla that he was going to surprise her but she wasn't aware of what kind of surprise Frank meant.

Later that evening as they were watching TV, Kayla and her mother had a door knocking and both looked at each other as "who will it be this time?" her mother went to open and behold Frank was standing on their door step. Kayla's mother was surprised shouted "Kayla I think you have a guest" Kayla went over and Frank greeted Kayla's mom and asked if he could get in and of course She wasn't going to stop him from getting inside her tiny cubic crib, surprised as she was, she even forgot to render her usual greeting to Frank. Kayla was astonished to see Frank. She went over hugged him and let him come in. Frank for once sounded calm and small not knowing whether Kayla's mother would appreciate his visit or not. Frank had a bottle of red wine and a paper bag of popcorns he gave the bottle of wine to Kayla's mother.

"Here's for you" Frank handed the bottle to Kayla's mother in a gentlemanly voice. "Kayla told me you drink something like this" he joked and looked straight onto Kayla's mom's eyes.

"Thank you Mr Sinclair" as she received the bottle.

"Please call me Frank" he begged with his deep romantic voice looking at Kayla's mom.

"Hey Frank come let's play this" shouted Kayla launching a play station game for them to play.

"Should I get you anything Mr Sinclair oh Frank?" she sounded shy and low toned

"If you are going to drink with me we could open the bottle?" Frank looked straight on to her eyes

She was totally confused and very shy at that moment not thinking straight or at least thinking slow. She had silky pajamas on, no bra underneath and no panties either. You could see her silky blouse stung her nipples yet see the movement of her round ass as she moves. She was totally beautiful at her own special way, very natural, her skin was as light as milk and her hair braided as usual but tied up a knot, she was off make up and looked purely naturally beautiful. Frank couldn't stop looking at every inch of her while engaged with Kayla. So she got a wine opener and opened the bottle, as she was busy opening the bottle at the kitchen counter Frank couldn't resist offering his help. He went very close to her that she couldn't move an inch.

"Let me do this" said Frank at a very lower tone in his deep voice and raised his hand to take the opener from Kayla's mother whom just handed the opener to Frank in a silent mode.

"How was your day?" asked Frank as he took the opener and tried to open the wine cock

"Very fine Mr Sinclair, we were about to play a game before we sleep" she said in a very polite tone looking straight at one angle of her kitchen whereas Frank couldn't stop looking straight at her.

The house was filled with Frank's scent.

"How do I get you to call me by my name?" asked Frank in a very seductive way.

Kayla shouted at Frank that the game is about to start. Frank managed to open the wine and passed the bottle to Kayla's mom for her to pour some on glasses and he left to join Kayla on the couch for their game.

Kayla's mother got a glass for Frank and served him at the couch where he was.

"Thank you" smiled as he said to Kayla's mother.

"You're welcome and thanks for the bottle. It's a good one" said at a very low tone and shied away.

She went to her room closed the door and called Pam.

Pam: "hey girl what's up?"

Her: "you can't believe who is at my house!" said in a lower tone trying not to be heard.

Pam: "are you okay?" she queried on her loud voice

Her: "I am fine, I am saying Frank Sinclair is at my house playing some video game with Kayla. He brought a bottle of wine and popcorns." She added, "girl I think you were right one of this brothers may have a move on me coz the way he looked at me and talked to me is no joke he's into something"

"Damn right! Girl, I knew it! One of them was into you" she added "now listen go into your bathroom put on your best cologne and change those pajamas. I have a feeling which ones you're wearing, please change and smell good and look good, will talk later" Pam was very excited from the other side of the phone.

She did exactly what her friend advised, switched into better silky pajamas and wore some cologne. She looked more breathtaking than before.

She went back at the living room and both Kayla and Frank were shouting over their video game. She poured some wine on her glass and went to join them at the living room before she could sit she went for the whole bottle from the kitchen counter since Frank had his glass almost running dry. She poured more in Frank's glass and looked at Kayla enjoying her game with Frank.

"You have saved me the trouble of playing the game" said to Frank as she sipped her wine.

"Oh really? I told her that I will surprise her today but didn't tell her how" Frank kept playing the game.

A siren from the TV and the game was over. Kayla won over Frank and she felt good about it.

"I told you I would bit you up!" shouted Kayla excitedly.

"Yeah right, had I known, I'd have been careful" replied Frank with a smile

"Okay time to brush your teeth and prepare for bed" she said to Kayla.

"Thanks Frank!" she hugged and kissed him on the cheek and added "the best surprise ever" and left the living room.

"Oh yeah? Goodnight young lady" Frank smiled back at Kayla.

Her: "Mr sincla." before she could finish.

"Please call me Frank" Frank insisted in his deep romantic voice.

"Yes Frank, thanks for everything you have been doing to Kayla and I" at first I must say I was a bit uncomfortable wondering what you two might be talking about but it all came to add up seeing how Kayla is happy and looks up to you." She added "she really likes you, again thank you very much"

"I must say I have never come across a kid that drew my attention as how Kayla did, she is a very smart, special girl and I feel like with me she has a platform for her to say what's on her mind, not saying she can't tell you but I found her being too conservative until when she opened up to me and I am glad I can be there for her. On the other hand I am proud of you for raising her the best way possible" Frank looked straight at Kayla's mom.

"I am trying and I am glad it's working on my favor" she said in a polite and again shying away Frank's direct eye contact.

Kayla had finished brushing her teeth and came back at the living room.

"You good for bed kiddo?" asked Frank, as he walked up heading for the door.

"Yap! Thanks for coming best game ever!" Kayla hugged Frank.

"Take care of yourself and take care of your mother!" Frank looked straight onto Kayla's eyes.

He then looked at Kayla's mom.

"Thanks for having me an announced and thanks for being the best mom to Kayla" Frank smiled and squinted his eyes towards Kayla's mom.

Both Kayla and her mom walked Frank out of the door and waved goodbye as he got to his car. Fadhil switched the range rover on and they left.

Kayla went to bed, as her mom was busy putting things in order and called Pam on the phone and told her all that had happened eventually they were both certain on Frank's intentions.

The next day the kids were taken to school by aunty Pam. When it was about time a black range rover pulled at the front door and he came out looking smart as usual all dressed up in grey suit and black shinning shoes had his phones on his hands and his shades on. He walked up to the front desk she saw him coming and stood to greet him it seemed a bit awkward for both Kayla's mother and Frank. Frank asked him to sit and he leaned over the desk and asked how she was doing, it was so much unlike of him but you could tell from his squinted sexy eyes and the movement of his lips that he was a bit coy. Her on the other hand caught her seat pretty well and faced up directly at Frank's eyes listening to him attentively as he explained how his previous day ended. You could tell from pulsation of her chest that she was not calm but her eyes shied away and yet looked very beautiful. She kept biting her lower lip and smiling from far as Frank kept explaining.

A moment later Freddy passed by and Frank had to wish the lady a good day and proceeded walking with Freddy towards his office.

"I see you're trying to get familiar with the lady huh?" teased Freddy.

"What are you talking about? I'm not allowed to greet my employees?"

"Since when do you stop and greet back?" asked Freddy sarcastically.

"Since right now as I had a time at the their place with Kayla last night" replied Frank majestically.

"So yesterday you were at their place? And why were you there to begin with?" asked Freddy as they entered Frank's office.

"I told Kayla that I would surprise her and so I did by going at her place for a game date" Frank explained.

"Oh so you were there for Kayla and not otherwise?" Freddy looked suspicious yet sarcastic.

"Yes, I was there for Kayla!" replied Frank and added "I'm sure none of this is your business Freddy" he grabbed his chair and logged into his Macintosh.

"Alright. I get you. Next time when you need a company for some video game I am in" Freddy joked and left the office.

Frank smiled and went on with his business.

That day Frank hardly stayed in his office as he was busy attending meetings with clients from one meeting to the other that way he got to see Kayla's mother so often as he got in and out of meeting rooms. She on the other hand seemed pretty busy not to have noticed the coincidence of them all and kept being at her natural best.

Later that day Kayla showed up at her mother's office and as usual she went from hugging her mother to snatching some candies from the candy bowl to slowly climbing the stairs to Frank's office.

Frank was so pleased and looked happy to see Kayla. They hugged and she ordered him to sit still as she was going to rehearsal her presentation to him.

"I couldn't agree more" replied Frank and sat at the oval couch anxiously waiting for Kayla to start. "Oh wait!" he interrupted before she started "do you want something to drink?" he asked Kayla.

"No! I am good, thanks" Kayla showed Frank a bar of candy meaning she was sorted.

"Ok go ahead!" Frank anxiously smiled and leaned back the couch to listen to Kayla.

Kayla began:

> *"On a bright sunny day, she met a friend*
> *Talked her to think big, and believe in masses*
> *Opened his door for her to dwell*
> *Offered his ears for her to orate*
> *Played part for whom, she didn't possess*
> *Made her feel, among the folks*
> *Hence led him in, her tiny abode*
> *That is, her wholesome bosom friend"*

"Wow! Wholesome?" Frank exhaled with a big smile and clapped for Kayla "Thank you! You indeed a bosom one" he added.

Kayla sat down and went on biting a candy swinging her legs.

"Has your mom heard it?" asked Frank.

"Not yet, I was going to say it to her over her shower" replied Kayla.

"Why over shower and not over supper or over a drive home?" Frank smiled.

"I think over shower she's more attentive than on the road" Kayla explained.

"Great!" Frank added "I bet she's going to like it" "speaking of your mother, I want Fadhil to bring you and your friends over my place. There is a pool and lots of other things for you guys to play. Would that be okay?" squinted straight onto Kayla's eyes.

"Yes yes yes that sounds fun, when should we come? Saturday?" Kayla questioned excitedly.

"What about Saturday? Works fine for you guys?"

"First let me ask Mom if it's okay with her but for me and my friends we are fine with Saturday" Kayla excitedly woke up and was leaving.

"Where are you going?" asked Frank in his deep voice.

"Going to talk to Mom and will be back" Kayla smiled and let herself out of the door.

Frank made some calls and called the house and spoke to MaryJohn to find out if the house was available for the kids on Saturday. MaryJohn was the housekeeper in the Sinclair's mansion. She was more like a female butler. She knew and had all the schedules for the house - expected occasions that will engage the house and she organized and worked with the rest of the team. After a call from Frank they were on standby to preparing the expected Saturday kids' party.

On the other hand Kayla asked her mother if she was fine with the Saturday arrangement and if she could also ring aunty Pam and ask for the twins as well.

Her mother was surprised with the non-stop revelations that kept popping from her boss. She rang Pam and told her what was ought to happen Pam agreed to the arrangement and asked if she could put Kayla on the phone.

Pam: "hey little girl, you're good?" asked in a loud voice.

Kayla: "I am good aunty Pam. Is it okay with …" before she finished Pam interrupted.

Pam: "yeah yeah yeah, it's fine with me ask your friend if aunty Pam is invited as well okay?" she lowered her tone.

Kayla: "ok I will, thanks aunty Pam" sounded very excited.

Her: "what did she say?"

Kayla: "to ask Frank if aunty Pam can come as well"

Kayla's mom shocked her head and went on with her work. Kayla climbed quietly to Frank's office asked Wanitha if she could go through and went on.

"Good news or bad news?" asked Frank.

"Good news and no bad news" Kayla added, "Mom agreed and aunty Pam also agreed but asked if she was invited as well?" and she went to her seat.

Frank smiled and squinted eyes on Kayla "ooh yeah? She is invited. As a matter of fact they are all invited. I didn't want to disrupt their schedules but if they find time they can join us." He added, "what about your mother, what did she say?"

"She said it's fine but I don't know if she wants to come because I know what she does on Saturdays."

"What does she do on Saturdays?" asked Frank attentively.

"She sleeps till noon and when she wakes up we will go out either to salon or shopping or checking on her new shop" Kayla explained.

"New shop huh?" Frank asked as he kept typing.

"Yes. My Mom wants to open a shop so she goes there and looks at the place and leaves" Kayla spoke politely.

"Good. Good. So how many will you come on Saturday?" asked Frank as he concentrated on his computer.

"Me, Jayda and Jayden and may be aunty Pam" she counted her fingers.

"Can aunty Pam come without your mother?" Frank kept working on his computer.

"I don't think so, if aunty Pam is coming I bet Mom is right there with her" Kayla said hilariously.

After a while aunty Pam came to pick Kayla and Frank had to escort Kayla out to see aunty Pam.

Kayla's mother stood beside the door waiting for Kayla to pass by and collect her school bag after she saw both Kayla and Frank dropping down the stairs she went to her desk and waited for Kayla from there. Kayla went over took her bag and hugged her mother and Frank smiled at both and opened the door for Kayla to pass and both went out to meet aunty Pam. Pam saw Kayla walking beside Frank towards their car she got out of the car and greeted Frank.

"You must be aunty Pam, I am Frank Sinclair, very pleased to meet you" Frank shock Pam's hand and remained squinting his eyes directly to Pam.

"Pamela Anderson, pleasure is all mine" Pam smiled at Frank as she pat Kayla's head and shoulder.

"And these must be the twins, hey guys you good?" said Frank in a different tone "" he smiled.

Jayda & Jayden: "good thanks, hi" both responded simultaneously.

"So Pam very nice to meet you, I feel like I know you all and I just have to say Kayla is a good friend of mine and it didn't occur to my mind that you may be available for Saturday but hey, you are more than welcome. We will be pleased to have you on board." Said Frank

"I was just joking but again will not refuse the offer, my girlfriend and I will take it into consideration" flirtatiously replied Pam as she jumped into her black Volkswagen Touareg.

"Alright guys be good." Shouted Frank as he waved goodbye.

Frank went back to the office building and hopped to find Kayla's mother at her desk so he could thank her in person for the Saturday arrangement and also to invite her but unfortunately she was no where his sight. He climbed the stairs back to his office and felt unsatisfied by his move. A phone had been buzzing for sometime but Frank kept ignoring it. Shirley had been calling Frank since he came back from his Europe trip with no success. Both had a misunderstanding that made them part ways but Shirley couldn't hold the silence anymore hence decided to call bad enough Frank had been occupied by his mysterious ladies.

Days went on being tense at SinEnterprises the next week was ought to be the week of the event benchmarking their successful year. Tense was among co-workers and yet business as usual.

Frank and Freddy came together on a convertible Mercedes that day. Freddy pooled over to the door and both came out looking smart and magnificent as always. She was on a call probably with a client she looked serious and a bit tense but kept going. Freddy looked at Frank wanted to see if he was going to make a stop at the reception but Frank noticed how busy the lady was and he kept moving towards the stairs to his office. Later that day she had to step out of office for two hours during lunch time and went to a nearby store to get herself a pair of stockings and met with Pam for lunch. They talked over on what had been happening lately the Sinclair(s) crashing their home unannounced and Kayla being put in the middle of the saga. Pam advised Kayla's mother to let the kids go ahead with the Saturday plan and they should stick to their usual errands. Pam was hundred percent sure Frank was making moves on her friend. Kayla's mother couldn't believe it and yet kept insisting that Shirley and Frank had been together since forever but Pam was not convinced. They had their chat over their lunch and both went back to their offices.

In her return she found a memo on her desk that she was urgently needed on one of the meeting rooms. It was difficult to identify the writer on the memo. She didn't waist no time and went through only to find Freddy and one other gentleman were inside the meeting. She knocked and went close to Freddy to inquire if she was still needed.

"Yes please, Thom here wanted to see you, he's been asking for you since his arrival" Freddy looked at Thom as he spoke.

"How are you my dear?" Thom asked and went for a handshake.

"Very fine thanks Mr Thomson" and she wore a fake smile.

"Well I am pleased to see you," Thom responded as he looked at Freddy.

"Should I offer you something to drink?" she asked politely.

"I am very fine thanks" replied Thom in his deep voice.

"Well guess now we are good to talk business, there she is you have seen her, safe and sound" Freddy turned to Thom.

"Excuse me!" She begged and left the room.

Thomson had been their great stakeholder of the firm for long and he developed interest on the front desk lady. Their meeting went on for more than half an hour and as he left he made a stop at the front desk and wished the lady a good afternoon. Freddy shock his head and left Thom doing his thing. Freddy jumped into Frank's office and told him how Thom behaved upon his mysterious lady, Frank took it easy for a moment but jealousy grew inside him. Kayla did not show up at her mother's office that day. The mother decided to call school and found out Kayla had remedial to attend to. On the other hand Frank felt the difference in time and no sign of Kayla quickly he called Kayla's mother to find out if Kayla was coming. He took advantage of Kayla's absence and the mother told Mr Sinclair that Kayla was not going to pass over that day due to her remedial classes and hanged up. She did not wait to hear Frank's response hence Frank felt the pressure the lady had. Later that day Pam went to pick the kids from school and took them back and Kayla's mother received a message from her account that the loan had matured and money was in the account. She went home with a happy mood. Passed by the liquor store and bought her favorite bottle of wine and went home took Kayla from Pam's were she had to share the good news with Pam and the day ended admirably.

The following day was granted half-day for all staff so as to prepare for next week's event so the day went on to being as short and things went very swiftly before they could all disperse. Kayla's mom left right after half past noon. Most of the staff had already left and most of the management team remained in the boardroom they had a last minute catch up but released the rest of staff off.

Kayla's mother went to do her hair, she helped Pam collect her laundry from the dry cleaner and went for some shopping that she would have done on Saturday instead handled them a day before due to half-day off from work. She was in a good mood from a day a go. After running her errands she passed by the school collected her team and off they headed home. Pam joined her loved ones at home after her usual c.o.b time. They had a perfect gathering at Kayla's mother the nana had grilled some chicken breasts and chicken wings in the oven and they baked some pasta and fried some potatoes like a party theme, Kayla's mother was in a very good frame of mind that evening, she changed the usual dish to everyone's best dish, blended some juice for the kids and popped up a bottle for Pam and herself. The kids were on video games at the living room while Pam and Kayla's mother had their wines at the kitchen counter preparing supper. George rang Pam to ask if they had plans to go out that night but she turned down and so George promised to pass by later that day. Pam and her friend kept having their girls chat and planned to go visit the site for her new shop.

On the other hand the Sinclair had their evening spent in the boardroom of their office they revised their speech, report and statistics for press release for the actual day of the event. All seemed exhausted and left office at 08past midday went to start their weekend as how they normally do except for this time around Shirley was missing out.

"I think we are good to go, everything is on set, what do you think?" Freddy asked his brother.

"Yeah man, we are good, just have to pass through the speech once more, may be Sunday evening" said Frank to his brother.

"So I have been wanting to ask you since" Freddy looked at his brother on a serious face.

"Aagh! You have really waited longer than I expected" Frank interrupted his brother "she's out of my life bro, I can't deal with unsecured woman" he faced Freddy.

"So talk to her, tell her how you feel and end it well" Freddy insisted "are you enjoying the back and forth calls she's making?"

"You can do that for me right?" Frank joked

"You such a jerk!" Freddy punched Frank on the shoulder "you better end this well or else it's going to ruin your reputation to everyone much less to your mysterious lady, I hope you don't want that to happen?" Freddy sounded sarcastic.

"What lady?" Frank pretended to be unaware.

"The one you're yet to officiate, by the way her loan is out they must be somewhere celebrating with the baby daddy.

"What loan?" Frank surprisingly queried.

"She requested a loan from the office a month a go" Freddy added "speaking of which, do you know anything about her baby daddy?" sipped his drink.

"No I don't. What's there to know about?" asked Frank.

"None" Freddy added, "is there something you have not told me yet?" he looked at Frank.

"I think I like her. I don't know. I haven't heard a chance to talk to her anything about herself and I kinda feel like I am loosing it when I'm around her. It's totally not me. I don't know bro but ain't rushing" Frank spoke honestly.

"I know. I see the crazy things you're doing lately it's never you at all" "just take it easy bro, take it easy" Freddy pat Frank on the shoulder.

Freddy and Frank were the best twins one could wish for. They were very honest to each other, friendly and yet quarreled most of the times but their bond was unbreakable. They had the night to themselves talked much about their love lives and went to another joint to join their friends.

Whereas at the coolest condos down the lane they finished their supper, kids went to Kayla's bedroom and let their mothers and uncle George use the living room. They had their wines and George had his usual drink throughout, they laughed, loved and lived their night to the fullest.

After a while Kayla's mother put the kids to bed whereas George and Pam took advantage of one another in the living room. They started kissing George's hand was underneath

Pam's dress and the other hand kept caressing her all over, you could tell from Pam's look that she was feeling good. George's boner protruded. Kayla's mother had to chase them away for she couldn't allow another sex game in her couch especially when the kids were asleep in the next room and so they left to their condo. She locked her doors and went to sleep.

The next day Kayla and the kids woke up earlier and excited for their trip to Sinclair(s). Her mother was still on bed fast asleep. The nana helped the kids get ready and by 10 am Fadhil was at the doorstep when Kayla got the door she saw Fadhil, greeted him and knew time was up for their cruse. She told Fadhil to wait as she went to wake her mom up. Kayla's mother got up cleansed and went to meet Fadhil and released the kids. Afterwards she got back to sleep.

Kayla and the twins reached at Sinclair's mansion after half an hour. The mansion was located at the very most expensive real estates. It was along a private beach, very huge house and other houses within the compound, a swimming pool and a pool house, there were basketball court and a huge garden. From far you could see tiny houses that looked like dogs / rabbit house. The estate was amazingly beautiful inside out. MaryJohn received Kayla and her friends and told them Frank was not up yet but they should feel at home and enjoy. There was a carousel, jumping castle, swings and slides at the garden, kids' bikes were parked at the garden. The house was parked with kids play and toys. Kayla was shocked to see all that and the twins were excited as well. They were happy to be there.

"Wow! When do we start playing with all this?" Kayla asked looking amazingly astonished and excited.

"Anytime you are ready, you can change from the pool house and when you need anything there will be a lady or two outside ask them for anything." MaryJo added, "there is the counter for you to get any drink you want the barbecue will be set out soon for you guys to start eating so enjoy and feel at home." Said MaryJo and left

Kayla and the twins ran to the pool house to change.

At quarter to two Frank came to join the kids out he could barely see them as they were scattered. Everyone enjoyed her own favorite play. He went for a drink at the counter and sat beside the pool and made some phone calls. After a while Kayla felt hungry and was heading to the barbecue buffet for something to eat and happened to see Frank at the poolside. She was excited and ran over hugged Frank and thanked him for everything.

"I love everything, I don't know if I can finish playing with all these" Kayla talked energetically.

"I am happy you like it. What were you playing?" asked Frank.

"I was at the carousel, but I feel hungry, I want to eat something and will go for a swim later" she said excitedly.

"Good. Go ahead get something you like. Where are your friends?" Frank asked Kayla.

"Jayda! Jayden!" Kayla shouted

Good enough they heard and went over to greet uncle Frank.

After a while Freddy joined the group he got his massive hugs and kisses from Kayla and the twins and Brenda came along later on so the group was big except for the kids whom were not at one place, they were scattered all over at different places. They really had a blast you could tell from their laughs and talks. Frank asked one of the maids to switch some music on and the party eventually began.

"We have never done this before" Frank said to Brenda, "these kids are really enjoying and they seem happy, I like it."

"Oh yeah? I guess you like more than that bro?" Freddy hinted.

"What do you mean babe?" Brenda asked looking at Freddy flirtatiously.

Brenda was a very beautiful and smart girl but also very close to Shirley hence Frank was not comfortable to speak about what was going on inside his mind in front of Brenda assuming that it will all end at Shirley and Freddy realized the discomfort of Frank and changed the subject.

On the other side of the world Kayla's mother and Pam went to check on the soon to be shop and they had some serious business talk on how she was going to renovate the place and what not. At sunset they headed to a nice restaurant and began sipping their favorite red wine and had some more talking. Pam was curious to know how the kids were doing but her friend was sure that they were fine. Pam wanted Kayla's mother to call Frank but she didn't.

At the Sinclair's - Freddy asked Frank if he had talked to any of the kids' mothers and insisted to call them. Frank was excited about the idea and stood up went close to where the kids were playing while making the phone call.

Kayla's mom's phone rang as they were in the middle of their talks and laughs over their drinking at a restaurant. The number did not display and she was unaware of the caller. Pam looked at her like.

"mmhmhh girl, it's them" Pam looked at Kayla's mother in a funny face "you have to answer may be something is wrong" she added.

Her: "hello"

Frank: "hi it's Frank Sinclair, is this Kayla's mother?" in his deep gentlemanly voice

Her: "yes it is, Mr Sinclair, how are the kids?" in her sweet voice

Frank: "please call me Frank, the kids are fine. They are in deep plays right now." Maintained his deep voice "I just called to let you know they are in good hands enjoying as we speak, unless you want to speak to any of them?"

Her: "I am happy to hear that, no need let them play and thank you so much" she smiled at Pam as she talked.

Frank: "don't mention I am happy to have them around, never done this before but it still going on well" he added "so what made you not be around?"

Her: "I heard some errands to run with my friend, I think you met her before" her heart was pounding as she spoke.

Frank: "oh yes Pam, I did meet her, please pass my regards, her twins are adorable" he still sounded so gentle.

Her: "thanks, I will do." Smiled at Pam and made funny face.

Silence prevailed for a second. "Am I going to see you later as I drop the kids back?" Frank begged.

"I think so." She replied in her seductive voice.

"Thank you! Just in case you are done with your errands before the kids, I will be glad to pick you up or Fadhil can get you and join the kids" Frank tried to convince her one more time.

Her: "thank you Mr ummm Frank but it wont be necessary we will head home after we are done here." in her sweet tone.

Frank: "well thank you very much, see you later." He hopped for better than that but remained patient.

Frank felt good and went back to where Freddy was he seemed satisfied and kept his drink on.

After the sunset kids had to go shower and were told no more swimming. They lit born fire outside, Kayla and her friends joined after they had changed. They seemed exhausted but very happy. They had their supper outside in a cool evening. On the other hand Pam kept insisting that Frank was in love with her friend. She went further advising her friend not to resist Frank's move. On the other side her friend was not sure what to do next or how to behave when Frank's around for she already was convinced hence felt uncomfortable. They drove back home refreshed and kept drinking at the living room waiting for the kids to be back.

A while later they had a sound of engine next to their house and she went to open the door only to find Frank's car parked and the kids came out looking exhausted and sleepy it was beyond their usual sleeping hours.

"Hey guys did you enjoy? And did you thank uncle Frank?" she asked the kids as they were heading in but none responded than a smile from their faces and went straight to their rooms.

"Hello there, the kids are awesome and they were asleep on our way here" Frank sounded very fatherly.

"Oh they can't even speak, come on in" she let Frank in confidently.

"Heey Frank, how are you?" said Pam in her deep voice

"Pam, I'm good thanks. Your kids are amazing. I surely will have them next time" as Frank got comfortable on a couch.

"We are having Boschendal merlot red dry, should you wish to join us" she held the bottle up showing it to Frank from the kitchen and smiled.

"Yes please, I would love to" Frank was impressed. "So ladies how was your day?" as he got comfortable.

"Good, easy, you took the trouble from us, what do expect?" Pam smiled as she responded.

"I'm glad I did" said Frank in his deep voice "but was no trouble to me at all"

"Where is Freddy?" asked Pam and before she got the response "I like him" and she sipped her wine.

"Oh yeah? He's actually at home with friends. We were all around with the kids. I will pass the compliments" Frank turned and smiled at his mystery lady.

Her: "Pam is always the charmed one just get used to her" she told Frank in her lower seducing tone. "*AllICareIsYouBabyGirl*" Frank spoke in his mind and sipped his wine then added "Pam, I'm officially inviting you to our office event" he looked at his mystery lady

"Oh thank you very much. I'm not going to miss it" excitedly replied "furthermore the preparations have been eating up my girlfriend. I feel I need to experience it"

"I know preparations are always tense especially the last days but we are good now, right?" Frank gazed at her.

"Yes we are good." As she shied away from Frank's direct eye contact.

"How's your school? I'm told you had a paper to submit." Frank squinted his eyes at her.

"Yes almost done, I'm just waiting for results" she still sounded shy.

"Yeah girl, get that paper fresh and we celebrate" Pam added "so Frank you were told she had a paper to submit? What else have you been told?" as she smiled at Frank.

"Pam, I'm told she had evening classes for three years, she's a single mother of a beautiful smart girl whom I have met, her circle is small just her friend who happens to live the next door with her twins, she has been at Sinc for more than three years right?" Frank kept going "I'm not told much" he smiled at them.

"Mmmh they must have told you a lot. Do they tell you about everyone else in Sinc?" Pam sounded sarcastic and smiled at Frank.

"hahaha absolutely not!" Frank laughed out loud and sipped his drink "I just happened to need more details about her and not the rest" he looked straight at his mystery woman.

Her: "okay, enough Pam with your questions, we are not in court." She looked at both of them.

"No further questions your Honor" Pam teased

"But honestly speaking, I'm daily drawn slowly into you guys, your families, your lifestyle and Kayla has a lot to do with this but in a good way and you (pointed at Kayla's mom) may be wondering the CEO is at your couch at this time of the night and sipping your wine trying to make conversations with you guys but I'm simply enjoying this, especially you (looked at Kayla's mother) I just enjoy being around you" Frank confessed in his gentlemanly voice.

"Oh la la! You sound like you're proposing, and she may say yes!" Pam kept teasing Frank.

"You're right Pam, I feel the same, call it a proposition." Frank kept his confession going. He looked at Kayla's mom as he spoke

"On behalf of my friend consider your proposition granted!" Pam kept teasing and raised her glass "to our new friend!" she looked at Kayla's mother as she raised her glass for everyone to toast and so they did.

Her: "guys enough with this, um Frank thanks for everything you are already a friend from the moment you started entertaining Kayla in a special way so yeah thanks." She hardly looked at Frank's eyes.

"Great!" Frank sounded excited in his deep voice "so let's celebrate then" he quickly stood up and went for the door.

"Yeah right, that's what I'm talking about" Pam sounded excited wanted to see what Frank was up to.

Frank went out and came in with more bottles of red wine and his usual whiskey bottle.

"Yeees let's do this" in Pam's loud voice.

Her: "shh Pam kids are asleep" she shook her head went into her room to pee and came back.

Frank and Pam were having a chat at the kitchen counter while Frank was opening the bottle for the ladies.

Frank: "how are the kids?" he asked

Her: "I didn't check on them let me go check" she went back to check on the kids in the other room.

"She's very shy but I like her" Frank told Pam.

"It's very hard to digest, your boss blending with your girlfriend at your place for the first time and things are going like a flash of light in a good way - so I understand her, give her sometime." Pam made funny faces to Frank as she spoke and they head to the couch.

"You're right, where's George?" Frank squinted at Pam.

"Wow! They even told you about George? Did they tell you about Robert as well?" Pam teased Frank.

"hahaha very funny, no! They didn't, they must have skipped that" Frank teased right back.

"George is on his way coming, that's what he keeps saying for the last hour" Pam rolled eyes.

Frank: "I see" he sipped his drink.

She came back and found her guests comfortable at the couch with some more drinks in their glasses.

"Here's yours (raised a glass at her) I poured some for you" Frank squinted at her.

Her: "Thank you" she went over for the glass from Frank and you could tell the tension from her sweaty hands and heart pulses on her neck. Frank felt all that and wanted to ease her but he didn't know how so he managed to make an eye contact whenever he talked to her.

They kept talked, gave more info to Frank about their lives, their interests and one thing she didn't talk about was Kayla's dad and luckily Frank didn't ask either so they were good. Freddy checked on his brother and he was surprised to hear Frank was still at Kayla's. Almost quarter to midnight, she had enough of the drinks and started feeling sleepy but Pam was on top of the stories and Frank kept enjoying every bit of it eventually he realized his lady was silent for a while and looked like she needed a sleep and so he decided to leave and call it a day. Pam was not ready for him to go since they were both at the same state of mind.

"I think we have had enough, ladies thank you for this wonderful night, you have made my night, Pam you're an amazing friend, thank you. We should do this next time" Frank smiled at his lady as he walked to the door.

Her: "thank you for everything Mr Sinclair" in her sweet little voice.

"Please call me Frank!" Frank smiled back at her.

"Ooh Frank you're leaving?" Pam jumped off the couch and went to the door.

Her: "haven't you heard what he said lately?" wondered at Pam "he's leaving, time to sleep" she added.

"Aw you were awesome today, thank you and good night" Pam waved at Frank.

And there was that moment Frank couldn't figure out how it was going to happen. He hugged Pam and went for his mystery lady opened his arms as if he was requesting a hug and finally she went for it and hugged Frank for more than a second. Frank wanted to go for a kiss but she seemed not to be set for it but he could smell her cologne from her neck if not hair and he felt the nipples out of her baby pink silky pajama top and for more seconds than the seconds on Pam's hug it felt good and so he went out and the ladies locked their doors.

Her: "what is happening?" she sounded uncertain.

"What is happening - is that your boss, yes damn boss likes you!!" Pam said it like she meant it

Her: "he's has a girlfriend, a cute lady named Shirley, why would he come for me?" she sounded shocked with all that had happened "and I think he was about to kiss me" she added

"Shut up! Stay put for the movie has just begun!!" Pam responded in her loud voice.

"Pam I don't think if he's real, we are like two different people, two different worlds, and perhaps you have forgotten he's Frank Sinclair. Honey! I'm not his type. He may use me and leave." She sounded worried

Pam said,:- "Baby girl, let's go sleep. No one is using anyone or leaving anyone, I feel some real thing here! "Frank Sinclair! I will motherf***** put you behind bars incase you mess with my friend!" said Pam in her loud voice as they went to bed.

Frank felt so overwhelmed on his way back home he couldn't stop playing in his mind the move he had on his lady over and over again. He went home took a shower thinking on her, thinking on how the night turned out to be and for once he smiled and said to himself "Frank Sinclair – You're on!"

The next day was a Sunday and more relaxed day for everyone. Kayla, and her mother together with the twins went to church and left aunt Pam fast asleep after church they passed by a bakery store and picked some muffins and pastries for breakfast and went home. Aunt Pam had already woken up and prepared some toast bread and omelets for everyone, they sat at the kitchen counter and had their breakfast while they recited on their day at the Sinclair. They had a lot to unfold on how grand the house was to the meals they had and did not leave a thing out. After the breakfast Pam and Kayla's mom did the dishes as the kids went to play. Afterwards Pam left and went to her condo and Kayla's mother took a nap until sunset.

Pam's nana stays with Pam she's a full time nana and hence in the afternoon she would prepare some meal for the kids.

At the Sinclairs they had their late breakfast at the garden but this time around it was just the three of them. Brenda, Freddy and Frank. They had a little chat and discussed business for a while and later Frank went upstairs in his private office to reminisce about the last day. He then decided to call her but unfortunately there was no response as she was napping. He felt like he needed to know how they had been since he left them at midnight and so he called Pam.

"Pam Anderson" Pam answered the call.

Frank: "hello Pam it's me Frank" in his deep voice.

Pam: "Hey Frank, how you doing?" in her loud voice

Frank: "I'm great thanks, I tried reaching your friend with no answer, are you guys alright?" he sounded concerned.

Pam: "yes we are, thanks. I just got home and she took a nap I think her phone's silence. I will let her know you called or try call her later if it's okay with you"

Frank: "yes, no worries. I was just checking on you guys I'm glad you're all fine. I will call her later. Thanks"

Pam: "hey Frank, thanks for everything and um about yesterday I hope you meant what you said." She rolled her eyes.

Frank: "I did! I meant every single word I said. Why are you asking?" he queried.

Pam: "because my friend, doesn't take all that seriously as she mentioned to me that you are seeing someone and she wouldn't want to be part of anything between you two and as you know she's your employee. She needs her job more than anything." In her advocacy tone she added, "well she didn't send me to tell you either of these but that's what friends are for and please for the record we didn't discuss this"

Frank: "well Pam, thanks for telling me all these but just so you know I meant and I'm serious on everything I said and as a matter of fact my relationship with Shirley ended few weeks ago and with your friend I wouldn't want to drug her into anything serious so fast hence I'm willing to take it nice and slow" he added "I will not mention a thing about this and I'm pleased to see she has the best friend anyone would have wished for"

Pam: "thanks for understanding, I will let her know you called, till then be good bye"

Frank: "yeah right, thanks and will call her later. Thank you very much my regards to the kids, bye"

They hanged up and both had some minutes to think through the conversation they had. Pamela was very protective of her friend and she wanted nothing than to see her friend happy and safe. So she decided she was going to tell her everything what she discussed with Frank and not hide a thing from her. She went at her friend's place straight to the bedroom where she was fast asleep.

"Hey girl wake up, wake up!" said Pam in her loud voice.

Her: "damn Pam your voice, when will it ever be low" in her sweet little tone.

"Frank called you, you didn't answer so he called me" said Pam.

Her: "what? I didn't hear" as she unlocked her phone.

"Yeah right. He was calling to check on us and I had to shake-him-up a bit." Pam rolled her eyes and made herself comfortable

Her: "what? What do you mean shake-him-up" she looked worried and surprised "No no you didn't!"

"Yes I did. I had to ask him if he meant what he said yesterday and told him how you don't take him serious because you know him and his relationship with Shirley and that you were not going to be in between all that and you love your job more than anything because that's all you have got and you wouldn't be ready to destroy it." Pam kept explained.

Her: "you said all these to him? Oh my God!" sounded worried and jumped off the bed went to pee and cleansed up.

"Damn right I did!, because I knew you could not tell him half the things I said or perhaps when it's too late" responded Pam on a serious tone.

Her: "what did he say?"

"He was calm and very explanatory of himself assuring me he meant everything he said" Pam added "but again I asked him not to tell you what I told him but later I thought it's best for you to know the gear I have pulled so that you take it from there."

Her: "wow! You guys." She went speechless for some minutes "I don't know what to do, I think I will be uncomfortable at work which I can't work at my best when I'm uncomfortable and yet I can't date my boss it's the worst situation ever!"

"I feel you girl. I told him you love your work and you need it more than anything, he seemed understanding and said he was hoping to take it as slow as you could ever handle and he doesn't want to force you into anything" Pam added "you know what? He hasn't asked you out yet, that was off record talk between me and him so ignore everything girl live your life and most importantly be at your natural best!" she smiled wide.

Her: "what's all that smile?" she looked at Pam.

"I can't wait to see you dating again, it's been a while and I began to worry you may have lost interest in a man's shaft!" Pam made a funny face.

Her: "Pam! I swear I may have forgotten all that shit" she added.

"Now I may offer you some revamp classes" "catch me every time I get laid" Pam teased.

They both laughed out loud and laid on bed facing up the ceiling.

Her: "but seriously Pam, I don't know what I will do or say." She exhaled.

"You don't need to do shit nor say anything girl for he ain't going to ask you a thing except a date." Pam continued, "Damn! Life can change in a blink of an eye"

They went on with their kinky chat and later George came.

"Where's my wife?" shouted George in his loud base voice as he walked towards the bedroom. "Where's my wife?"

"George stop shouting!" Pam shouted back.

"Hello, can I come in?" George knocked on the door and went in without waiting for reply.

Her: "hey G, how you doing?" she greeted George.

"I'm good sweet mama, do you happen to know where my wife is?" George teased as he got close to Pam and started tickling her.

"Your wife is in the next door, getting laid by your best friend" Pam teased back laughing loud "G please stop!"

"How have you been ladies, I have missed you badly" said George to the ladies.

"Start by explaining where you have been for the past twenty four hours…" Pam urged.

"Can we all go out please? Some where for sunset? I missed my squad." George begged caressing Pam's neck, playing with her tits all the way to her thighs kissing back n forth.

"Hahahaa not until you fuck me babes" Pam lowered her tone.

"Oh yeah that's my girl. Come hear!" George grabbed Pam's waist and rolled her dress off over her head and snatched off her bra and went on top of her, started kissing her all the way to her ears, her lips, her neck, her both tits playing with her nipples and went all over down to her abs and gave her a breathtaking head, he sucked her thick labia and Pam's cry went from lower to louder moving her body sideways enjoying every moment of it as she massaged George's hairy head. Kayla's mom had left the room immediately when George started unclothing Pam.

After they had their copulation both came out to join the crew looking and smelling as fresh as never before. I guess they took some shower.

"So guys where should we head for the sunset?" G sounded loud active and excited.

"Let's go at the park dad" Jayda's voice little and sweet

"No park's boring let's go out and have some music and games on dad" Jayden sounded like his naughty dad

"Anywhere just out of here uncle G" said Kayla.

"Great I'm not going to tell you where until we reach so get dressed up and let's Rambo" said G, loud and deep.

Pam and her friend were in the room changing the sheets.

Her: "I can't get enough of your love affairs" as she changed her bed sheets.

"I can't get enough of it either, he's just the best. I bet you and Frank will be the same." said Pam.

"Mom we are going out with uncle G, is it okay?" Kayla sounded polite.

Her: "Yes, ask uncle G if I can join"

"Me too, if I can crash your outing" Pam chuckled. A minute later Kayla got to her mother and shouted, "he said he would love that".

After a while, longer than expected they were ready and left in a black suv. George took his squad to a new Seaport restaurant – Levee Food Co a beautiful place with riverfront setting, delicious dishes from pizza, and steaks to seafood. They ordered food for everyone; wine as usual for sundowners and George requested a bottle of Limeburners and some ice, juice for the kids while they focused on the beautiful view.

Her: "twosome fresh" she teased Pam & G.

"Aagh believe you me penetrating her on her best friend's bed is the best feeling ever" G smiled as he cuddled Pam.

"Oh yeah? Soon she will be on my bed" Pam looked at G

"By who?" G asked anxiously.

Her: "don't listen to her, she's insane" she begged

"By Frank Sinclair" said Pam out loud and clear

"the Frank Sinclair? Your boss? He's making a move?" asked G in a shocked way.

"Yeah right, moves are damn fast, we had him at her place yesterday until midnight, he asked about you" Pam continued "you should have seen how he looked at her when he tried to make an impression so sweet and sincere"

"Oh yeah, but Frank's a good guy and good businessman as well. I don't know much about the rest but we did one deal together and man he's good." G added, "Wow so I guess our lady is officially off the bench" "I should really get you ready for Sinclair at least tonight my love" he teased.

Her: "you're crazy, I don't need to be ready for anyone we are simply friends and I wouldn't want to jump so fast" she said in her politeness.

"Yeah that's my girl let along not until me and you are done with our unfinished business" G winkled at her.

"G darling if you didn't have her then just count it a loss for you aint going to have her now or later" Pam made her funny face.

Pam and G had always liked the company of Kayla's mother and to no surprise they were ready since before to have a threesome although she was reluctant about it. Couple of minutes later their order was ready, kids got back to the table and they shared pizza and different seafood platters. After a long talk and of course delicious meal Kayla and her team went to enjoy the rest of the outer space and left their parents drinking, chatting and laughing. A phone in her purse vibrated and to her surprise it was Frank.

Her: "speaking of the devil" as she answered her phone "hello" in her sweet little voice.

Frank: "hello it's Frank, how are you?" in his deep voice.

Her: "I'm good thanks, how have you been?"

Frank: "not at my very best" in his deep voice.

Her: "what's wrong?" rolled her eyes.

Frank: "I have been wanting to hear from you since morning, I called but there was no reply, Pam told me you had a nap." A little silence "I miss you" he paused

Her: "yes I had a little nap and she told me about your call, we have been good, managed to go to church, thank you for missing me" she rolled her eyes.

Frank: "how's Kayla and the twins?" he asked politely

Her: "They're fine at a corner playing with other kids, she can't stop telling her story about your place, our kids have had a story to tell which hasn't ended as of now, thank you for entertaining them so well" she said in her serious polite tone.

Frank: "oh please don't mention. I didn't expect it to lit either but I'm glad they enjoyed" "where are you? I can hear some airwaves through the phone" he urged sounded jealous.

Her: "out and about with Pam and George and the kids, it's a new beach restaurant…"

Frank: "ooh I know the place, good place to be. So Pam is with George and who are you with?" just like that he asked.

Her: "I'm with both of them and the kids" she replied.

Frank: "can I join you? Or at least see you and Kayla for some minutes?" sounded polite than never before.

Her: "yeah, sure no problem" making some funny faces.

Frank: "great will be there soon" sounded excited.

Her: "Frank's coming over" she looked straight to G and Pam.

G: "I'm okay, the dude is dying for you we can't stop him" he kept cuddling Pam and caressing her neck.

Pam: "ooh yes let him come and give my girl some love" smiled back.

In not less than an hour Frank was approaching their direction from far holding Kayla and Jayda on his hands.

"Mmh someone's someone has arrived" G looked from the direction where Frank was coming.

"Oh Jayda can't have enough of Frank, she keeps saying mom uncle Frank is the best uncle ever" Pam responded looking from the direction where Frank was.

They all stood when Frank got to their table.

Hey guys, thanks for letting me crash your party," Frank joked.

"No worries man, how you doing?" G patted Frank on the shoulder.

"George long time no see, hope you're good bro" Frank went over to Pam hugged her and kissed on her left cheek he then hugged his lady for more than a second and kissed her on both cheeks "you smell nice" he whispered on her ear.

Her: "thanks, so do you" as she tried to ease on his arms.

Pam was smiling like a baby.

"How's SincE doing?" G eased him with a talk.

"Very well so far so good, about to end another year, you must have received an invitation to the event" Frank said trying to ease around his lady friend.

A waiter came over their table and Frank joined George's whisky that was on the table, they went on with their stories. Kayla and the twins kept coming to their parents' table to check on them. The kids sipped their juices and left to play. As George and Frank talked about business for a while, Pam was chatting with her friend re: lady's stuff. During their business talk George went for Pam's shoulder caressed her neck gently as he kept his conversation going. Whereas Frank couldn't bit that up since he was supposed to take it slow with his lady friend hence managed to hold her left hand while caressing her gently through out and squinted his eyes every time he looked at her. She on the other hand was extremely calm and quiet most of the time listening to Pam, George and Frank talking. Frank whispered on her ear every time and later she excused herself and went to the ladies' room with Pam.

Her: "I can't take this Pam, I'm so nervous and uncomfortable" she exclaimed.

"You are letting yourself be so, take it easy girl, he's trying to get used to you and so should you" Pam rolled her eyes and both went back to their table.

"Is everything ok?" Frank asked as he kept caressing his lady's arm.

Her: "yeah everything's fine" in her little voice "guys we shouldn't over stay, kids have school tomorrow and we have to work tomorrow – it's going to be a busy day tomorrow, how do you see if we leave soon?" she begged the rest of the crew as they all looked at her attentively.

"Yeah girl, busy day for you tomorrow huh?" Pam teased.

"We get you sweet mama we're leaving soon" G looked at her and smiled.

"Can I take you home?" Frank begged.

Her: "won't that be trouble for you?" she asked in her lower toned voice.

Frank: "Not at all" he looked straight into her eyes and squinted his eyes "guys should I save you the trouble and take my lady at home and the kids if it's okay?" he asked Pam & George.

"Your lady huh? I like that, please save my baby some trouble take her home but will have the kids with us" Pam insisted looking at her friend in a funny face and sipped her drink.

Frank excused himself from the table and went over the counter cleared the bill and came back and went on with the stories.

"I'm told someone is interested with my sweet mama" George teased Frank.

"Yes I'm" Frank squinted his eyes to her mystery lady and caressed her back.

Her: "guys, stop talking about me, I feel uncomfortable" she begged in her sweet little voice.

George asked for the bill and the waiter informed him it was cleared by Frank.

"Guys we can leave I'm told Frank sorted the bill, thanks man, take my sweet mama at home" G woke up hugged Kayla's mother and patted Frank on his shoulder "hey kiddos it's time to go get yourself ready" shouted at the kids.

"Pam thanks for everything" "can we go? Should we go with the kids?" asked Frank.

"No no no we will come with the kids, guys just go ahead. Take care of my friend" said Pam.

Frank left with his lady to his car. Pam and George came with the kids with their car.

"Here's for you" as Frank opened the car door he couldn't help to smell her cologne.

Her: "thanks" sounded sweet calm and collective.

"Do you want to make a stop anywhere or it's straight home?" asked Frank as he started the engine of his black range rover.

Her: "straight home please" she said in her low toned voice.

He drove her lady back home, it was almost fifteen minutes drive, on their way he extended his hand towards her wanting to touch hers as well, they had pretty much long hand cuddles and he caressed her hand throughout the entire drive back home. They arrived sooner than Pam & George. He parked next to her condo went to open the door for her and they went straight in.

Her: "thank you for the ride, do you need anything?" she whispered.

"No thanks, I'm good. I guess the kids are not here yet?" said Frank in his deep voice.

Her: "not yet but will be back soon" she replied and went for a glass of water at the kitchen leaving Frank beside the kitchen counter.

"*YouShouldLeaveFrank*" Frank thought in his mind and said "I think I should go we do have a long day tomorrow" he went over the door, she followed him back and at the door he turned around hugged and kissed her gently on both cheeks and whispered in her ear "thanks for everything" he couldn't stop feeling her heart beat.

Her: "thank you and goodnight" her voice sounded like she needed more and almost turned red.

Frank couldn't handle the chemistry he felt and so he opened the door and left. She locked and leaned back at the door wondering what was actually happening inside her body. The feeling was abnormal!

The kids came back, Kayla wanted to go home and not sleep over at her friends. She found her mother on bed but awake, she took shower and joined her on bed. They had a little chat before they could fall sleep. Kayla wanted to know if her mother was okay and why she left earlier but her mother told her she had some work related issues she had to discuss with Frank and so she understood. They said grace and slept.

SincEnterprises was busy. Lots of cars were at the parking lot. A huge long red carpet ran from the entrance door to the lobby of the office building. Beautiful and well-dressed ushers stood at the entrance and inside you could spot a pair of ushers in their uniforms at every corner of the building. Just beside the entrance there was a huge poster with the name SincEnterprises set as a background for snaps and videos. The office was immaculate and decorated with natural plants and magnificent décor on the walls and every corner, at the corridor of the first floor top offices was a podium and a projector screen was set just beside behind the podium and on the ground floor was the large area for guests to stand watch and listen. There were cocktail stools scattered. Guests kept coming in the building. They were received by ushers at the entrance and taken at the reception were there were other ushers who offered visitors' book for signing, a big glass bowl was placed on the reception desk for business cards and yet fliers about the schedule of the event were on the front desk as well. Low music was heard from the ceiling, the lights and the reflection of the lights on the ground tiles were amazing. Everything was flawless and spotless, the employees were well dressed. Half an hour before the commencement of the scheduled event Frank and

Freddy pulled over in their black range rover they dressed in dark blue suits and they looked smart and perfect. They were in deed the best looking twins one could wish for. They smiled and greeted everyone they met and came across with. Guests were scattered everywhere from the meeting rooms to the lobby having group discussions and group chats as they waited for the event to begin. Waiters and waitresses were moving around to offer light drinks and snacks to the guests. Frank seemed to look happy. Freddy went to meet with the event organizer to find out if everything was in order while Frank got busy with his clients, guests and the rest. On the other hand the front desk lady of the firm was all around the place looking stunningly beautiful and smart ensuring ushers were on point. Ten minutes to time the guest of honor arrived Frank went to receive him at the entrance door and led him to signing of the book and went upstairs to his office. The master of ceremony announced that it was about time; most of the guests and visitors gathered at the lobby. In Frank's office the guest of honor was offered a drink and was being briefed on the schedule of the event. Frank sipped some of his usual whiskey from his drinks' tray in his office to gain momentum.

Ten, nine, eight, seven, six, five, four, three, two, one -second to action - Frank and the guest of honor walked through and stood next to the podium facing the guests from up, the mc began the event and thanked everyone for showing up and invited the CEO of the firm for further acknowledgement. Frank went behind the podium, he looked confidently smart and magnificent, he thanked the guest of honor, stakeholders, invited guests and everyone else for their presence, he started with a joke and the whole room went laughing, introduced about the firm, the reason of their gathering, explained on the firm's prospective and he later concluded by thanking all the employees for their massive efforts and welcomed the guest of honor. Frank had been in the business for more than twenty years and you could tell from his public speech and persona that he was the right CEO for such best firm in town. The guest of honor went close to the podium and expressed gratitude for everyone and mostly the firm for their massive contribution in national development. He concurred with the designated plans of the firm and offered support and cooperation from his office. His speech was shorter than Frank's but very drift. Afterwards the master of ceremony announced that there was going to be after party at the ballroom of the best hotel in the next block and everyone was invited. Frank and the guest of honor went downstairs to mingle and chitchat with other guests as they were preparing to walk out to the next block for after party session. George and Pam were in the building with the rest of invitees and all looked amazingly smart. She was up and down ensuring everyone was moving towards the other venue. She hadn't come across Frank that day and was hoping not to.

After a while guests started leaving the building and headed to the ballroom of the hotel in the next block others left with their cars while others walked down the street. Ushers were on point in the ballroom-receiving guests and leading them to their seats, waiters and waitresses were also on duty doing their best.

At SincEnterprises Frank climbed the stairs to his office pulled off his coat and made a phone call at the reception asking to see her lady only to miss her. He then rang Wanitha and requested the same. Wanitha ran up and down looking for the lady. After some last minutes before he could give up and leave the office to join his guests at the hotel there was a knock on the door and she came in.

Her: "Good afternoon Mr Sinclair, did you want to see me?" she sounded very professional as she went inside Frank's office.

"Please, call me Frank" Frank said as he moved closer to where she was standing, he opened his arms and hugged his lady.

Her: "I don't think if this is right" she said in her sweet little voice trapped by Frank's arms all over her body for more than a minute.

"It doesn't have to be right" Frank whispered on her ear and kissed her hair "I am happy to see you" still held her tight.

Her: "me too" her sweet little tone came out from the trapped arms. She was feeling somewhat good and yet very shy.

For once Frank kept holding her tight and kissing her hair left and right, massaged her back whispered words in her ears which none of us could hear. At last he said out loud:

"I've missed you" Frank stopped hugging his lady and squinted straight into her "how was my speech?" he asked.

Her: "perfect. You were stunning." She comfortably replied, "You're supposed to join the guests at the ballroom" she sounded professional one more time.

"Yes mam, I couldn't have gone further without seeing you. Stay closer and don't go far from my sight" squinted his eyes to her "ok?" Frank ordered.

Her: "yes Mr Sinclair" she replied with a gentle smile and headed for the door before she could leave.

"Excuse me um." trying to remember something. She stopped walking and looked back at him attentively and realized what was happening;

Her: "Victoria" she said in a professional tone "it's a high time for you to get used to my name" she sounded serious.

"Yes Victoria, I'm sorry" Frank begged as he walked towards her, he held Victoria's hands and said "I'm sorry my dear Victoria" in his deep voice.

"It's okay" Victoria sounded sweet and calm as she tried to exit from Frank's hands. Frank pulled her back and kept Victoria's hair well and smart and whispered on her left ear. "Thanks for understanding, please stay within my reach" romantically said Frank as he held Victoria's both cheeks.

A door opened very fast and it was Freddy almost banged into Victoria as he opened the door.

"Heeey Vicky" Freddy faced Frank "you are supposed to have left the building". Said Freddy.

"Excuse Me," said Vicky loud and clear as she wanted to exit the room but Frank couldn't let her off his hands. "Give me a second Freddy" Frank begged his brother for privacy as he got hold of Victoria's hand. "Okay wind up and get down" said Freddy as he left the room.

"Is there a problem?" asked Frank, as he looked straight into Vicky's eyes.

"No, I wanted to give you both some room" Vicky explained in her sweet little voice "please let me go and let you join the rest" she begged him.

"Okay, don't forget what I told you" Frank looked at Vicky as he let her walk out. Frank left his office a minute later, Freddy was next to Frank's office and said to Frank; "Fadhil will drive you please go straight." Frank left with Fadhil and got to the ballroom in few minutes. Victoria went later after Frank had left. She ensured things at the front desk were kept well for tomorrow's business day and parked up her stuff in her beetle and walked down to the hotel.

"Hey Vicky, hold up" shouted Frank, as he walked fast towards Victoria. "I thought I was the only one left behind" Victoria sounded honest as they walked towards the hotel.

"I just want you to be a bit far ahead of Frank, like advising him more than letting him decide for himself" said Freddy, in a serious tone as they walked down the street "I'm not saying he can't make the best decisions on his own but I want to know I can count on you to do so, especially now that you're more closer to him than any other person or at least any other woman." Freddy looked at Victoria as they both kept walking.

"I don't know what to say" said Vicky in her little voice looking straight in front as they walked.

"Say that you understand me and you will do your best. See I have a responsibility to take care of my brother but I want to cooperate with one other person whom might be closer to his life other than me, if you know what I mean." Freddy tapped Vicky on the shoulder and added, "and don't give me that crap that there's nothing you can do or there's nothing going on while we both know there is and for as long as he's happy I'm all supportive" he let her pass first through the door of the hotel and came behind her and they kept headed to the ballroom. "Thanks for your understanding, later" he patted Vicky's shoulder and went to join his friends at a corner table.

She passed slowly and quietly at the side of the room looking at the ushers' positions and conducts and went to greet Pam and George and the rest of other people on that table.

"Hey girl, you look good and smell multiple cologne as well" Pam teased Vicky.

"I know, I have a lot to tell you, will catch up later" Vicky held George's shoulder "hey G, you good?" in her sweet little voice.

"Oh yes sweet mama, I'm all good, nice event as well" G smiled at her.

"Thanks" she replied in low toned voice, greeted the rest of the people and left the table.

She went close to Frank's table and went to stand not far from his sight as how Frank ordered. Frank saw his lady and smiled at her as he sipped his drink and kept conversations going on. After meals and other lots of entertaining shows the guest of honor left the ballroom and was escorted by Frank. On his way back to the ballroom Frank stopped at George & Pam's table, he thanked them for coming and sat with them for a while made some jokes and chat. He later asked them not to live soon for they had another after party to attend. George was impressed and couldn't agree more and so was Pam. Frank went back to his seat and on his way he raised his hand tried to call his lady over, Vicky realized and went closer bent next to him and he whispered to her ear: "You are the most beautiful woman in the room" and squinted at her. She nodded and left. Freddy had been following up his brother's moves after catching him getting touchy with Vicky so he couldn't stop prying on him for the rest of the day. The party went on well and guests had really good time, eventually people started leaving one at a time. Vicky went over and sat next to Pam.

"What are you having girl?" Pam asked her friend.

"I don't need anything just my shower and my bed" Vicky sounded tired with the event.

"Here have some water" Pam passed a glass of water to Vicky "drink this, have you eaten anything today?" she sounded concerned.

"Not at all and believe you me I don't feel like having anything" Victoria replied in a lazy tone.

"Should we leave?" asked Pam.

"I wish" Vicky rolled her eyes.

"What do you mean you wish? – of course you should be able to coz things are over unless there's something else" Pam added, "and what was that you wanted to talk about?" she whispered close to her friend.

"Long story girl, I'll tell you when we are just the two of us" she whispered back to Pam.

"Then let's go home, myself I have heard enough. Guess what, Frank just told us to remain back for there's more after party than this. But I guess I can't, let's just leave with your car, I'm guessing George is still around" claimed Pam.

"Yeah you're right let me see Patrick and Marian then we leave". Responded Vicky.

She went at the table that Patrick and Marian were and sat next to them and told them that she was about to leave and they were fine about it.

Meanwhile Pam asked George if she could leave with Victoria since G was not ready to leave and he was okay with that. All that time Freddy at his corner table kept prying while maintaining his conversation with his guests. Victoria went back at Pam and told her that she was good to go anytime. Frank looked around only to realize his lady was out of his sight. He stood up and looked around and saw Vicky next to Pam. He went closer in between the ladies and whispered "guys please don't leave we are about to go some other place." Pam told Frank that Vicky and her were tired and Frank was not buying their story. After some minutes Pam and her friend had to leave. George and Frank escorted them out.

"You're very silent, are you alright?" Frank whispered at Victoria as they walked out of the hotel.

"I think I'm tired nothing is wrong" Vicky kept it short and while walking out.

"Guys you can go back, we can take it from here" Pam looked at George and Frank.

"Why are you chasing us away? We want to escort you guys unless there is someone else who will take it from here?" G sounded upset.

"No there's none, thanks G" Vicky responded politely.

"How are you guys going, can I get Fadhil to drop you at home than having the trouble of driving?" asked Frank, holding onto Victoria's hand.

"I left my car at the office" replied Victoria, trying to escape the offer.

"No problem, let Fadhil get you home and he will come for your car". Frank ordered. He took his phone from his pocket and called Fadhil to bring his car at the office and Fadhil did so right away.

They all stood at park lot of the office building waiting for Fadhil to bring the car.

"Are you sure you want to leave? Or can I pass by at your place once I'm done with the guests?" Frank begged smoothly as he got closer to Vicky.

"I'm fine, you don't have to do so, just go straight home and get some rest. You had a long day and tomorrow is another day which needs you" Vicky tried to put some sense in him just like what Freddy had asked earlier.

"No I'm passing by once I'm done with these people unless you don't open for me" Frank whispered at Vicky's ear as he got really closer to her and laid his other hand on her back "where's Kayla sleeping tonight?" Frank asked.

"At Pam's, please don't do that" Vicky begged Frank to stop caressing her waist from her back.

Meanwhile Pam & George had an argument at low tone regarding leaving him at the party and going home all over a sudden. Pam was insisting it was for the best interest of Vicky and George couldn't understand.

Fadhil pulled over, Frank opened the door for his lady and got her to buckle up and George did the same to Pam and the car left.

"I still don't get her, we were all good for a longer night out but changed her mind abruptly. Said G as they walked back to the hotel.

"I think it has to do with Victoria. She seems out of mood" said Frank.

"Anyway let's go back man, these ladies are fragile." Said George.

They walked back to the hotel and pounded their night.

On the other side Pam and his friend got home safe. Fadhil left Frank's car at Victoria's and went fetch the beetle. Vicky and Pam got inside and the stories began;

"Thank God I'm home" Victoria exhaled putting off her clothes and jumped in the shower.

"So what's up girl? It better be something for I have quarreled with G for you and he didn't understand me at all" Pam yelled across the bathroom as Vicky was showering.

"Please come get some shower" Vicky begged.

Pam went over the bathroom and jumped in the shower while her friend was done and brushing her teeth. They both finished showering and got to bed. Vicky started telling Pam how her day went to when Freddy caught her at Frank's office to Freddy's conversation.

"I feel like he's going to use me and leave me shamelessly and I can't handle that. I think I should talk to him Pam" Vicky sounded worried.

"Come on, I don't think if that's how he will be" Pam eased her friend.

"And the way he touches me it's as if we are officially dating the way he controls me it's as if I'm his" Vicky added, "the feeling is super good but what if it's not the way I'm thinking. May be that's how he is and I'm here busy turned on every moment he gets close to me and puts his hands on me. This is ridiculous! Moreover have you realized I can't be with him publicly? What will people think of me or say behind my back?" she talked with her hands in a serious tone.

"You're worrying too much, do you think he doesn't know all that? He knows, he has to create a good image for you to the society just calm down let's see his move if he wont upgrade himself by having a lengthy discussion with you that's where you come in" Pam responded back.

"Well let's wait and see" said Vicky, in her sweet little voice. They laid on bed and fell asleep.

Fadhil came back with the beetle parked outside and rang the doorbell to drop the keys of the beetle but no one responded. He switched the range rover and drove off with the keys to the beetle. When he got back to the hotel he had to let Frank know that he couldn't return the keys for there was no one answering the door bell. Frank got worried for a bit and called Pam to no reply and called Victoria to no reply as well. He went over close to George and told him. For once they felt something weird was going on and they both went out. George drove his car with Frank up to the apartment and when they reached they rang the door and there was no response. George went at Pam's apartment and took Victoria's house keys from where Pam keeps them. They went over at Victoria's place opened the door and went straight in to Victoria's bedroom.

"They are in here fast asleep" G shouted to Frank as he got closer to the room none of the ladies was awake both were deep asleep and they couldn't hear a thing. George went over at the side of the bed close to Pam and tried to wake her up.

"Babes, babes" G moved Pam. Frank was starring at his sleeping beauty while Pam was being awakened.

"What's up" in Pam's unusual low toned voice, she moved her body and looked up "what are you guys doing here?"

"You both slept dead not answering our calls we had to come check on you" explained G as he caressed Pam's hair.

They were both half naked in their silky mini nightdresses. Pam woke up and took the men to the living room.

"Come on let's go this way" as she moved with the guys outside Vicky's room and switched off the lights.

"Is everything ok Pam?" Frank asked.

"Yes everything is fine, she had a long day" "remember I asked her if she ate anything and said that she didn't and was not in the mood for anything?" Pam turned to George "we got home took shower, had a little discussion and we fell asleep" she explained looking severely hot in her silky nightdress with nothing underneath.

"The driver came to return the keys for her car, he rang the bell but there was no response and so he came to tell us that's why we decided to come" Frank explained heading to the kitchen for some water.

"I swear for once I thought you two had your mission and I was so upset the whole way, thank God!" G went over to Pam and hugged and massaged Pam's ass gently as he kissed her.

"Ok guys get some room let me see if I can get to kiss my lady before I leave" Frank went inside Vicky's tiny bedroom for the first time, he sat on bed beside Vicky and massaged her hair and caressed her cheek, neck all the way to her shoulders and she woke up only to find Frank beside her.

"Hey, sorry if I woke you up" said Frank in his romantic deep voice.

"What are you doing here?" she looked aside to see if there was any other person in the room "you had to come?" in her sweet voice "where's Pam?"

"At the living room with George" Frank kept massaging Vicky's cheeks and neck and shoulder "it's a long story us or perhaps me being here on your bed without your permission but will explain later"

"No it's okay" she woke up went to the washroom cleansed and brushed up and came back sat on bed.

Vicky's nightdress was no different from Pam's only the colors but very short silky and very see through. Frank saw almost everything through the dress from her round raunchy boobs to her supple nipples her round soft ass and thick thighs he almost had a clear view of how she looked underneath that piece of silky dress.

She got back on bed and tried to cover up with a duvet but it looked like too late. He got more comfortable on her and her on him.

"You didn't have to come all the way here" said Vicky in her soft voice.

"I'm glad I did." Frank caressed Vicky's right hand and kissed her hair "can we go out sometime tomorrow after work just the two of us?" he begged in his deep voice.

"Are you asking me out for a date?" Vicky questioned rolled her eyes but Frank couldn't see her from his direction.

"I guess, I'm" Frank held Vicky gently and added "it's time for you and I to know more about one another" he added, "I will pick you up at 7pm sharp" in his commanding tone.

"I didn't say yes though" said Vicky with a smile.

"I know when it's a yes" Frank replied confidently as he kissed and caressing her gently.

Vicky instantly developed goose bumps. Frank felt them on her hand, neck and shoulder.

Frank: "easy baby girl" as he massaged her

She couldn't help it as the goose bumps kept emerging and Frank felt her arousal and didn't stop caressing her.

In the living room George and Pam were doing what they do most rumpy pumpy except this time it was at the kitchen counter. Pam's whine voice was head from the corridor to where Frank & Victoria were.

"Oh my goodness, that's my friend" said Vicky, shamefacedness at Frank.

"Calm down, they are having their moment, let's have ours as well" Frank slipped deeper into the duvet and laid his head on Vicky's shapely gamy boobs.

For a second Victoria's heart was pumping faster than usual she thought on what to do next and started massaging Frank's bold head gently. A phone rang out of his trouser pocket he took his phone from his trouser and laid it on his left ear while laying on his lady's chest.

Frank: "what's up man?" in his deep voice.

Freddy: "where are you?" said Freddy in his serious tone.

Frank: "at Vicky" he answered deep and slower.

"You left without saying, are you coming back?" Freddy was angry with his brother.

Frank: "I don't know Freddy, let me see" he turned to Victoria and said "babes should I go back?" squinted his eyes on her.

"Yes you should" Victoria kept caressing the bold skinned head.

"I'm coming back but wont stay for long and the after party people can go ahead without me, I'm all good" Frank replied to his brother.

"Alright" said Freddy, and hanged up but felt really disappointed on Frank.

Frank kept laid on Victoria's flirtatious boobs for few more minutes enjoying his head massage.

"Thank you" Frank posed.

"For what?" Vicky asked in her little voice.

"For what you're doing to me" he replied romantically.

"You're welcome" she added, "now Freddy is officially going to hate me?" sounded concerned.

"Why would he hate you?" Frank asked holding Victoria's waist on one hand and on the other caressing her thigh.

"On our way to the ballroom he asked me to help him take care of you and if possible advice you the right things" Vicky added softly massaging Frank's boldness "I think after catching us at your office that time he had to talk to me"

"What?" Frank sounded surprised "you guys should take it easy. I'm okay and can make way better decisions than all of you put together" as he made himself comfortable around Vicky.

"Oh yeah, then start proving, get up and get yourself going, you can't leave your guests at your own party and go elsewhere unless it's a matter of life or death" Vicky softly convinced Frank to let her off.

"I swear I don't feel like letting you go, I'm super cool on here" Frank confessed as he kissed Vicky's left and right boobs and rose out of the duvet "so what else did Freddy tell you?" he asked in his deep voice.

"Nothing just gave me some induction on how to deal with you in your both best interest, and I feel he was right" she sounded loud as she stepped out of the bed.

Frank was tacking his shirt and dressing while Victoria had to freshen up in the washroom. Frank went through the washroom to take a leak while Victoria was on the other side drying her face.

"I wonder what Pam & George are doing right now" Vicky said politely and smiled at Frank.

"Sat butt naked" replied Frank, as he got closer to Vicky and hugged her tight.

"You need to get going" she posed softly.

"I'm trying baby girl" Frank whispered in Vicky's ear.

"Try harder, let's go" as she held Frank's hand and both walked out of the room.

"Should we bounce?" G sounded like nothing happened.

"Yeah man, we bounce" Frank replied as he held his lady from her back and kissed her neck "I'll miss you" he whispered.

"I'll miss you more" Vicky replied.

"I'm going to call you every after ten minutes stay close to your phone" Frank ordered as usual and kissed her forehead.

Victoria: "I will" in her little sweet tone.

Pam was on top of George busy texting on the phone. George had to let her off and walked out with Frank jumped into his black SUV and both left.

The ladies kept their night going. They opened a new bottle of red wine and went kinky with stories.

"He asked me out, tomorrow at 7pm after work" Vicky sipped her wine as she sat on a couch close to Pam.

"Oh yeah?" Pam widened her eyes as she talked "that's better, see I told you he was going to man-up" she continued "now whatchu gonna wear girl?" sounded excited.

Victoria: "I have no idea"

Pam: "I guess you gat no idea of where you will go either"

Victoria: "ooh yeah"

Meanwhile Frank had been calling his lady several times to check on her. Pam and Victoria decided to get back on bed and call it a day. The night for the boys went on till 3am. Frank and Freddy got back home at 4 in the morning.

The next day was a bit lazy for everyone at SincEnterprises, people got in late and some didn't show up at all. Cleaners were all over the place tiding up the office and putting everything in order. Victoria got in late as well but more energetic than the rest. Frank and Freddy didn't show up neither did the management as well. Pam took Kayla and the twins to school at their normal hours since in Pam's world it was business as usual. Victoria got an ample time to sneak out of the office and went to several boutiques near their building to search for something to wear for her date night with Frank. She managed to pick two dresses since she wasn't sure of which one to rock on.

Few minutes to close of business she had to leave early pick the kids from school and went home. The kids went at Pam's house and she laid her clothes on bed and took shower during all that time she kept having flashes of Frank in her mind wondering what was going to happen smiling at herself and running her best playlist at low volume. She blow dried and styled her hair, this time her natural hair was free from braids and looked thick, healthy and shining. It was 6pm in the evening her phone rang;

Frank: "hello beautiful, how you doing?" in his gentlemanly voice.

"I'm good thanks, how are you?" Vicky responded sweetly.

"I miss you" Frank paused "and I can't wait to see you in the next hour."

"Me too, although I don't know where we are going" Victoria queried seductively in her little voice.

"Leave that to me, somewhere comfortable just for the two of us" he responded.

Victoria: "it's okay, see you then"

"Alright" said Frank and hanged up the phone.

She went to the kitchen opened a bottle of red wine and poured some in a glass and went for her phone and rang Pam.

Victoria: "hello"

"OMG girl was about to call you, just thought of you like right now" Pam's loud voice

Victoria: "still at work?"

"Yeah, I'm caught up with a huge doc to review and needs to be submitted today, I'm afraid I won't be able to see you before you leave for your date." Said Pam.

"It's okay, Frank just called a while ago, I asked him where we are going but he couldn't say, I feel butterflies" she sat on her bed as she talked to Pam.

"Go for a glass of wine and start making up yourself I told you he gat this! Everything is under control baby" Pam added, "What are you doing right now?"

"I'm having some wine, but I wish you could see me and help choose a dress" Vicky sounded disappointed.

"I can't girl, sorry, just be you and rock your taste" Pam encouraged her friend as she smiled over the phone "I will check on you later today, enjoy and remember to take it easy and be yourself" and she hanged up the phone.

Victoria went on sipping her wine while trying her dresses. She later decided on one of the two dresses she picked from a store down town and that was above the knee laced baby pink flare dress with mini hands sleeve, She accessorized with black 5inch heels and a black oval fur clutch. Victoria seldom wore make up but she perfected her eyebrows, eyelashes and on her lips with a nude shining matte, she came out amazingly naturally beautiful than ever.

A few minutes later she heard a doorbell and went for the door, it was Frank.

"You look stunning!" Frank was amazed to see Victoria transformed into a sexy beauty.

"Thanks and you look perfect as usual" said Vicky in her sweet little voice as she paved way for Frank to get inside.

"Is anybody home?" Frank asked as he looked around.

"Yes, that's me" she smiled and shied away.

"Come here" Frank pulled Vicky closer to him and hugged her gently for a minute and whispered, "I can't have enough of you" and looked at her with his squinted eyes.

"We should go" she escaped from a major kiss holding Frank's hand as they walked out.

"We have a bit of a long drive before we sit for dinner" Frank walked out with Victoria sounded excited. He went on the passenger side and opened the door for his lady, Victoria jumped into a metallic colored Ford Ranger and he closed the door. Frank went over to the driver seat and as he was starting the engine Victoria asked Frank if they could pull over at Pam's door to check on the kids before they left. Without hesitating Frank agreed and Victoria jumped out of the car and Frank followed her as they went inside Pam's house.

"Mom! You look beautiful" Kayla exclaimed

"Thanks honey, where's Jayden?" Vicky asked as she walked towards a room next to the living room

Kayla: "hey Frank"

Frank: "hey baby girl, you good?" he went over and hugged Kayla

Kayla: "you guys are going out?" she asked in her little voice.

"Yes I'm taking your mother out for a date" Frank smiled at Kayla.

"Really? That's awesome! So you two are dating?" Kayla sounded excited.

"Yes if she ends up loving the night, I think we will be dating and if that's okay with you" Frank smiled as he explained.

"I'm okay, very much okay. Wow! That's cool" Kayla turned at Jayda "Mom's going on a date".

Jayda was busy playing on her pad and smiled at Frank.

Frank: "you good little J?"

Jayda: "I'm good"

"Great, take care of yourselves and be good girls" and he went over the kitchen counter where the nana was busy setting dinner for the kids. Victoria came out of a door and walked towards Frank smiling beautifully.

Frank: "is everything ok?" he asked pampering Vicky's waist from her back.

Victoria: "yeah, Jayden is on his video game" She smiled at him and waved goodbye to the kids and the nana, and they left. Pam's house and Victoria's are all designed the same except Pam's has one more room compared to Vicky's.

On their way Frank leaned closer to Victoria and held her hand while he drove. The sun had set and dark began emerging. They talked over their drive and Frank couldn't get enough of Vicky's hand, he told her about his family, how and where they were raised and he told her about his mother who lived in USA and his late dad. Frank managed to present himself and not left a thing out. Victoria most of the time was listening at Frank looking at his eyes and looking in front as Frank kept driving. And when Frank felt like he had said enough about himself he asked Victoria about her story. She did not have a lot to say a part from what Frank already knew. She also mentioned about Kayla's dad whom was upcountry living his life as a farmer and livestock keeper. She was slower in speaking and on her low tone voice. Frank asked about the limits on the relationship Vicky had with George and Pam. She didn't know what Frank meant but she said it out and clear that Pam & her were good and extremely close friends to an extent of sleeping together but she neither had threesome nor slept with George. Frank was pleased to hear that and ran a smile over his face as he kept driving. He later asked Victoria if George was good for Pam and she candidly responded to Frank that Pam's happiness was all what mattered and Pam seemed happy. An hour and a half they entered into a village with lots of eucalyptus trees and forest atmosphere the roads were narrow covered on leaves that shade off the trees. It was windy but wonderful environment fresh minty smell from the trees kept blowing towards their direction. She asked if that was where she thought it was and Frank nodded smiled and kept cuddling her hand. A few minutes later Frank drove in front of a black gate and pressed on a remote the gate opened it was a long driveway to the front of the building. It looked like an isolated house with no one in it but lights were on and he drove over to the front, parked the car and got out went on the other side to open for his lady, she got out looked and wondered her eyes around.

"Here we are" Frank paused, hugged Vicky tightly, kissed her hair and whispered on her ear "welcome baby girl"

"Thank you" Vicky whispered back as she eased around Frank's hands

"Let's go in" Frank held her hand as they walked in. The house was big and spacious with huge glass doors and windows, wooden floor and very illuminating ceiling. She couldn't help staring at each and every thing from top to bottom, left to right, Frank kept holding her hand and walked her pass the living room to the dining room and emerged on the other side of the house at a terrace through a big glass French door. There was a table for two with candles and glasses and beside the table there was a set up buffet table everything was immaculate, out of the terrace you could see a blue pool within the compound and farthest one's sight there was a riverbank. The place was quiet and beautiful at that time of the day you could hear birds chirp from far. He pulled a chair for his lady and she sat down yet staring at everything. Frank was silent and let his lady take her time getting amused with what she was seeing. He took a sit opposite her and started looking right at her with his squinted eyes. A man came over greeted the lady and Mr Sinclair and asked if they were ready to dine and it turned out they were both starving. They had shucked oysters, farmed salmon, and lamb steak for their choice. In between their romantic time Frank paid attention to every little detail on Vicky as she maintained her persona like shying away, avoiding eye contact with Frank and smiling as she talked. Victoria had one of the best red wines she never had in her entire lifetime along her meals, she let Frank refill the glass as it almost ran dry. Frank had sparkling water alongside his meal and once he was done he went for his brandy on ice. They had their dinner nice and slow and once they were done they moved closer to the blue pool on a couch near fireplace and kept their stories going. She developed goose bumps and Frank felt her skin and went for his coat and covered her up. Pam called to check on her friend and found out everything was super fine. Frank made a phone call as well to let Freddy know that he was at the river house and everything was fine. He later cuddled Vicky on the couch across the pool with fire on and birds chirping from far and began his smooth gentle talk as he lay against Vicky's chest feeling her heart pulse. Frank was way more comfortable with Victoria than Vicky with him. She had some more wine at the couch and she got lighter and easier on Frank. She could caress Frank's bold head and smell him from his head to his neck. Frank loved that. He asked Vicky why she smelled him and she replied softly that he smelled really good. Frank couldn't be happier likewise Victoria couldn't be freer and ease on him at that moment. They both had quality time to discover one another. Frank passed un noticed inspection on his lady looking attentively over her body and he discovered a dot close her left thumb and a scar on her right hand and asked her about them and it turned out to be some birth marks. He went further caressing Vicky's thighs and her flare dress was short enough to reveal her thick light skinned thighs and Frank loved everything he saw. Surprisingly Victoria was way comfortable on everything Frank was doing they kept their Q&As going as they kept cuddling one another. She felt the need to use the restroom and Frank had to escort her through and once she was done Frank gave her a tour on the house. The house was insanely beautiful; wooden floor except the stairs were shinning on marbles up to the upper floor in the rooms. The house had a built-in gym and a theatre, there was a huge library and office room in one and underneath the stairs there was a cellar with plenty of wines and precious family best drinks (in Frank's voice). He took her around the cellar and she kept starring at the drinks and wines showcased. He then led her out on the other side of the house where there were cottage houses indeed the estate was amazing the neighborhood seemed like it didn't exist and very quiet. You could only hear sounds of birds, ducks and moving grass. All this time Frank held Vicky's hand if not he put his hand over Vicky's shoulder if not he held Vicky around her waist from behind. Victoria loved the place. After the tour they landed at Frank's room. You could tell it was Frank's by the set up; there were huge glass walls, his favorite color grey and white on bed. They sat on the floor on a large white fur carpet in front of the bed and Frank passed her some of his family pictures and he started showing Vicky his family, family friends and family events' photos. She liked everything she saw. They later slept on the fur and did some more talking. You could see from Frank's eyes he was about to make a big move on Vicky and she realized that and decided to dissolve the situation by waking up from the fur pulled Frank up and forced him to go out. Victoria did not want to indulge Frank further than she already had. She was an old fashioned lady whom seemed comfortable with her ancient love vibes. She was concerned about time and asked Frank if they could start heading back. Frank kept having his drink on while talking to Victoria he couldn't agreed more yet wanted to have more time with her. He pulled her at the counter and popped another bottle for her. Indeed Victoria had stamina on red wines she knew how much to consume before she could took some water and kept going. At half a bottle she got very ease and tipsy but when she took a certain amount of water she diluted and kept going just like that. Frank led her through the stairs back to his room out the terrace she stood on the terrace and faced a beautiful night view of mother nature the view was amazing, very tall trees and a riverbank. The smell of minty wind across was far way different from the city.

"Oh My God! Look at this beautiful view" Vicky exclaimed as she kept feeling the breeze.

"I know" said Frank as he got closer and grabbed Vicky from the back both looking at the same direction.

"It's so beautiful" she commented yet in her little sweet voice "thanks for having me here and thanks for everything, I still don't believe if all this is true" said Vicky softly.

"What is?" Frank asked yet grabbed Vicky's waist and leaned on her as they faced outside enjoying the view.

"Everything, from you meeting Kayla to being part of our lives and now me standing on your terrace enjoying this beautiful view, I still don't know what to say or even what to think of" Vicky kept talking while Frank was busy kissing her neck and grabbing her waist from behind it was the best feeling in her as much as it was in Frank.

Frank went inside and put the glasses that they were holding and came out the terrace and kept cuddling his lady as they enjoyed their view, the breeze and the stars, far from where they stood they could see the river and it was breathtaking.

"I really like you Victoria" Frank whispered holding her out and gently "as a matter of fact I'm falling for you" he added, "I don't want you to say anything just sit back and enjoy"

Victoria smiled and kept being submissive to what Frank was doing that time. It's like she was on for it but couldn't tell. Frank turned her around and held her right and left cheek and went closer to her and just like what was been waited for so long was that deep romantic tongue kiss. He did it like never before, deep kissed her pale pink lips while holding her cheeks, he later went for her soft bubbly ass and grabbed them tight while kissing her. It was the best feeling ever for both of them. She was very responsive on all Frank was doing and made him go further kissing her lips back and forth while massaging, grabbing, holding, and caressing her body through the laced flare dress. Frank turned red and so was Victoria. After minutes of kissing and holding her they went for their drinks. Victoria was silent for a while and Frank went closer to her and held her in front squinted his eyes

Frank: "I promise, you will never regret this day" he kissed her right back and kept on kissing her.

He could feel the pulse from Victoria's flirtatious boobs he even grew bigger underneath his trouser even Victoria felt the stiffness and enlargement of Frank's knob. That was so epic for both of them he turned her back to the great view while adjusting himself, still that couldn't help for he was on zero distance with Victoria hence she still felt his erected dick on her ass. Victoria couldn't care less; she as well was running wet underneath her panties. They hold onto each other for sometime trying to ease their hormones and after a while she whispered to Frank if they could leave since tomorrow was a working day.

"About that, we need to discuss how we are going to handle your work situation" Frank raised it out loud and clear in his deep voice (I guess things were cool underneath)

"What do you mean?" asked Vicky softly bearing in mind her wetness underneath her panties doesn't dry that easily.

"I want you to step up, you have been in the firm for so long doing the same thing which I'm sure it might be boring, you need an appraisal or else I want you be a boss of your own life, run your business and forget be employed for I can't help it when I need you is when the firm needs you as well" Frank added, "I just don't see myself able to deal with that, so please think about it and come with the way forward." "You don't need to say anything about it right now, take your time and make the best decision considering our relationship as well" he sounded like business talk.

Victoria nodded back and they went down the stairs and got out of the house. Frank put his lady to her car seat fastened her belt, kissed her one more time and went over to his seat started off the engine and drove back home.

Victoria was all the time smiling looking at Frank and looking on the road it was almost midnight and Frank had to concentrate on the road due to the darkness outside and the narrow road which was slippery and full of leaves.

They took lesser time to reach back than when they were going. Frank pulled over her entrance and before he could jump out.

"Can I ask you something?" Frank begged.

"What is it?" asked Vicky as she held and caressed Frank's arm.

"Don't go to the office tomorrow for any reason you can get, I need to have you for lunch" and there! Frank sounded like he was begging for more than lunch.

"I'll try" she kissed his hand.

"Please do. I will call you when I wake up and will take it from there" Frank jumped off the car and went to open for Victoria, they both got out of the car and went inside Vicky's house.

"Do you need something" Vicky asked softly

"As a matter of fact I do" replied Frank and went for a deep tongue kiss while massaging Vicky's bubbly ass.

"I meant something else other than this" Vicky teased while kissing Frank holding him around his neck.

"Yes please some other thing I'm dying for" Frank teased back.

"Well Mr Sinclair sit back don't say a word" said Vicky as she squat down closer to Frank; unzipped him and took it all in her wide wild mouth.

Despite of her old fashioned lifestyle Victoria could give the best blowjob ever. And to Frank's surprise he went hard-on until about to explode Victoria stopped zipped him and rose up begged him to drive home safely and hoping to see him tomorrow. That was insane!! Frank was hell surprised and for a moment he went starring at Victoria as she unzipped her dress in front of Frank and remained with her white matching lingerie.

Victoria: "Mr Sinclair is there a problem?" she acted "the meeting is adjourned until tomorrow" as she went over her kitchen for a glass of water.

Frank followed her still amused by her character and yet hopped to get her on bed that night.

Victoria: "some water for you Sir?" still acted.

Frank: "no, some you for me please" still looked excited.

Victoria: "Mr Sinclair our meeting is suspended until tomorrow" she held Frank's hand and walked him close to the door.

Frank couldn't stop starring at Vicky's amazing body and couldn't stop touching her soft ass, squinted his eyes and kissed her one more time and went out. She locked her doors picked her dress from the floor and went to her room, jumped into shower smelling Frank's essence all over her body was the best feeling ever.

Frank drove back thinking on the show Victoria pulled for him. He smiled all the way as he drove back home and said to himself: "Game's on Frank!"

The next day was a normal day to almost everyone except the new couple in town. Children were dropped to school by aunty Pam, the nana came in for her daily work at Victoria's, Freddy went to the office more energetic since he didn't show up to work yesterday, the rest of the employees and people out on streets were business as usual.

Frank and Victoria were still on bed both at their zones. Few minutes past noon she woke up and realized that she did not make any excuse as to why she wouldn't show up to work, she grabbed her phone and made a phone call to Patrick telling him that she had food poison and won't be able to show up that day. Freddy heard the news regarding Victoria's absenteeism and decided to call her. He almost believed on her made-up story because he knew she and Frank were at the river house last night so probably she might have ate something bad.

"Hello this' Victoria" Vicky answered to a general office line.

"Hello Vicky it's Freddy, I'm sorry to hear that you're unwell" Freddy sounded serious "I understand you were with Frank at the river house last night, was it something you ate or drunk may be?" he still sounded serious.

"Hello Freddy, thanks for calling, I can't really talk right now" Vicky hanged up.

Freddy was shocked on Vicky's brief response and decided to drive at her place. After few minutes a doorbell was heard and the nana got the door and Freddy greeted the nana introduced himself and asked to speak with Victoria. The nana went over to Victoria's room and came after a minute. She invited Freddy to some fresh blended pineapple juice and Freddy went for it waiting for Victoria at the living room. After couple of minutes she came out in a set of bronze silky nightdress and a silky rob on top looking freshened up and smelling good. He saw Vicky approaching Freddy stood and hugged her.

"Hey you, how are you feeling?" Freddy looked concerned.

"I'm fine, thanks" Vicky replied and sat on the couch.

"I decided to come, you didn't give me much of a choice, you didn't say much over the phone" Freddy continued "was it something you ate or drunk last night? Coz Frank told me you were with him over the night at the house" he kept being concerned.

"No Freddy that's not the case, I mean I was with him yes but the food poison thing was just a made-up story because I couldn't make it to the office in the morning" there she said like it was.

"What? You serious? Frank put you into this?" shit I thought was real thing and got worried perhaps some meal went bad or one thing or the other" Freddy smiled at her "so you're pretty fine huh?"

"Nothing went bad everything was good, your house is beautiful the place is nice I liked everything and I had a good time just that I think I had too much to drink and overslept" she smiled back at Freddy as she explained.

"You people should learn to alert me when you're about to cheat the world because Frank just sent an email at three in the morning to our potential client excusing himself from attending the meeting due to unforeseen business trip he had to encounter" Freddy shook his head and stood up "I have to go, you take care lest you don't end up falling for a real food poison" he stood hugged Victoria walked out and left. Before she could jump back on bed her phone rang and it was Frank from waking up but sill on bed. They had their romantic phone convo and she told him how Freddy fell easily for her made-up story and Frank couldn't care less, he asked Vicky if they could have their late lunch some place for he was starving and wished to see her at the same time. A little later, Frank picked Victoria from her place and drove to a wonderful restaurant down town. He couldn't stop smiling and when Vicky questioned the reason to his frequent smiles; he replied he's in love with an award-winning actress. Frank was all over Victoria he never stopped kissing her, caressing her hands and massaging her body. Victoria on the other hand began to get comfortable with Frank and she reciprocated her love by leaning and caressing on Frank's muscular arm, she got more comfortable playing with Frank's bold head, smelling him around the neck. They had their rump steak while catching up on yesterday terrific stunts and Victoria felt shy when Frank imitated him on her yesterday's scene. At the end of the day he took her at his place the mansion that Kayla and her friends were invited a week ago. Frank gave her a pleasing tour Victoria met MaryJo for the first time and she thanked MJ for attending the kids very well. After the tour Victoria begged Frank if they could stay outside at the poolside, you could tell from her preference how she missed exterior home environment her place had no compound rather confined condos with small parking space. She really enjoyed staying outside a lot. Frank opened another one of their best red wines for his lady and he got his brandy on ice drink for himself and stayed out cuddling and kissing. It was by no surprise Frank was the happiest man alive at that moment and Victoria was the most shy away yet very horny and loving lady in the compound. They kept their romantic stunts going on for a while she asked him all what she reserved for him and he did the same. Frank also brought the matters he discussed with her yesterday regarding her work situation and it turned out Victoria had put some thought to it and came with her final decision which was to quit working at SincEnterprises and start her own venture. Frank was pleased to hear that and offered his maximum support. They stayed out for the sunset and after a while Frank asked Victoria to join him for a swim she was shy to agree but seemed like she could go for it. He stood up put off his polo shirt and his jogger and jumped to the pool. Victoria was busy smiling and sipping her wine wondering if she was to swim what was she going to wear later after the swim. Frank swam to the other end of the pool and begged his lady to come for him. Victoria denied and kept other stories on. After some minutes he got out of the pool and grabbed a rob which was brought by a maid and went sat with his lady he kissed her deeply and gently while penetrating his hand under her flare dress just to feel if she had panties on and so she did, he felt her boobs by his other hand and felt her swollen round nipples - it was magic! Victoria didn't resist any of that in fact she was responding well by her sexy postures.

"Come with me" Frank demanded, extended his hand to Victoria.

Victoria got up and gave her hand to Frank just at her surprise she was pushed into the pool she couldn't help and started laughing.

Victoria: "you could ask me?" laughing out loud and floating on water.

Frank: "I did" he unrobed and jumped in as well.

Frank got close to his lady he went behind her and unzipped her dress removed it from her body she was way responsive. He turned her around and kissed her passionately, Victoria was flexible and sexy, and she swam away from Frank for him to chase her. Frank got her in a second on the other side of the pool on her back he snatched off her push up bra hooks and there for once her coquettish boobs were free from its bra cups he massaged her round supple nipples while kissing her neck, she felt really needy and didn't resist a thing. Frank kept playing with the nipples and the luscious boobs kissing Victoria back and forth, the tenderness from Frank's hand job was pleasing Victoria whereas Frank was filled with lust of ripping off her matching bikini. He kept playing with her, touching and feeling every part of her wet body he penetrated his hand to her labia gently strummed her clitoris with one hand and the other was on her left nipple. At some point his rod was rigidly upright in his Calvin Klein briefs, she could feel him on her ass. He float her on water facing up and kept kissing her right and left pink nipples she on the other could not do much than responding with a pleasant cry. Frank got out of the pool he went for a rob and took another for Victoria he then went for Victoria asked her to come out of the pool in his commanding deep voice. Victoria swam and got out of the pool and Frank covered her gently with the rob. He then held Victoria's left hand and walked with her up to his room. Victoria was silent throughout. In his room he ripped off the rob from Victoria's wet body carried her and laid her on his giant bed that was the most gigantic bed Victoria has ever seen but she couldn't think more of what was in the room than what she was undergoing with Frank. He laid on top of her, Victoria untied Franks rob from his waist and removed it softly while she received numerous kisses around her neck. Frank got free from his rob and began sucking Vicky's nipples, holding her hands above her head, he went to her belly burton and got more deep to her abdomen Victoria had a pleasure cry throughout and it kept Frank proceeding with giving her a head she louden her cry it was one of a kind, her soft little voice yet in a cry manner stimulated Frank, he sucked the hell out of her cunt and his tongue played with her pink clit she cried out loud and swung her body slowly left and right. Frank did not stop he kept going with his tongue around Vicky's clit, labia and in her vulva, eventually Vicky turned pale blue and goose bumps appeared all over her body as Frank kept kissing her and giving her head, she turned red and the cry increased gradually her hands were held up her head by Frank, she had no control of her body, Frank dominated her inside out, after few minutes of sucking and leaking Vicky's jelly roll, Vicky lost her cry and there she was "I'm coming baby" she cried out loud, splash of water ran out of her. Frank stopped and rose looked straight into Vicky's eyes, damn! She was reed! Her lips pink and looked so wasted and sexy. She discharged back-to-back waters and Frank couldn't be more happy to see his lady in that state of mind he kissed her as the waters came out and she hold his erected penis and inserted in her ready made vagina. He gently fucked her tight wet pussy she couldn't stop shaking as Frank penetrated into her in slower motion and the pace kept increasing, Frank did what he does best screw her with passion and love and kept whispering how much he loved her inside her ears and she kept responding with a cry of pleasure. Frank increased the pace of his intercourse and they took a doggy position kept pounding her hard and sexy, she loved it never complained her cry revealed, they went for a missionary position he fucked her like never before, she loved it. He got her on top for a cowgirl position she made it. She reversed cowgirl style, he loved it and he spooned styled her, she screamed and just before he felt about to explode he went for A-spot stimulation position and he whispered to her ears that he was about to come and there he was his deep voice cracked out of him while she screamed her little soft voice. He came in her, kissed her and laid on her for few seconds before he rolled a side. They went silent and fell asleep for few minutes. After half an hour she woke up. Frank was still on bed she walked around the room and got to the bathroom washed herself out and came with a hot soft mini towel went over to Frank and wiped the cunt out of his shrank penis and kissed him on his lips nice and slow and left. She did that for two more times and the fourth time as she was about to return to the bathroom he clung her hand and pulled her on top of his chest and kissed her back and hold onto her tight on bed. It was already half past eight and it was dark outside. He cuddled his lady and both fell asleep. They slept for more than an hour, Freddy got home with Brenda went on with their business but he was told Frank was with Ms Victoria in his room. He was surprised and didn't want to disturb, went on with his business. MaryJo organized for a dry clean of Ms Victoria's garments which were found floating on the pool. Another hour passed both Frank and Victoria had numerous missed calls they slept for two and a half in total that was the longest after-sex-sleep Frank had in ages. Freddy was taking Brenda back home and decided to knock on their door but before any of them could hear he went in found the restless couple in bed under bright white duvet and shouted: "hey guys, dead or asleep?" Frank opened his eyes only to find Freddy standing next to the bed.

Frank: "what's up?" he asked sounding shocked and confused "what time is it?"

Freddy: "quarter to ten" he replied looking at his brother and starring at the beautiful Victoria who was dead asleep "mmh so it's official huh?" "She's beautiful" he smiled and walked close to the door.

Frank turned around and found his beauty sleeping beside him, her curly natural hair spread out on bed, her skin so flawless and her naked body covered on his duvet he smiled at Freddy.

Frank: "yeah man, she's the most beautiful thing that has ever happened to me" he raised his naked body up and went for a rob. Freddy couldn't care less; both left the room and went down stairs. MaryJo informed Frank that Ms Victoria's clothes were dried cleaned and ready for her re-use. Frank went to the bar poured some brandy on his glass greeted Brenda with a fresh smile on his face, Freddy and Brenda left and Frank went for a cool air on a balcony and attended his missed calls. One of the calls was from Ms Shirley he didn't return and further blocked her officially. He called Pam assuming she might have called several times on Victoria's phone and told her that he was with Victoria since afternoon and she's asleep by now so she shouldn't worry. Pam was pleased to hear that for she had called Victoria zillion times and was going worried. They had further discussion over the phone; Frank thanked Pam for believing in him and supporting their relationship from day one and promised her that everything was going to be fine. Pam was very pleased to hear that her girlfriend was officially dating a man and a half.

Inside Frank's room, Victoria slept like a baby her body was immaculate and her natural hair color blended perfectly with her flawless skin tone. She was indeed beautiful. Frank climbed back to his room sat on a single sitter next to the balcony French door of his room facing his lady sleeping on his bed. He didn't want to disturb her sleep even for a second. He then called MaryJo and asked if Victoria could get something to eat once she woke up. Frank had never brought a lady up to his room before; all the ladies including Shirley had been attended in the guestroom, which was down the lobby on the right near the stairs. Hence Freddy and the rest of the house crew were surprised to see Ms Victoria engaged in Frank's bedroom and that was a message to everyone. She turned around like a baby and opened her eyes only to find she was on bed alone. She rolled over to the end of the bed and got up, Frank was facing her with a huge smile.

Victoria: "what are you smiling at?" in her little voice.

Frank: "at my love, the best thing currently happening to me" in his deep voice sipped his drink "let's go for a bath" he stood took her hand and drugged her into his huge bathroom. Ran the tub for a bath and kissed her nude body and whispered, "let's get wet babe" as he untied his rob on the floor. They got into the tab, the water was nice and warm, the lavenders were nothing she had ever experienced before, the fragrance for the bath gel was amazing she laid in front of him and he massaged her back nice and slow kissing around her neck. He sponged her tits nipples all the way to her abdomen, he let his hand massage her labia and clitoris he played on her as much as he wanted and she humbly let him. Later after they rinsed and got out of the tub. Frank got Vicky his favorite polo shirt to wear and asked her to join him for dinner down the dining room. Victoria was worried with time and wanted to get hold of her phone which she left out on the pool as well as her dress and bra but Frank told her all were taken care of and will be brought in nice dried and cleaned. For the case of her phone she got her pulse down at the living room when they dropped for their dinner. She found fifteen missed calls and six messages from Pam but Frank told her to worry less for he had made a phone call to Pam on her behalf and she was very pleased to hear that.

Victoria: "I need to go home, I have work tomorrow morning" she explained.

Frank: "I think we passed that already? – Work issue" in his serious face.

Victoria: "yes babe we did, but I have to hand-over in a right way" in her little voice.

Over their dinner they discussed on how she was going to resign. Frank told Vicky that he will clear the loan for him first thing tomorrow morning and she shouldn't worry on the loan anymore. Victoria was pleased to hear that. They had their dinner at a big square dining room and later she went up changed to her dress and her lingerie and she was good to go. Frank wanted Vicky to sleepover at his place for he knew Kayla was not at home but she couldn't agree later he drove Vicky back and asked if he could get in and lay for some hours, Victoria welcomed him and both went straight to the room, she changed to her silky nightdress, brushed her teeth and went to bed where Frank was already on, she led a prayer and both went on talking for a while before they fell asleep.

Her alarm went off only to check it was the next day that was the longest sleep Frank had in history, he woke up kissed his lady and jumped in the shower he decided to use Vicky's toothbrush. She also woke up went to the bathroom and found Frank using her toothbrush she liked it and smiled and leaned on his back and said;

"Next time your toothbrush will be available" in her little sweet voice.

Frank: "I'm-comfortable-with-this-one" as he kissed her on both cheeks, on both sides of the neck, on the forehead and on the lips word by word.

Frank had to leave and go home prepare himself for work whereas Victoria prepared herself and went to Pam's check on the kids, greeted her friend and everyone was early and ready to leave hence she took the kids onto her old beetle and released Pam for work and she left with the kids.

Kayla: "Mom," looking straight to Victoria as she was driving.

Victoria: "yes baby" she smiled and looked at Kayla through the rear-view mirror.

Kayla: "how was your date?" she posed.

Victoria: "It was very fine baby" she smiled and looked at Kayla once more as she kept driving.

Kayla: "I'm glad you're happy Mom" there again in her very concerned sweetest tone.

Victoria: "Aaw baby, I hope you're happy as well" she replied with emotion.

Kayla: "yes Mom" and just like that she fulfilled her mother's day.

Few minutes later the kids got to school and Victoria drove off. An hour or so she settled on her desk. Frank got in forty minutes later he was in his usual magnificent smart suits he walked to her desk she stood wanted to offer him the usual greeting.

"Babe, I don't need that. I feel like I should kiss you right now" Frank spoke on a low toned deep voice "I have never slept quite early and had a lengthy sleep like yesterday, thank you" he squinted his eyes on Vicky.

Victoria: "You're welcome Mr Sinclair, shouldn't you be in your office by now? I feel uncomfortable having you stand in front of my desk for so long talking to me" she had a professional tone.

Frank left Vicky's desk climbed to his office and greeted Wanitha before he got in. It was a busy day for Frank, first thing he had Wanitha call his dealer and connect him through, Frank inquired prices for latest BMW X6 SUV and its specs, he then chose a white one looking at it on his Macintosh and ordered the dealer to deliver it at Victoria's place, he gave them the address and that was done. A brand new BMW X6 SUV was delivered at Vicky's apartment and was parked just next to her door. The security guards at the apartment acknowledged the receipt of the car. Frank called Freddy and had a meeting with him at his oval sofa.

Freddy: "how are you sneaky boy?" he teased his brother as he walked into Frank's office.

Frank: "I'm good, let's sit here" he walked to the oval seat and both took their seats "Freddy, I thought you should know, I love Victoria so very much, I'm still getting to know her but she has no much of a story though" he continued "We saw fit for her to quit working for the firm and start her own thing. So I want you to clear her loan from the system, I also want you to organize a debit card from my account. Is that possible?" he asked looking straight into Freddy's eyes;

"Yeah very possible. So are you comfortable with her? And where were you last night?" asked Freddy as he sounded concerned.

Frank: "I have never been more comfortable, I passed out at her place. Freddy I love this woman and I mean it and I want you to support me just like how you have always been doing but don't put her under surveillance please, you did it before and came out with nothing." He faced him and you could tell that was an honest truth from his twin brother "I have got a BM delivered at her place"

Freddy: "ok! I think she's welcomed to the family, I'll keep an eye on her for I don't fall for your stories easily" he stood up "anything else?" he asked Frank

Frank: "no that's it for now, and thank you" he smiled at his caring brother.

"I'm watching you guys very close" said Freddy as he left the room.

Freddy went over to his office first thing he called his private investigator and told him to resume keeping an eye on Ms Victoria and her family twenty four seven, he wrote an advance check and had it delivered to the investigator's office. He then called the bank and inquired Frank's statement of account and pressed an order for a debit card for Ms Victoria under Frank's account. He also called their car dealer to check on the delivery of the BM at Victoria's. He then logged into SincEnterprises high clearance account and altered the figures on Victoria's loan account statement. All was set and in order. Victoria was working on her resignation letter and part of it was an explanation on her monthly loan returns to the firm. She forwarded it to Frank for a review, Frank saw an email from Victoria he read it on the spot and track changed the whole part of loan situation and sent it back. He called her extension number and explained that he handled the loan matter and she shouldn't include it on her resignation letter or elsewhere. Later that day she requested a meeting with the HR that was Bob and rendered her letter to him. Bob was aware of Ms Victoria's situation and didn't ask a thing rather smiled at Vicky and wished her luck. Victoria met some of her colleagues and told them that she was leaving the firm most were surprised except for Ms Wanitha and few others who already had rumors regarding the Frank and Victoria's affair. Patrick sent an email to the team offering after office drink to bid farewell to Victoria.

Victoria drove to pick the kids and took them at home for she had office drink up to attend to. She drove at Pam's entrance the kids got off her beetle and went in the house. She saw a beautiful car at her drive way and it didn't cross her mind that was hers, she thought there must be a guest from another house who used her park space for some time, as she was leaving the compound the guards at the gate wanted to inform her on the new arrival but she was in a hurry and didn't get the memo. On her way back she called Pam and updated her on what was happening regarding her resignation. Pam was pleased to hear that for she had a call last night with Frank and realized Frank was there to stay. She also offered her friend a party to celebrate a huge step of her life. There was an incoming call as she was on the phone with Pam - it was Frank's, she told Pam that she would call back and accepted Frank's call:

Frank: "hello beautiful, where are you?" in his deep voice

Victoria: "driving back to the office I went to drop the kids at home" she replied in her little sweet voice

Frank: "you realize they are throwing a drink up for you in the office?"

Victoria: "I have heard so"

Frank: "do you want me there?" "I mean will you be comfortable?" he added

Victoria: "no please, thank you for asking, I wish I could be but I can't and you know that" smiled as she kept driving

Frank: "okay, I get you then I guess I'm leaving let me know once you're done or back at home"

Victoria: "I will, thanks"

Frank hanged up. Victoria drove back few minutes after c.o.b and Patrick was chasing people to head to a bar in a restaurant near their building. Freddy joined the team and they all met at the bar. They had their drinks and snacks on, chatting around, their drinking game was slow everyone was concerned on tomorrow being a working day. Patrick tossed for Victoria for the best years they had her in the firm and wished her happiness and blessings ahead. Freddy on the other hand was just wondering how perfect will his sister in law be to achieve all these at a short period of time. He kept drinking and observed Victoria from far. A few minutes later Victoria had a call on her cell and stood aside, it was Frank checking on her and asking her to finish up with the drink-up and get home, he missed her already. Freddy went over to Victoria and held her hand to a seat on a table, Victoria told Frank that Freddy was with her at the moment and asked if she could call him back and they hanged up their call.

Freddy: "I'm proud of you, to have managed working in the firm and coming out a hero" he said to her eyes.

Victoria: "what do you mean Freddy?"

Freddy: "I mean getting my brother to love you to this much is a blessing as much as it is to him having you, so please do not Fuck it up!!" he sounded serious yet had a smile on his face.

Victoria: "Freddy, thanks for the talk but rest assured I do not intend to!" she seriously responded back.

Freddy: "good then, I guess I should say welcome to the family" he held Vicky's both hands and had a genuine smile in his face.

Victoria: "thank you" she smiled back and went to join the rest of the team.

There was no chemistry between Freddy and Victoria at all. Freddy was trying to protect his brother and at the same time getting used to Victoria that obviously was not working but he was a patient smart unbothered man. The drink up went not for long, Victoria had to leave she went to everyone who was there shook hands hugged and thanked them for everything and went to Freddy did the same.

Freddy: "let me know when you're leaving, I want to escort you to your car" he said in a low toned voice

Victoria: "as a matter of fact I'm leaving right now Freddy" she replied in a serious tone looking at Freddy's eyes.

Freddy: "alright let's go then" he stood up and walked out with Victoria.

Freddy escorted Victoria back to the office building and made sure she got in her car and safely drove off.

Victoria got home but her parking space was occupied by a white BMW she squeezed her beetle to fit in the space got out wondering who would have parked his/her car for so long without being considerate. As she was about to get inside her house security guard followed and informed her that the car at her parking space came in the afternoon addressed to her and they received it and gave her the delivery package. Victoria was not sure what she heard at that moment and asked the guard to rephrase. The guard one more time explained to her that the car parked in front of her drive way was delivered for her in the afternoon and there was a delivery package addressed by her name. Victoria thanked the guard for the information took the package and got inside called Pam and shared the news. Pam was shocked and pleased to hear so and told Victoria that must be Frank and so she should call him and ask him about it. Victoria called Frank.

Victoria: "hello babe" in her little sweet voice.

Frank: "yes babe, what's up?" in his deep voice.

Victoria: "I just got home in my parking space there has been a car parked since afternoon when I dropped the kids from school, I thought some neighbor might have parked for a while, now the guard is telling me it was delivered to me" sounded surprised.

Frank: "do you like it?" in his deep voice.

Victoria: "like it? I love it! I haven't taken a closer look but I love it, why didn't you tell me?" smiled and jumped up and down like crazy.

Frank: "I wanted you to be surprised, now that you know do you mind doing me some favor?"

Victoria: "name it babe?" in her sweet voice going outside to check it out.

Frank: "please come pick me up on your new ride Fadhil is taking ages to reach here" he smiled as he ordered.

Victoria got the address of where Frank was, she went to see how the kids were doing at Pam's house and then left in her brand new car.

Frank was at a friend's place a very nice estate Victoria got there on time, Frank went out and got in her car and both left.

As she was driving, Frank was busy inspecting the car they went at Frank's place parked the car and left out. Frank was busy kissing his lady and caressing her body throughout. Victoria didn't want to stay for she had a long day Frank insisted her to come in. MaryJo greeted Ms Victoria and Frank ordered not to be disturbed as they both climbed up in his room.

Frank's room is the hugest and well designed, the walls are super clean white colored and so was the floor tiles his bed sheets were most of the time white, grey or both. His room was spotless with big windows and a French door outside the balcony. Victoria loved to be in there. As naughty as he was he had never taken a lady into his room. There was a room down the stairs called the guest room that Frank used to entertain the ladies he happened to posses. Every housemaid and employee of the house knew that the room was specific for Frank's entertainment but with exception of Ms Victoria that room hadn't been used since her appearance.

Frank and Victoria fling off each other's clothes while French kissing, he lit the room with a playlist of songs on a remote and took her into his huge bathroom, he ran a bathtub and both got in it. She sat in front of him and as usual he couldn't keep his hands off her instead he kept kissing her neck while playing with her boobs, this time her neck was on red spot she loved it, kept nodding with pleasure changing poses of her neck, he scrubbed her back, her hands couldn't go as far as to his neck and his bold head as Frank played with her boobs, massaging and pinching her nipples, Frank washed Vicky from neck to her back and to her thick thighs down to the vulva, he kept massaging and playing with her like never before, he strummed her clitoris while gently scrubbing her other parts, Vicky's ass was soft and bubbly Frank couldn't resist to massage it, she turned around and faced Frank got hold of the scrubber and started with his bold head down to his neck and his muscular toned chest and arms and went down to his knob, she tightly massaged it played with his balls and they kept it neutral rinsed their bodies and came out of the tub, he dragged her to the balcony it was dark outside he bent her over the glassy balcony separator and came from her back hard and thick, she screamed out with a cry of pleasure. Frank had the best view of Victoria's long curved back and round medium bubbly ass, his penis kept penetrating back and forth, he laid on her back, kissed on the back of her neck, he stood straight pounded her in and out holding her hair and sometimes round her waist she loved it, her body turned pale blue before it could be red, her cry for pleasure increased as he kept pounding her harder, and she bent more and curved her ass more sexier, they couldn't hold any longer both came at the same time, the best feeling ever as she climaxed her voice cut and you couldn't hear her scream anymore but trembled and Frank broke silence and gave a deep exhale as he exploded holding Victoria's boobs tighter and whispered her name into her ears that she was the sweetest thing alive. He leaned for a minute on her back as he dispensed his last drops into her. They both went to bed and passed out for some minutes.

A phone rang out of Victoria's purse that was her friend - Pam eager to see her friend's new ride, she woke up from the sex nap went for her phone spoke to Pam and went to the washroom took shower and got back on bed with a small hot towel sponged Frank around his pelvis, his shrunk penis and around his balls. She went rinsed the towel and repeated sponging him two more times. Frank felt good on the warmth of the towel around his masculine parts. He woke up and got his robe on and Victoria put her dress back and he walked her out down the stairs. She really wanted to meet with Pam, her excitement for the car was still on Frank understood how Vicky felt. They went outside where Vicky parked her car, got in and started the engine on. Frank kissed his woman on the lips while his hand was underneath her dress playing with her bikini and her labia he wanted her more but he couldn't have her, Vicky always felt good on what Frank did to her body. Victoria had never said no to however Frank would touch her or play her around, in fact she loved every tip of it and Frank already discovered that. After a while she had to go back home met with Pam and showed her the ride. Pam was extremely excited and happy for her friend, she knew Frank was no joke or not like the rest and she believed on him from day one. Pam called Frank excitedly thanked him for the ride for her friend. Frank was pleased and happy to hear that. They popped up a champagne that Pam came with from work at Victoria's house sipped it as she gave her friend the whole story of what had happened with her and Frank lately. After a long chat and story telling Pam took shower and slept over at Victoria. Their stories prolonged on bed before they fell asleep. Frank called his lady before she fell asleep talked with her for almost an hour, Pam fell asleep and left Victoria on the phone with Frank.

The next day Victoria had to take the kids to school since she was loose and off work from her resignation. Frank got to work and behold there was another lady at the front desk. He was happy with the abrupt change and decision Victoria had made for their relationship now he got to have her anytime and anywhere he wanted with no exceptions. First thing he did when he got to his phone was to ring Victoria talked to her like twenty minutes he asked her to pick her up at one past mid day for their lunch. Victoria went over to her shop site and met with a contractor whom was renovating the place for her new business. They had some lengthy discussion on the work whereabouts and she left went to the city center for some window shopping and research before it was actually quarter to one she remembered her lunch date with her man. Victoria was feeling fresh and new, she had her brand new ride, she was about to start her new business venture yet had a powerful man in the whole city by her side. She was the happiest woman alive, her skin glowed gradually, she was transforming into a better woman. That day she wore a dark blue short sleeve above the knee pencil dress and her grey 5inch pumps. Her curves could easily been seen through the dress and her beautiful long legs were outta seen and shaped by the heels she had on. Her blue purse was small and simple. Victoria was never a fashionable lady at least wasn't blessed enough to posses up to date fashioned wears and accessories. Frank noticed that and was organizing a serious shopping for his woman in the western hemisphere. She was like fifteen minutes late to their lunch appointment she got in the office building and didn't get out of the car, she rang Frank when she arrived and Frank left the building straight into Victoria's car and left. The security guards had seen Victoria in her new ride and moreover Frank being all over the place, office rumors spread regarding Victoria and Frank's situation. Freddy was asked by Patrick but couldn't confirm a thing.

Frank and Victoria went for lunch to one of the best hotels down town, they sat together discussed on how their day went and Frank asked her if she could escort her to US for his meeting and also get a chance to meet his mother. Victoria was shocked by the news and couldn't resist hence Frank told her that Wanitha will call her for further visa appointment hence she should be aware and ready. Frank also asked her if she could spend a night at his place for he missed her and wanted to experience a night at his room with her, more request that Victoria couldn't resist. After their productive lunch she dropped Frank off to his office and left went to finish up her errands on her site and went to pick the kids from school and got them home. She decided to make dinner for the kids something she didn't do for some days.

At SinEnterprises Freddy met with Frank and handed him Victoria's debit card as Frank requested. He also confirmed that Victoria's loan was cleared as discussed Frank was pleased with the updates, they discussed other work issues and both left work almost the same time.

Freddy got home and had a scheduled Skype with his mother. They usually had their regular video calls or Skype with Mrz Zoya F. Sinclair. Freddy updated his mother on what had happened lately with Frank and his new woman Victoria. And shared the surprising news of Victoria being attended at Frank's bedroom something which was unlikely than usual and so they thought Frank might be serious with Vicky than he never was with the rest. Mrs Zoya asked Freddy to inform Frank to call her and never miss out their scheduled calls unless otherwise. Mrz Zoya was a serious woman yet loving mother, she liked to be kept on the loop with regards to her sons' lives and their family business also she had always prayed for Frank to step up his love game and be more mature and committed for the sake of his life and the firm hence when she heard of Victoria's existence and the steps Frank had taken she was pleased and convinced that Frank might have stepped up. Frank had missed the call with his mother although his calendar reminded him every minute of it.

On the other side of the city, Victoria made dinner for the kids inspected their homework and were well attended. She went to take shower, Pam got back and went straight to her friend's place, kids were watching TV and on video game, she went straight into Victoria's room had a chat with Victoria whom was wearing her satin and lace ultra sexy lingerie and had her stockings on and covered herself with a satin robe. Did her hair out and as they kept talking she wore a light nude lip matte and sprayed her best cologne. Pam was surprised to see her friend's sex game up and strong she helped her tie her curly hair. Victoria carried some of the things she may have wanted for the night or the next day on her black purse and went out to the living room. The kids were done and it was almost bedtime. Kayla wanted to know what her mother was up to that night they still couldn't have enough of her mom's ride yet. Victoria came out sexy and about to leave. She told Kayla that Frank bought the car for them and she was going to meet him that night. Kayla understood and asked her mother to pass her regards. Pam went with the kids to her place as Victoria was locking up her place and got into her ride and left.

At the Sinclair mansion Freddy was already in the house but Frank was not. MaryJo welcomed Ms Victoria and asked her if she wanted her usual bottle of wine or anything else. Victoria was comfortable with her usual bottle of red wine; she had it at the balcony of the living room. Freddy went to meet Victoria he got to the balcony and called her name, Victoria stood up and Freddy went for a hug kissed Victoria on the left and right cheek while he grabbed her waist smiled and welcomed her. Victoria was pleased of Freddy's gesture they both sat at the balcony. Freddy went for his whiskey and got back accompanying Victoria while waiting for Frank. He laid some few stories on, he seemed easy and friendly to Victoria. They laughed and talked for almost an hour before Frank showed up. Frank saw Victoria's car parked at the driveway and smiled. Fadhil pulled over for Frank to drop, first thing he asked was where Victoria was and MaryJo informed him that she was with Freddy at the balcony. Frank went straight to the balcony he got closer to his lady, Vicky stood up they hugged and kissed immensely Freddy was just starring at both of them with a funny face. Victoria was partially shy and wanted to stop but Frank couldn't let her stop and kept kissing Vicky deeply and gently after a while he whispered to her ears that he was happy to see her. She reciprocated by smiling and nodding as she sat down. Frank went for her brandy on ice from the bar and called MaryJo and told her in front of Victoria and Freddy that Victoria was part of him and so it's okay for her to access his room whenever she feels to. Freddy was just listening looking at Victoria as Frank was giving out updated status of Ms Victoria. All said and done Frank apologized to Freddy for missing the call with their mother and grabbed his lady and both went up to their room. Victoria was a creative woman she unrobed herself and behold Frank was much pleased to see what Victoria had underneath the robe. He went for his playlist on a remote lit up the fire and shut the blinds on his large French door and windows, she then scratched off Frank's tie from his neck, doff his shirt and trouser and pushed him to lay on bed. She then pulled off Frank's boxer brief and went for his penis got hold of it tight and strong sucked it in and out nice and slow in circular and vertical motions yet licking it nice and slow her pace kept increasing as she rotated the motion of her sucking and licking deep throating his hard penis and kept sucking. Frank felt heaven on earth he couldn't say a word was just feeling every bit of it, he kept nodding tried to touch Victoria's hair but the feeling was so strong that he lost control, Victoria doing what she does best kept her blow job up and strong, sucking and leaking Frank's penis all the way to his balls deep throating it back and forth the vertical and circular motions of his hard penis in her mouth kept him feeling waaay good. He didn't want her to stop and she wasn't going to stop either, her pace increased her game went on strong, Frank lost it and shouted that he was about to explode Victoria went on winning the match she did her circular motions around her tongue deep throat it once more and suck it hard, vertically and there his hands were holding her hair tight and vigorously, he exploded on her mouth holding her head not to let her off. The discharge was lump some, her mouth was full of Frank's sperms and right after he could release his penis from Vicky's mouth Vicky got up and went straight on him swallowed all that in her mouth looking straight into his eyes and with her seductive eyes kissed his lips and laid beside him on bed. Frank was cursing throughout the after-party situation not believing what just happened. He put his hands on her bubbly round ass playing with her bridge on her ass and the black lingerie she had on. After he regained his strength he went to shower leaving Victoria laid sexy on bed he got out put a robe on and asked her to go with him to the dining for a meal. Victoria obeyed and both went down for some meal. Frank couldn't stop touching his lady all the time. Freddy joined them for a meal and all he could see was two people kissing and touching each other insanely. They had a discussion over their meal Freddy was filling up Victoria about family schedules and activities such as the one he was supposed to have earlier with Frank to Skype their mother but Frank ended up on no show. Frank was also filling up Victoria on how protective and organized Freddy was and so she shouldn't wonder seeing him up on her ass. Victoria enjoyed the dinner with the two twin brothers. It was soccer time that night Frank Victoria and Freddy went to their home theatre to watch the game. Soccer was one of their favorite games. Frank asked a maid to bring over their drinks at the theatre. Frank and Victoria sat close to each other while Freddy was one row in front of them as Brenda was few minutes late. Frank and Brenda had been dating for almost four years despite their lengthy relationship there was no signal of them taking their relationship to the next level. Brenda a very confident blonde six feet tall with curly hair had some reservation for extra commitments in their relationship, whereas Freddy had been a frequent survivor of Brenda's infidelity acts hence both kept their affair static. So after a couple of minutes Brenda was in the mansion, she knew about the soccer night and so went straight to the theatre and met Victoria for the first time and apologized to Freddy for running late and the couples went on enjoying each other's company kissing and caressing one another. Frank and Victoria couldn't care less, Freddy and Brenda the same although Freddy was a bit concerned of Brenda's late coming. They both exchanged good night vibes and left to their rooms. Frank had a wonderful night with Victoria that day. He closed the blinds and switched some lights on for he wanted to see Victoria in every move she makes. Victoria went to change and refresh in the bathroom and came out sexy and ready for whatever in her transparent baby pink silky nightdress and tied her thick hair behind and had a headband on. It was no joke Victoria was way cute and sexy than possibly all the women Frank had ever dated the only difference was that she lucked exposure of good and luxurious life other than that Victoria was one big deal of a woman. Frank followed Vicky in the bathroom, he kept holding her waist kissing her neck and lips and cheeks and massaging her boobs and pinching her nipples. Frank was way free on Vicky and she liked every move Frank laid on her, she enjoyed every bit of the massage and the kisses and the sex. Victoria was good on feeling the pleasure from what Frank was doing on her and Frank knew how pleased Victoria felt hence he couldn't do less. They both jumped to bed, Victoria made a phone call at home to find if everything was well and to wish her people good sleep.

After that she turned back to her man and their romantic sexiest night began. Over their night Frank suggested Kayla to move to a better school and also Victoria to get a better place of her own or instead do an interior house change. Victoria couldn't agree to that since her budget on the loan she had was for her new business and not house renovation but Frank cleared her doubt and asked her to consider his request as he finalized her debit card situation with the bank. She couldn't agree more.

Alarm went off at 5am Frank immediately shut it off and turned over to Vicky, he grabbed her from a side and held her tight and went on to sleep for about thirty more minutes. Later Frank began kissing Vicky's neck, massaging Vicky's boobs and nipples and eventually Vicky was turned on. Frank took his hand down to Vicky's vulva between her labia and she was extremely wet and ready. Frank couldn't hesitate penetrating his middle finger in her, the sound of her vagina rubbed by his finger was out loud and clear he penetrated his finger back and forth, kissing Vicky's neck and rubbing her boobs. Victoria got way wet and ready, she cried out as Frank kept fingering her in and out and lastly he turned her around and faced on top of her, kept kissing her on the neck to her boobs and raised her legs above in a missionary position penetrated his cock in her vagina and gently fucked Vicky's wet vagina back and forth, the pace of his penetration increased as she increased her screams and cry, Frank was stimulated by Victoria's sweet little crying voice and so went hard on her, she loved it and came earlier than usual the spattered water out of Vicky's vagina made Frank happy and more needful he kept going in and out of her, holding her legs tight and squeezed way inner than usual eventually he whispered "I'm exploding babe" and there he came in her, dispensed all his semen silently his heart beat faster than usual and he breathed heavily. Afterwards Frank freed Vicky's legs and he kissed her nipples and went straight to shower. Victoria was exhausted and couldn't wake up instantly. She lay on bed and Frank covered her with the white duvet.

After thirty more minutes Frank was ready to go and well dressed for office he went over at Victoria kissed her on her forehead and left quietly as he didn't want to wake her up. He dropped down and ordered MaryJo to attend Vicky at all times. Frank and Freddy left in one car. On their way Freddy was teasing his brother for he seemed fresh and energetic for a good cause.

On that day Freddy submitted Victoria's debit card to Frank along other assignments. Frank dropped an appointment to their usual home décor and furniture store for Victoria's shopping. Where as at Sinclair's mansion Victoria woke up with a phone call that was Pam checking on her they had a chat on how her night went Pam couldn't be happier for her girlfriend. Victoria then went for a long beautiful bath and MaryJo organized a proper breakfast for the lady and went knock on the door to inform her that breakfast was set for her and also to say where she would want to take it. Victoria was pleased and asked it on the balcony of the room and after some minutes all was settled for her. She had her breakfast over newspapers and Frank called her, they both had a long happy call and he informed her on the shopping appointment. Victoria couldn't agree more. She got ready after two hours and went to meet the best interior designer of the home furniture store down town and explained how her house was and planned a site visit so that they could select the some furniture and electronics for her home. After the furniture store appointment she went on with her daily schedule on her site, met some contractors and had few reviews and decisions to make. It was almost lunch hours Victoria had asked Frank to go meet Pam over lunch time and when time was up she headed to Pam's office took Pam in her car and went out to a nice restaurant and had their long talk over their lunch whereas Frank had to stay in and kept working. After an hour Victoria left with a lunch box for her man, dropped Pam at her office and took the lunch box to Frank but again she was not ready to be seen by her ex co-workers hence she asked Freddy to come out of the building and asked him to assist pass the lunch box to Frank. Freddy did the same. Frank was pleased to see a surprise lunch from his lady of course Freddy had taken some of it and both went on with their work schedules. He then called Vicky thanked her for the surprise lunch and asked if they could go for dinner in the evening with Kayla for he had not seen her for sometime and Victoria couldn't agree more. She went pick the kids from school and got them home she spoke with Kayla about dinner arrangements and Kayla was excited, ran her assignments quickly and got ready for the dinner where as Victoria cooked supper for the kids including Pam's kids ensured that they were all attended and had their homework on at Pam's house and went back at her place got ready for the dinner. Frank came to pick the ladies in his Mercedes Benz C Class he looked fine and smelled waay good in his Roberto Cavalli jeans trouser and black Armani bodycon cotton long sleeve slim fit T-shirt. Kayla let the door for Frank she hugged him as he came in and was very happy to see Frank. Victoria was in her room. Frank and Kayla had a little chat at the living room and both walked to Victoria to check on her. As usual they both kissed and left the room. Frank took the ladies out to an indoor restaurant and had a delicious cuisine that night. Over their dinner Frank had to announce to Kayla that he was dating her mother and Kayla was very happy to hear that.

Kayla: "I hope that makes you my dad then" smiled as she swung her legs underneath the chair.

Victoria: "we are just…" before she could finish up the sentence Frank interrupted.

Frank: "absolutely! I'm your dad baby girl" smiled and extended his hand and held Victoria's hand as they both looked at Kayla with a smile.

Kayla: "this is awesome!" smiled and sounded extremely excited "so we're going to have movie nights together, sports' days together" as she kept mentioning all her activities that may need Frank's presence.

Frank: "yes yes, as a matter of fact I want you to write for me your schedule for the whole week, what you do after school hours and on weekends and I will jump right in." he continued "I just want you to know that you're a very special young lady and your mom and I love you so very much" Frank smiled and squeezed Victoria's hand silently.

Victoria: "what are you supposed to say Kayla?" she turned to Kayla and looked into her eyes.

Kayla: "thank you" said to Frank and sipped her juice.

Frank: "anytime young girl, come here" he opened his arms hugged and kissed Kayla on the forehead.

Victoria was surprised with the discussion Frank pulled on the table. She smiled and kept having her meal. They had their dessert and just like that Kayla was done with her meal she thanked Frank and Victoria and left the table went to gaze on aquarium fishes. Frank and Victoria kept having their drinks and she couldn't stop thanking Frank for everything he had been doing for her family and Frank kept dodging the credits. He told Victoria how happy he had been lately and wanted their bond to mature and grow as strong as it could possibly be, he further explained that sooner she would have to meet his mother Mrs Zoya whom had been hearing about them from Freddy. Victoria couldn't imagine how fast things were going and asked Frank to slow down since she was loosing it but Frank insisted that it had to happen that way and not otherwise. They spoke about Freddy; Victoria told Frank how she misunderstood Freddy in the beginning of their relationship but as time kept moving she admitted Freddy to being the best thing in their relationship. They discussed about revamping her house and where to take the old stuff. After some time Frank requested for the bill and paid through his debit card and just before he forgot he gave Victoria her debit card. Vicky was surprised at least Freddy knew how to mesmerize her, and Vicky kept thanking Frank endlessly. Frank smiled went over to get Kayla and both exit the restaurant.

At her place Kayla said her thanks to both and went to bed. Victoria and Frank were still in the living room sipping some wine and doing what they did most, kissing and touching one another shamelessly. Vicky had to ask Frank to leave or else he was going to be held captive throughout the night something Frank wished for but eventually he had to go kissed her goodnight and left their place.

That night Victoria couldn't stop thinking of Frank from the first time they met and got close to each other and every other moment. She had flashes of their romantic journey in her mind she went to Kayla's bed and slept next to her through the night.

Days went by with same errands at Victoria's and same love intuitions with the couple. Frank got an office trip to West Africa he wanted to go with his lady but unfortunately Pam was away for an office trip hence Victoria was left with the kids. Vicky's shop was well set and ready to open and she was finalizing her business licence and other documents. The interior designers got her the best furniture yet cost effective for Victoria's choice and she managed to buy some bottles of Frank's best brand to add on her small bar at her kitchen. She also added grey color bedsheet sets for Frank in her wardrobe and some pajamas for Frank and in house slippers for Frank. Indeed her house was revamped and ready for Frank. In between Frank's stay in West Africa she Skyped him several times and had frequent phone sex, their affair grew wild and strong. Pam was more jealous with Vicky's sex life leave along other life. Pam got back sooner than Frank and managed to have quality time with her girlfriend before Frank came to take over. They went out for dinner and overstayed had some drinks and enjoyed their night just the two of them before her phone rang only to find Freddy checking on her. Freddy used to pay a visit once or twice on Frank's absence to check on the ladies. That day he passed by Victoria's place and she was not around he went to Pam's and the nana informed him that the ladies were out for the evening. He then decided to call Victoria on her cellphone she answered loud and clear her voice was not the usual one either it was the place they were or her current state of mind. Freddy asked her where she was and she replied he then told her he was coming for her and she couldn't resist. Freddy got to the restaurant fifteen minutes later he saw Victoria and Pam from far at their own table laughing and talking. He went close hugged Victoria and looked straight into her eyes just to check if she was tipsy or not. He then greeted Pam hugged her as well and went sat in between the ladies asked what they were having and stories kept flowing. Victoria easily blended Freddy into their conversations and just so you know Freddy was enjoying her night with the ladies, they drank talked and laughed the entire night. Freddy asked Fadhil to drive Victoria's car back at her place for he was going to take them home by his car. Frank called Victoria at their usual time and she had to excuse herself from the noise and went to Freddy's car to speak with Frank. Vicky told Frank about her night out with Pam and Freddy. Frank was pleased to hear that Freddy was with them. After their long phone call he asked her to go back home as soon as possible and have her call him back. Victoria obeyed as she always does so, got back to her seat and after some minutes she asked Freddy and Pam if they could leave the place. They had enough after all and agreed to leave. Freddy drove the ladies home he really had a blast night with Pam and Victoria given the fact that Pam was a very good entertainer and fun to be around with. They got home safely, Pam asked Freddy to come in for a glass of whatever there was before he left. He agreed and went in for the first time since Victoria had changed the look of her home. He loved the new look more modernized and chic for beautiful ladies like them. He went check on something to drink from the mini bar at the kitchen and got himself the brand with some ice. Pam went for another bottle of wine and both kept their stories going over the kitchen highlander. Meanwhile Victoria went straight in her bedroom took shower and eased herself on a chiffon nightdress but got some underwear on this time since Freddy was around. She came out smelling nice and fresh. She had her glass of wine as well and her phone rang it was Frank on video call. Had to say hello to Pam and Freddy and they went on with their business. Victoria went to her room where she was free to speak with Frank, they had their phone sex as usual revealed to him what she had on for the night and played herself around as per Frank's request and the rest was history. Pam and Freddy got pretty close to one another both enjoyed each other's company and she even confessed that Freddy was her favorite and wondered why Frank never told Freddy about it. They could hold hands and laugh and flirt like no one is watching. After her phone sex she came out joined the rest of the team. Only to find the very two separate committed people where coquetting. Victoria loved what she saw and kept the mood going. They laughed drunk and teased one another and eventually Victoria couldn't hold it for long and decided to go to bed she had enough of wine and enough of everything and also remembered that she had an early morning errand with the kids hence hugged and kissed Freddy goodnight and left. Freddy on the other hand didn't seem to have signs of leaving any sooner. He kept his drinking and flirting game on for a little longer with Ms Pam whom also enjoyed the company they got to know each other shared their stories, criticized one another but all was for good. He asked Pam to go home for it was almost three in the morning and Pam informed him that she was already home. She stood went in took shower and changed to a nice sexy see through nightdress sprayed some cologne and after twenty minutes she was back at the living room. Freddy was on his phone replying to his messages and emails and was amused to seeing Pam in a whole lot different ensemble. He smiled and didn't want to believe if he could see through Pam nightdress, the music from the TV went on they had another glass of their drinks and Pam agreed to Freddy that time was up for him to leave and for her to jump to bed something which Freddy was not looking forward doing. He posed some questions about George and where he was and for a pause she replied with feelings not sure was the alcohol in her brain or an intended stunt for Freddy but bottom line their relationship was regular offs and ons and there he finally understood why Pam was behaving that the way. Pam with her advocacy character she also posed a question to Freddy regarding Brenda and Freddy didn't hesitate to reply that both had different night plans that day but most of the time they were together. It was time for Freddy he got up put things in order and returned the bottle of the brand he was having to the mini bar shelf and let other things in order, took the wine glasses to the sink after he was done with putting things in their right position he then went for Pam extended his hand for her to hold and stand and hugged her softly kissed her left and right cheek and walked with her to bed wanted to see how the two slept, he got Pam on bed next to a sleeping beauty Victoria, Freddy kissed Pam one more time on the forehead and whispered; "you sleep tight will check on you later today" and covered her with duvet same with the one Victoria had on. Freddy switched the lights off closed their bedroom door and went switching other lights off as he exit the house he locked the house with the spare key he had and left. He had a naturally fun night and a memorable one. Freddy had always been a one-woman-guy unlike his brother but he saw himself being a two-woman-guy going forward. He drove carefully and reached home safely. Got to his room and was not seen until ten in the morning the next day. Likewise Pam got to office late she dropped an email to her office that she was going to start with external meetings only they knew the truth the only external meeting she had was between the duvet and the bed. Victoria ran her early morning errands took the kids to school and left Pam on bed. She went to one of the offices in town to follow up on her business licence something that Frank had wanted to assist her on but she refused since she wanted to have the know-how on her business opening. Freddy got up late than never before he quickly got himself ready and drove to the office, good enough he had no pressing matter that morning he had a pretty bad hangover and asked his PA to assist him with a cold orange juice. He had his orange juice and felt better than before and called Pam to find out how she was doing. Amazingly Pam had already treated herself with her diy hangover cure and was already in the office rushing her tasks out. They had a few moments of recap and laughed and Freddy admitted that he had a wonderful night with Pam, likewise with Pam whom she already confessed before that Freddy was her favorite she couldn't deny a thing. Freddy then promised to check her out later that day and hanged up the phone. Pam called Victoria to check on her and gave her the remaining part of last night's story.

Two days had passed by and Freddy didn't get a chance to see his ladies apart from phone calls and text messages. At one evening on a weekend were kids had a sleep over at their other friend's house Victoria and Pam had ordered some take outs and Freddy got home refreshed and changed to a better sexy look he had his pony tail rolled and tied a knot on the back of his head. He smelled good and indeed the twin brothers were insanely beautiful. He came with the barbecue orders that Pam had pressed from one of their favorite local bar, Victoria blended some fresh juice and made it chill in the freezer. Pam was busy making stories with Victoria whom was busy juicing. It was already night somehow eight thirt-ish and Freddy came in unlike Frank, he just gets to open the door and never knocks. Pam and her lovebird hugged and kissed each other. Victoria got the barbecue off Freddy's hand and went place them in the oven, Freddy got ease on their kitchen lander and made stories with the girls as he poured some drink for himself. Later that day there was a knock at the door and to everyone's surprise Frank was standing at the door in Victoria's house. Victoria was astonished to see Frank since she was expecting him the next day and so was everyone else. She went hugged him and had their prolonged kisses and made Pam and Freddy feel jealous. Frank was happy to find all of his best people at one place he was also impressed to see the magnificent new look of Victoria's house. He kept holding and caressing her ass as if no one was watching Victoria poured some juice for Frank although he wanted some brand but she insisted to take a glass of juice before he jumped to alcohol. Fadhil knocked and came in with a bag some duty free bag and a big suitcase. Frank took it from there and released Fadhil. Victoria took the bag in the room Frank followed her kissing and wanting her so badly, she couldn't let it happen since Pam and Freddy were at the living room and would get suspicious but Frank could care less of what Freddy and Pam would think. He flung off his t-shirt and trouser and she doff his boxer brief kissing him in a flirtatious smile and look, Frank turned his lady from behind kissing her neck vigorously and massaging her boobs and her supple nipples she couldn't help it and began to cry her pleasure out he kept his fingers going every place of her; to the waist, the bubbly ass and her vulva. Vicky got wet like never before, Frank loved it pushed Vicky on bed and sucked the cunt out of her vagina. Vicky screamed even louder she kept going holding and playing with Frank's bold head and that even turned Frank more on and vigorous, Frank licked and sucked Victoria's pussy like he never done before, Victoria screamed and moved her body, her thighs were even sexier, thick and light skinned. Frank had it all at his disposal and eventually got himself in Vicky hard and strong, he gently squeezed in her. Victoria loved it and wanted for more. Frank was a sexy maniac and there was nothing off limit when it came to bed game. He massaged Vicky's ass and caressed her soft ass bridge. It was the best feeling ever. He repeatedly massaged Vicky's ass as he fucked her passionately. He went for her nipples and boobs, he went for her lips kissed her deeply, he got back turned her around and penetrated in from her behind, she loved it like never before, Frank couldn't stop, he kept pounding his cock in her tight vagina holding her boobs, her hair periodically. She screamed loud and louder. She loved every moment of it, he loved her cry, he increased his pounds as the scream increased and she cried out loud that she was coming and before you know it Frank whispered to her ear that he was about to explode and so he did as he finished mentioning the word. It was the best feeling ever the two have never got tired of their game. They laid on bed for some minutes and she woke up took shower and Frank joined him he showered with his lady wanted to penetrate on her during the shower but Victoria asked him to reserve the play for after party. They changed put some clothes on Victoria got thicker lately, her ass was growing big round and sexy and so was Frank's knob always unsettled around Victoria. He gave her the suitcase which was full of perfumes, shower gels, bath lavenders for her glowing skin, some cologne for Kayla and matching lingerie for Victoria, he asked her to bath with and wear the cologne and lingerie he gave her for as long as he existed and it turned out to be the best gifts ever. Victoria was excited and grateful, Frank then told her when they go visit his mother she will have to do a full closet make over. She sprayed some twilly d'Hermes from the fragrance packages she received from Frank and walked to join Pam and Freddy at the living room. Pam started teasing Victoria's sound of cry and Vicky denied that to be her crying sound they had their drinks on, laughed and talked. Frank talked of his successful trip Freddy told Frank how Pam had been interestingly fun-to-be-with since he left. Frank was accused of being selfish of not conveying the compliments Pam offered to Freddy and the night went on happily until George knocked on the door, Victoria went for the door. George hugged his sweet mama and walked in

Frank was happy to see George he went close and pat him on the shoulder welcomed him and introduced him to Freddy whom he already knew and met sometime back. Pam on the other hand was not pleased to see George there but she gave a fake smile as he tried to kiss and hug her. They all noticed some negative vibes between the couple and Victoria kept entertaining her brother-in-law as if nothing was sensed. Freddy had to join Victoria at the kitchen for a little low chat as to what was George doing there but Victoria tried to calm Freddy by reminding him that he was the father of Pam's twins hence he might be here for one reason or the other. Brenda called Freddy and to their surprise Freddy told Brenda where he was and Brenda requested to crash the party and Freddy wanted to bit-up George's move and let her. Victoria asked if she was going to come and if that was what Freddy wanted and Freddy admitted that it was good for everyone. That was a hell of a stunt. Vicky kept entertaining her guests and her man, Pam came over at the kitchen counter where Freddy and Victoria were and she posed to Freddy but Freddy was not up to her play. Victoria mentioned to Pam that Brenda was on her way coming. Pam didn't like it either, she looked at Freddy and asked if that was what he wanted and without hesitation Freddy confirmed that was good for everyone. It was not good for Pam obviously you could see it on her eyes and the reaction afterwards. Pam went over to George sat close to him and leaned on him to George's surprise his woman was way cooperating and ease than before. George's night was going directly as he wished except for Pam's and Freddy's. Frank had no idea what was happening except he kept stories going with George and both had a good time. Freddy was actually calling Brenda to hurry her up and Victoria couldn't take the drama out of her home. She kept silent and in between everyone's mood and tried to entertain all. Brenda arrived, Victoria welcomed her with open arms hugged and kissed. She introduced Brenda to George and Pam whom she had never met before. Freddy took his lady into his arms and just like that the room was filled with couples. Pam didn't like Brenda being there at all and Freddy didn't like George around Pam. But both kept their feelings reserved and the night went on perfectly fine. Victoria served the barbecues for everyone to chew as they kept talking. Frank got up and went help Victoria serve their guests, Vicky was the happiest woman in the room and all she wanted to do was to update Frank on what had been happening behind bars but she didn't find the best time. George had his hands around Pam kissing her and whispering somethings on her ear and Freddy couldn't take it he also exposed some romance with Brenda. After lengthy talks, laughs, bites and drinks George had to step out, attended a phone call Pam followed him out they had a long conversation which didn't go well and so George had to leave and Pam got back not very settled she went into the bedroom. Victoria followed her and they were talking Pam was upset of George's action not showing up for some days and getting back as if nothing happened and weird phone calls from his mistresses that kept him uncomfortable until he stepped out of the house to attend the calls and when Pam questioned about it G became furious and left. Pam explained to Victoria while shading tears and looking extremely upset. Victoria calmed her friend down. Freddy couldn't help it, he went to the room where Pam and Victoria were, he got in a little earlier when

Pam leaned on Victoria's chest, he asked if everything was alright and Victoria told Freddy that Pam and G had a little meltdown outside and that was what upset Pam. He really felt touched and wished to have done something. Both pulled themselves together and Victoria left the room first Freddy lagged behind pulled Pam against the wall and kissed her passionately, he held her head up right and grabbed Pam's face and kissed her lips rolled their tongues over and kissed one more time and he let her off and walked out. Pam couldn't leave at the same time she was even shocked of Freddy's naughty and romantic move she loved it but at the same was worried not to be caught by Brenda whom happened to be in the next room. Freddy got back went to the kitchen poured some drink for himself and went sat closer to Brenda whom was busy laughing at Frank's jokes. Victoria joined the happy group and sat on Frank's lap and enjoyed a massage by her man's hand on her waist and ass as they kept their stories going. Brenda had enough and wanted to leave but Freddy was way enjoying given that George had vacated the premises. After some more minutes of talking Brenda left. Pam decided to sleep for she wasn't really sure of how she was going to appear in between Freddy and Brenda after the kissing situation at least she had some lump of shame in her. Brenda left and Freddy went to the room and found Pam changed in her nightdress and under the duvet he pulled out the duvet and looked at her closely she slept like a baby on her belly her curved body and shaped ass was half way out of the transparent nightdress. Freddy leaned on her back and kissed her neck touching her both hands and smelling her. Pam felt Freddy from behind and went silent Freddy took his hand to Pam's waist like massaging her ass and her shaped body. Pam wanted to turn and face Freddy whom did not let her. Freddy kept playing with Pam's sexy body from behind kissing her neck and penetrating his hand to her left and right boobs. Pam liked it, Freddy got on top of her from behind he grabbed a pack of rubber from his jogger pocket and loosened his jogger and boxer put on the rubber and slowly went in. She was wet like a fountain Pam moved her body slowly as the cock screw her in she loved the situation and kept playing a long. Freddy shamelessly got in and out of her gently to vigorously he altered his pace according to Pam's body response he pounded her from behind she pulled her ass up to accommodate his knob properly he penetrated deeper and she elevated her ass to receive him more, their game kept going meanwhile at the living room Victoria was putting everything back to its original place doing some cleanness and washing dishes as she kept talking to Frank whom was helping out. Frank and Victoria had the rest of the house to themselves hence he laid his hands on her on every style possible they kissed massaged and enjoyed each other's company since no one was watching. Victoria tried to distract Frank by updating him on Freddy and Pam's situation but it turned out Frank could care less on what Freddy and Pam were up to. He pulled his lady against the kitchen counter carried her and put her on top, made her lay on the counter and gave her a head licked and sucked Victoria's pussy back and forth Frank widened Vicky's legs and took closer look of her genitals he played with her clitoris as he observed how wet she gradually became. Frank kept his investigation going, playing with Vicky's clit and fingering her back and forth. Victoria was feeling high above the heavens as she kept getting wet and wet. Frank had no rush he kept playing with his lady's genitals pinching her nipples by one hand as his other hand was busy on Vicky's vagina, her legs wide spread on the kitchen counter as if she was about to deliver and oops before you know it she started squirting as Frank kept the pace of his fingers going he made sure she squirt as much as he wanted her to. Frank was a sex machine or sex starring he knew exactly what to do and how to do it and Victoria's body was so submissive to him and very responsive which kept Frank loving her more and more. She kept squirting every after a minute or two just by Frank's fingers in her. His cock grew bigger harder and needful he freed Victoria from the counter top and made her lean against the counter pulled his knob out and took it in her. She was trembling due to frequent squirting and overwhelmed yet let him in, Frank pounded Vicky harder without delay, he kept his motion stronger and going spanking her bubbly ass and Vicky loved it and kept going, the harder Frank got the quicker he felt to explode and with no time he whispered in Vicky's ear that he-was-about-to-explode! And there he was discharged in her, feeling every moment of it. Victoria was exhausted and Frank was insanely happy. They held each other and kept on their clothes wondering what will Freddy be doing in their room. Victoria gave the whole story to Frank whom was shocked to hear all that. So they both snitched to see what they were doing only to find they were dead asleep. Frank went next to Freddy and yelled that Brenda was coming. Freddy woke up looked straight at Frank and knew that was a lie, he went to the washroom cleaned up took a leak and cleaned up again and came out. It was time for the twin brothers to leave Pam was fast asleep and didn't hear a thing. Frank looked at her and smiled hugged his lady and told Freddy to go start the engine likewise Freddy went on the other side of the bed kissed Pam goodnight and kissed Victoria goodnight and went to start the car and got ready going. Frank hugged his lady asked her to go straight to bed for she looked exhausted he switched the lights off as he kept exiting room after room locked the door and left. Victoria changed to her nightdress and jumped to bed. Freddy left with Frank on the same ride and on their way Freddy had to explain his situation to Frank. Frank already heard of it yet wanted to hear it from Freddy and all was good they reached home safely and the rest was history.

The next day Frank got up quite early gymed up, showered and left around five thirty in the morning. He drove to Victoria's place, he got in and walked into the bedroom and Kayla was zipping her mother's dress they were shocked to see him at that time of the day he looked fine smart and happy to see his ladies he kissed and hugged them and helped out zip Victoria's dress and announced that he was going to drop the kids to school, Victoria was very pleased to hear that and told Kayla to go finish up her breakfast. Pam had gone back to her place that morning to prepare her kids as well Frank asked where Pam was, he went to her place the nana opened the door for him, greeted the nana and asked for Pam and the kids, he went to the kids' room and Pam was dressing up the twins for school, she was surprised to see Frank standing by the door the twins were happy to see uncle Frank they ran to him hugged and kissed him and he told them he was going to take them to school they were happy. Frank hugged Pam the kids rushed for their breakfast and all went to Victoria's place everyone was ready to go Frank hugged kissed Victoria whispered in her ear that he loved her, he hugged Pam and told her that they will catch up later the kids got in Frank metallic black range rover Kayla sat in front at passenger seat and the twins sat at the back buckled up and they left. Pam was touched by Frank's moral support, she thought loud when was the last time George took the kids to school and never caught the memory. Victoria ignored Pam's thought and they jumped into a serious discussion over the kitchen counter on how they shouldn't pay much attention to George's action. Victoria discussed her day plans with Pam that she had an appointment at the embassy for her visa and small touch ups at the shop awaiting for the licence and Pam shared her day scheduled as well she had to go prepare for work and Victoria had to leave to catch-up her appointment at the embassy.

On the way to school, Frank made jokes and discussions with the kids asked questions on what they like and dislike about their school. Kayla loved the school due to the friends she had and nothing else. Jayden loved school due to his soccer team friends and Jayda loved school due to her musical classmates they kept their stories going Kayla confessed how comfortable she was after her mother got a new ride. They finally arrived to school Frank got out opened doors and unbuckled the twins and Kayla unbuckled and dropped out and waved goodbye to Frank as he got back to the car and left. His day was lightened by the stories and excitements from the kids. Victoria arrived on time for her appointment at the embassy she was attended and was scheduled a day for her visa collection. She then went to her shop sometimes she had job interviews trying to get an assistant for the shop a little later she received a call informing her to collect a letter from the college. She went over her college and took the letter at the administration desk it was a confirmation that she passed her finals and was going to graduate. Victoria was filled with joy and happiness she jumped up and down got in her car called Pam and shared the good news she then called Frank and shared the news with him, both Pam and Frank were happy for her and all proposed a call for celebration which she couldn't deny. Her day was way too good to be true, she thought in her mind that soon was going to be a graduate, her shop was almost on the finish line to opening, her love life revived, her Kayla happier than ever and tears ran down her cheeks as she kept thinking and driving back to her shop. It was afternoon she went to pick Frank for lunch but unfortunately Frank had a meeting that extended, Freddy dropped down and left with Victoria went to pick Pam and the three of them went out for lunch break, Victoria shared her news regarding her final results both started discussing how the graduation party was going to lit. They had their lunch and Victoria ordered some take away for Frank. After they had finished Freddy took care of the bill and Victoria started dropping one after the other back to their offices Pam was dropped first and Freddy was next and took Frank's lunch box with him and Victoria left.

Later that day Victoria went for the kids from school and got home earlier made supper and supervised the kids' homework. Pam got back early went to her place refreshed and came to Victoria's place and food was ready and all had their supper together with their kids. The kids went to Pam's for video games and later bedtime. Frank passed by from work with a bunch of fresh white roses and a big round glassy vase with a note on Frank's handwriting "congrats! You made it" she loved the flowers took them put some water into the vase and settled the roses in. They looked beautiful at the kitchen counter. He had some of Victoria's cooked meal and had their discussion on how her graduation was going to be. Pam and Frank wanted a big thing with people and friends over but Victoria wanted a little thing. Frank had some readings to do for his early morning meeting with a client the next day and so he left, Victoria walked him out into his car, kissed and freed him.

The next day Frank did the same routine of taking the kids to school and got in the office earlier for his meeting, Victoria ran her errands and so did Pam. In the afternoon kids were picked from school by Victoria whom kept her routine going. It was a movie night for Kayla and Frank didn't forget about it, hence few minutes before the movie he got at home and had the movie going with Kayla at the living room while the twins had their video game on with Victoria at Pam's home. After an hour or so Victoria took the kids to bed and got back at her place, Frank did the same to Kayla covered her with the duvet and kissed her goodnight. They both went to the kitchen to have a little chat and plan for the trip to US. Frank updated Victoria on the duration, his meetings and activities they will encounter without forgetting meeting Mrs Zoya. They also discussed on how they will settle everything on their absence. Frank suggested on tasking Fadhil the kid's routine to and fro school until Pam feels otherwise. Freddy was also available hence he assured Victoria that everything was going to be fine. Victoria had been researching about Mrs Zoya so as to know more about the woman but couldn't find much and decided to ask Frank how his mother was; what she liked and disliked and if she had allergies and so forth but it appeared that Mrs Zoya was a regular woman and had no complications or whatsoever. He later moved closer to Victoria.

Victoria: "not tonight baby" in her sweet little voice.

Frank: "why not?" while grabbing her waist, kissing her neck.

Victoria: "I'm tired and you should get going, you have a meeting to catch tomorrow morning" she posed while feeling Frank's hands around her boobs, waist and thighs.

Frank: "I know but I want a quickie." Kept playing around Vicky's body, he squeezed her nipples as he unbuttoned her pajama top.

Victoria couldn't resist Frank's hands around her, she stimulated whenever Frank caressed her. He dropped off her pajama cotton trouser and made her lean against the kitchen sink and penetrated from her back. Vicky widened her legs passionately allowed Frank to plunk his hard-on phallus into her punani. They made love at the kitchen against the sink. From her back, apart from the pounding cock and his muscular hands on her, she also felt Frank's heart pulse and his luxurious signature smell from his front. Frank felt the bubbly shaped ass and curvy body while penetrating his boner back and forth. They had their quickie very quickly he exhaled deeply got off her and went to wash-up.

Frank: "what? You look doleful" squinted his eyes on Vicky.

Victoria: "nothing, just go" in her little seductive tone.

Frank: "oooh I get it, someone doesn't want me to go" he smiled kissed and hugged her passionately.

Victoria: "you're damn right" exhaled deeply as she walked him to the door.

Frank: "listen" he stopped and turned to Victoria.

Victoria: "just go please" she begged Frank to leave in her sweet little tone.

Frank: "Vicky!" loud and squinted his eyes "I'm feeling exactly the same but will be all yours tomorrow night, okay?" he grabbed Vicky's face and kissed her deeply in her lips and walked out of the house.

Vicky locked the doors went to check on Kayla and jumped to bed. On his way back home Frank felt sorry for Vicky on how she needed him for the night and couldn't managed to be there for her yet tried to figure out how to deal with the situation going forward. He called her and they spoke throughout his drive. Frank told Vicky how much he's falling for her and she told him the same. Victoria's tone over the phone was a million sexier than usual. They kept talking over the phone until Frank got home and she fell asleep.

Two weeks later her visa was ready for collection at the embassy and their US trip was around the corner. Frank managed to play his daddy role on Kayla, attended several movie nights together kept taking Kayla and the kids to school and for once he attended Parents-Students assembly where Kayla had a poetry presentation. Kayla grew happier and smarter. She had a feeling of possessing a father for once in her lifetime and her class teacher was impressed of her progress.

Frank and Vicky left the country to US. He had meetings in New York City for three days and had to visit Mrs Zoya in

LA afterwards. It was the first time for Victoria to visit US, she was excited and had a lot of fun from her business class flight to landing in JFK. They checked in Hotel Brooklyn Bridge. She was glowing, smiling and enjoying every step of the way. For three days at Brooklyn Bridge Hotel Victoria managed to do a thorough wardrobe shopping designer brand shoes bags dresses accessories. She was as busy as Frank with his meetings. She got herself some spa treat and got some gifts for Kayla, the twins, Pam, Freddy and Mrs Zoya whom was looking forward to meet. In between her busy shopping spree on daytime her night was fully occupied by Frank they fornicated throughout the nights, their sex game grew stronger and wilder, Frank taught Vicky a lot to do with sex game and Vicky was a good student she learnt a lot and coped with every lesson and situation. Due to time difference they called in the evenings, as it was early mornings at their homes. Three days down the lane and Mrs Zoya couldn't wait longer. They went to LA where Frank's mother resided. Mrs Zoya was above sixty but looked way younger than the number. She was colored six feet tall had her long natural thin hair down below her neck, her figure looked like a size 16 with some natural curves on her body. She loved herself so very much and had a fabulous luxurious life. Her mansion, the Sinclair home had been there since the passing of Mr Ferdinand Sinclair. A bungalow with huge beautiful garden big parking space, a swimming pool, in-house gym, in-house theatre, guesthouse, pets' house and maids' houses. The estate was insanely huge and beautiful. They were picked from the airport by one of their chauffeur an old man well dressed. Frank seemed to know him very well, he was happy to see the old man; they got in the car and off left to the residence. On their way Frank had to tour guide Vicky showing their closest mall, hospital, park and so forth. It was almost six in the evening Mrs Zoya had prepared a beautiful dinner for her son and Ms Victoria. The weather was beautiful approaching summer. They arrived, Mrs Zoya was standing at their tall huge front door of their entrance eager to see Frank and his lady, it was not Frank that she couldn't wait to see but the lady. She and Frank had their frequent meetings and phone calls and so the anxiousness was for Victoria. The car pulled over at the drive way and they got out, Mrs Zoya went for her son hugged and kissed him left right cheek and on the forehead.

Mrs Zoya: "and you must be Victoria" smiled and went for a hug kissed her on the cheeks and on the forehead she added "I'm so happy to meet you"

Victoria: "I'm pleased to meet you Mrs Zoya" smiled back and gave her the most warmth hug.

Mrs Zoya: "oooh please call me mom" opened her eyes out wider and held Vicky's hand as they walked in.

Frank just stood by couldn't help watching how his most influential women met for the first time. They walked in Vicky complimented Mrs Zoya on her house and of course she already knew how beautiful her place was. She gave Vicky a grand tour of the house from ground floor to above floors and outside to the marvelous garden of hers and to the farthest end where maids' houses were. Victoria couldn't help smiling and wondering. Frank went to his room upstairs and it was tidy and flawless just like how he wanted it to be, very white crystal clear with white and grey colored bed sheets everything inside was impeccable. He stood by the French door outside his room balcony and could see his mother and Vicky very far at the garden talking. Mrs Zoya and Vicky sat on a wooden bench at the garden. As they kept talking Mrs Zoya held Vicky's hand and caressed the back of Vicky's Palm with her other hand. Frank knew at that moment his mother liked Vicky. It was the happiest feeling in him. After a long tour guide and get-to-know-eachother-talks, Mrs Zoya took Vicky at Frank's room. He was at the balcony making a phone call. Mrs Zoya kept showing Vicky around as they waited for Frank to finish up with his call. Victoria loved everything she saw. The photo collection at their family library was amazing with different history and memories. Frank had finished his call and went to the library and found his mother explaining to Vicky about the memories the photos displayed, had he stood from far listening to his mother squinted his eyes with a big smile. They noticed Frank had been standing behind them. Frank went closer to Vicky he grabbed her on her waist and said to his mother that he was going to settle with Vicky and she shouldn't worry about him maturing and having a descent relationship anymore. His mother was happy to hear that and she complimented Victoria and loved her style (only if she knew how less of stylist she was before then) and her smartness. Frank kept caressing his lady on her back on her ass as they listened to his mother. They walked out of the room and went back to their room. Mrs Zoya left them to settle and refresh as she went to check if dinner was on progress. In Frank's room, their luggage arrived and Victoria couldn't help waiting any longer before she unpacked and gave Mrs Zoya her gifts whereas Frank couldn't help waiting to undress his woman and copulate her. He took her outside to the balcony and she stood consuming some beautiful air and he stood at her back held her waist kissing her neck took his hands on her boobs massaged them tightly while kissing her neck she wanted to turn around and face him but he couldn't let her, Frank kept dominating Vicky's body, her feelings, played with every part of her clothed body. He unzipped her flare dress from behind made it drop off her body, Vicky stepped out of it and they kept their romance going Frank snatched Vicky's bra out and released it from her shoulders. He went for her waist caressed her thighs and widened her legs as he kept playing with her, Frank penetrated his middle finger in Vicky's vagina, she was wet like never before, he squeezed himself in and out several times, she enjoyed, the wind blew to their direction and it felt good he kept going growing big under his trouser. Vicky could feel Frank from her ass. Frank's finger in Vicky's, his hand on her left nipple, his lips on her neck, her voice for cry and pleasure slowly emerged, he switched his finger with his hard cock slowly dived in her, Vicky took it, widened her legs and bent her curvy body and ass down, she looked amazingly sexy. Frank couldn't help it, fucked Vicky in and out holding her waist and looking at her curvy back ass and sexy legs, he pounded her hard and harder and before it was hardest he whispered on her ear that they should come at once and there he burst out Vicky's name and she orgasmed both paralyzed for seconds and they went for shower changed to better look and smelled good and dropped down. Mrs Zoya was doing some phone calls it looked like she was confirming on something. They listened and Frank already knew that there was something going to be held. He took his lady and went to the family library / office made some phone calls spoke to Kayla, Pam and the twins. He also rang Freddy and spoke to him and once his mother was done with calls they joined her. Mrs Zoya had to explain to them that there was going to be a party for them tomorrow evening at the house to introduce Vicky to her friends and so they should get prepared. Vicky almost forgot and rushed back at their room took a bag with some gifts for Mrs Zoya and brought down and handed it to her. Mrs Zoya was very surprised she told Vicky that she was the only woman out of his sons' women whom brought her something from their trips. Frank was surprised that his mother had memories and countdowns. Mrs Zoya hugged Vicky and blessed her. Vicky felt very welcomed and loved by Mrs Zoya's gesture and easily got comfortable with her.

They had their dinner, made stories and when it was time for Mrs Zoya to sleep she had to excuse herself Frank took his mother to bed kissed her and left the room. Frank went for Vicky, grabbed her and told her to get ready for they were going out to hit the club. Vicky couldn't say no. They went to their room, changed into more fancy look, Vicky wore a Givenchy leathered long sleeved black sparkling bandage mini dress with Giuseppe Zanotti heels, Frank got a pair of his Tom Ford ensemble from his wardrobe the transformation was amazing, they got on a Rolls Royce and drove off. It was almost midnight Frank took Vicky to one of the best night Clubs in town. It was an amazing experience, she laughed and loved made jokes with Frank kissed every time. Frank met few of his gang they seemed happy to see him. He introduced Vicky to his respectful longtime friends they loved Vicky had their night well and going until four in the morning they moved to some house party for a friend-of-a-friend Vicky seemed exhausted and slowly begged Frank so they could leave. It was almost five in the morning. Frank was straight-up fine he took his lady and they drove off home. Back in the house the maids were up and running their errands most of them knew Frank they greeted him and Frank reciprocated the gesture and ran up with Vicky, fling off their clothes and jumped to bed.

For six hours straight, they slept like babies. At noon Mrs Zoya knocked on the door and brought in some chicken soup for the couple. They loved it, had it on bed and their mother left. They had their usual wake-up sex, took a long bath in his huge glassy bathroom and dressed casually went down to allow the maid to clean their room. They were plenty of workers moving around the house at that time those of which Frank had never met. He asked his mother why he had many maids and it turned out they were hired for the day to organize the party. It didn't occur to their mind that the party was going to be that massive until then but Frank was used to his mother's parties, always were extravagant and fun. He decided to take Vicky for a walk to see the neighborhood and other places. Most of the neighbors were good with Mrs Zoya and of course welcomed for the party. Victoria had the happiest time of her life she was indeed enjoying every bit of it. They walked further to the park and walked along the path that Frank used to have his morning runs. He showed Vicky around different places he grew up in, and Vicky couldn't be more excited. After a long walk they went to a café had some cold beverages and walked back home. Frank kept playing with Victoria; his hands were all over her shoulders, kissing her neck as they kept walking back home. He had some calls and emails but kept the romance going.

After a little while they got home, Mrs Zoya was nowhere to be seen. Vicky wanted to refresh and help out, Frank wanted her to stay around but eventually they compromised he escorted her in the bathroom as she took her shower they kept their stories going. She changed to a loose silky top dress with her indoor fur slippers wore a pleasant chic fragrance, tied up tight her thick natural curly hair and were good to go. Frank could notice his lady transforming to Sinclair typa lady. He smiled held Vicky's hand and walked down. Vicky went over to the kitchen, there were maids looking at her with smiles, she asked to help out and they resisted but she insisted and went over to a baker who was baking some sort of pastries, she worked with him for a while and went over to another one who was marinating some meat she worked with him as well. Meanwhile Frank was making some phone calls perhaps trying to get his friends over the house for the party. He walked with Vicky to the winery room and selected a bottle for her. He opened it and poured on glasses they took their bottle and their glasses went to sit at the garden as they had their wine. Frank told her a story about their dad and his love for wine. They had their sundown at the garden over a bottle of wine, shared some family stories, Victoria never talked much about her family, most of her family stories were about the people she was surrounded with at that moment that was to say Pam's family and hers. Mrs Zoya was back from wherever she was, went over to Frank and Vicky gave them some hints about the party invited guests, theme, and so forth. The woman filled them in and asked them to enjoy the night for it was purposed for them. Mrs Zoya had asked for hair and make up artist from her personal salon to come over and glam Victoria and so Vicky was surprised and couldn't thank Mrs Zoya enough.

Later that evening Victoria was busy in Frank's room trying some of her dresses she bought in New York for the party, she picked two, one was Alexander McQueen champagne sequin long dress and Versace coral pink ruffled above the knee backless dress both looked amazing on her. After she had her long bath got on her robe and Mrs Zoya knocked and got in to tell her the glam person had arrived she was ready for him. Mrs Zoya walked with Vicky to a guestroom down the stairs and introduced her to Tommy the glam doer. He already settled in with his facilities Tommy was charming and fun to be around. He quickly eased with Victoria asked her how she wanted to look that night and Victoria had two looks in her mind that matched her dresses she explained to Tommy and decided to go for with the dress above the knee – the Versace dress. He then styled her natural hair and took a bit longer. Vicky had thick natural curly hair by then was wet from being washed. After the blow drying and styling she was glammed up and in between the make up Frank got back he went to his room didn't find Vicky but saw the two dresses lying on bed he picked the coral pink one and went out with it. He knew Vicky had lay them on bed for him to choose he got downstairs and asked if anyone had seen Vicky and he was told she was in the guestroom doing some make up he went through kissed her from back and laid the dress on bed

Frank: "that's the one for tonight baby" in his deep voice.

Victoria: "ooh I thought so" she smiled and looked at him through the mirror.

Victoria and Frank came out looking magnificent she had a long ponytail and a perfect glam Mrs Zoya looked beautiful in her white Givenchy dress she was glammed up by Tommy as well. Guests kept coming and everyone had a good time. The garden was sparkling with lights people came in and met Victoria and Frank – they talked, asked them questions others were longtime family friends, longtime clients to their firm, neighbors, member club friends of Mrs Zoya and so many. They had a wonderful night to midnight Frank was filled with smiles on his face he grabbed his woman everywhere he was. Kissed her around and introduced her to some of the people he happened to know. At some they had their spot in the garden with Frank's friends where they drunk laughed talked teased all night long. Mrs Zoya kept introducing Vicky to her old friends back and forth. Later on, people kept vacating the premises and Frank had a huge company at the poolside of the house where they kept the music up and running and friends called other friends and in a blink of an eye the house poolside was filled up. The night lit Vicky went up to refresh and changed to a pair of Calvin Klein leggings and bodycon top. Mrs Zoya had her bedtime soon after her guests left. The night went on till five in the morning. Vicky was exhausted, Frank got a little tipsy and for once he wasn't on the same page with Victoria since she wanted to call off the party and let people leave so that they could get to bed but Frank seemed to enjoy. She couldn't take it anymore and had to go up to bed. Frank kept hosting his guests until they all left at six in the morning. He went up doff his clothes and jumped to bed.

It was half past two in the afternoon Mrs Zoya knocked for some chicken soup for the two, they hardly woke up had the soup on bed while Mrs Zoya sat on the sofa talking to her beautiful couple. She asked if they could have dinner later that day in one of her best restaurants and they couldn't refuse since they had a day left for their trip back. Mrs Zoya left and the two kept enjoying their afternoon in bed. They had some catch-up to do since Vicky left the party earlier than Frank. After a while they had their bed game on except for this time the game was held on a wide bathtub. Vicky ran a bath with some lavenders and music on went to stand in front of the bed where Frank was facing she pulled off her sexy nightdress and walked away naked, her round ass bumping as she kept moving. Frank got up and followed her in the bathroom. They got in the tub and they scrub one another kept their romantic kisses going, he scrubbed her back and she reciprocated. He massaged her tits her nipples. Her thick thighs, her ass, her vagina, her clitoris and took his long finger in her, massaged her inner space as well. Vicky didn't do much than rubbing her man's cock thoroughly massaged his balls, kissed his nipples and his neck and felt his muscular body around her, she kept maintaining her hand job throughout and sat on it after it got harder and upright. Frank supported her thighs and kept pumping her up as it went in her punani. She felt good sitting on it yet pounding her upwards. They switched positions and took it against the sink and against the window and lastly on the bathroom floor. They cleansed up and went to bed slept like babies for an hour or so. As the sun got down they woke up feeling hungry Vicky got down to check for something to eat she went back with a bowl of chicken salad shared it with Frank as they were about to leave for their dinner with their mother. After a while Mrs Zoya had to follow up on them to get ready for the dinner. They went out for dinner in one car Frank was driving Vicky at the passenger sit next to Frank and Mrs Zoya at the back seat. They had their talks and Mrs Zoya asked them to make sure they come back for the holidays with everyone Freddy and Vicky's daughter Kayla. She also asked Vicky if she wanted another baby and Vicky couldn't hesitate to answer that she wouldn't resist some more and that made Mrs Zoya's evening. Frank got the memo from his mother's question and Vicky's answer. The had their dinner at a wonderful Italian restaurant Frank told his mother one more time on how he met Vicky and how the firm was doing. He also told his mother how serious he chose to be with Victoria and how supportive and protective Freddy had been all along and he also mentioned of Pam – Vicky's friend. Mrs Zoya felt like she already knew everyone better enough. After their dinner they drove back home it was bedtime for Mrs Zoya, Victoria escorted her to bed and they had a little lady chat, Mrs Zoya complimented Vicky that she was a smart lady and of course naturally beautiful she urged her to take care of Frank and advice him what was good for both of them. She also asked her to abstain from contraceptives if at all she wanted some more kids like a mother-to-daughter advice and Victoria couldn't agree more she kissed Mrs Zoya goodnight and covered her in duvet switched her bedside light off and left. Frank was in the living room watching a game on TV sipping his brandy he saw Vicky coming nice and slow he went to the bar popped out a bottle of red wine and served his lady. They sat on the sofa cuddling and she kept thinking on what Mrs

Zoya told her regarding having more babies she told Frank about it. Frank asked Vicky if she was ok with that and she smiled with assurance that nothing wrong with it. The game on tv ended they tuned into some other channel and that was like TV moment they kept touching one another kissing one another cuddling caressing here and there, she couldn't remain dry instead ran wet gradually as Frank kept playing with her, and he got harder and harder in his jogger as Vicky's hand job progressed. Frank couldn't hold any longer he got up kneeled on the sofa pulled Vicky's dress up and held her legs up to her head level and squeezed his hard knob into her, he pounded her in her tight wet punani, immerse his cock deep in and went back and forth, she cried out loud as he penetrated in her wet pussy, he felt his cock tight in her and kept copulating her, squinting his eyes on her as she looked beautifully sexy crying out for pleasure, the motion couldn't last for long before she cried out loud coming and splashed out. Frank turned Vicky around and went in from her back he too couldn't hold longer before he whispered about to explode and eventually he discharged in Vicky. The lights were off there was no one around the TV was on and so were their hormones. Frank stayed in her for a little longer this time, he held in there for some more seconds Vicky felt exhausted they lay on the sofa and kept their TV night going.

A day had passed quickly as they were busy shopping. Frank got himself some more custom made designer suits and Vicky bought some more stuff for Kayla and and for the twins. They got home, packed their suitcases and Mrs Zoya couldn't help noticing that it was about time for her people to leave. And when it was actually time she got the chauffeur ready and escorted them to the airport. Vicky was pleased to meet Mrs Zoya and promised to do her best, Mrs Zoya got onto her feelings and tears were almost shading her out. She insisted that all should come and be with her for the holidays. They reached to the airport hugged and kissed Mrs Zoya goodbye and left.

Frank and Vicky flew business class. After almost twelve hours of flying they arrived back to their country around midnight. Freddy went to pick them from the airport. He was delighted to see them back; they had long talk on their way home. Vicky went to Frank's place since there was no one at her place at that moment Kayla was sleeping at Pam's with the twins. They reached at Sinclair's mansion very jetlagged and had hundreds of suitcases to unload. Instead they passed out till morning.

The next day Freddy left early to work, Frank and Vicky were fast asleep. They slept till noon and woke up, she made a call to Pam to inform her that she was back and was at Frank's but will go back home later that day. Frank got his body up to the gym, worked out, went to swim and got themselves a meal at their grand dining discussed on their next step of the day. Later on Frank got Vicky back to her place. The kids were not back yet but the nana had her usual routine hence the place was tidy and organized. Frank helped his lady to unpack and sort gifts aside. As they were unpacking Frank got naughty on his lady, grabbing and kissing her vigorously, they had their romance going as she kept organizing her stuff. Frank loved to see Vicky naked or at least only with a matching lace lingerie on and that was how she was as they unpacked. Vicky grew sexier, confident and more comfortable with Frank. They had themselves organized and later Pam and the kids came over and spent the evening together at her place, she distributed gifts to everyone, Kayla was the happiest had a huge bag than the rest. Pam was filled with smiles and laughter as they kept feeding her stories about the trip.

Few days to Victoria's graduation ceremony and opening of her bakery store, Frank, Freddy and Pam secretly made arrangements for a party at Sinclair's mansion to celebrate Victoria. In the meantime Victoria was busy with ensuring her shop was set and ready to go. The hiring was done, the purchasing was complete and everything seemed to be in place for the opening. She expected to host her graduation party at the bakery store and to her surprise no one disagreed. The graduation was on a Friday, Pam had the kids ready and Fadhil dropped them to school. A day before Pam had spoken to the kids' class teachers regarding picking the kids earlier from school for Vicky's graduation. It was Fadhil's task that day to drop and pick them off. Frank went to work early in the morning, Pam drove Vicky to their usual salon for a glam-up and was all by her side, they had their hair, nails and faces done and took her to college ready for her graduation. Victoria had put some weight on, her thighs and ass grew bigger an inch or two, she had that curved body with a small waist, she wore Alexander Wang black bandage dress to her knee and a pair of metallic grey Brian Atwood pump, she looked amazingly beautiful. Pam had to leave after she dropped Vicky to the college for the ceremony had not commenced. She went to the Sinclair's mansion to see things through from the decors and so forth. Frank called his lady to find out what was going on at the college and to assure her that she will have the best graduation ever.

Victoria had no idea of the arrangements behind her back, she thought after the graduation at the college her family and friends will go to her bakery store pop some champagne and cut a cake which she ordered and Pam was aware of it and they will eat drink and call it a day. She wasn't expecting anything more or less to that, but in her absence a lot was going on. Pam and Freddy had everything put together, Freddy was partly working and partly organizing the party with Pam, he was in his casual wear except for Frank whom had several meetings that day but kept himself on the loop with the arrangements. At noon sharp Fadhil fetched the kids from school and dropped them home. The maids made the kids ready for the ceremony. Kayla and the twins were in Gucci casual outfits, they looked cute and organized, waiting for Pam to pick them and head for the ceremony. Frank had winded up his meetings made a phone call to Freddy to find out about the arrangements and went for the kids.

Frank got at Vicky's home took the kids in his black range rover and left to the ceremony whereas Pam drove with Freddy from Sinclair's mansion to her home refreshed and changed to a beautiful above the knee flare dress and left passed to a florist collected bouquet of flowers for Vicky and headed to the ceremony.

They all got right in time before Vicky's name got mentioned they had back bench seats. Freddy walked passed some seats and got an angle where he took some snaps at Vicky. Victoria was glowing and happy to see Freddy. Freddy kept taking pictures of Vicky and others around her and waited for her name to be mentioned. When it was actually time Victoria's name was mentioned by the Dean, she stood up in her brown gown walked straight up to the stage near the Dean and was awarded a medal and degree with distinction which was read by the Dean from the presentation card, she walked over to the Chancellor whom congratulated her with a handshake and capped with the academic cap, she walked over to another Chancellor whom hanged the academic sash over her shoulder and walked off the stage to the table and received her degree framed document and went back to her seat. All that time Freddy had been taking pictures in every step of Vicky's way. Kayla and Frank were happy to see Vicky on stage. Freddy went to take pictures at Frank, Pam and the kids. Later after the end of the ceremony Kayla and the twins handed the bouquet of flowers to Victoria, she was so happy to seeing everyone she expected, they hugged kissed and moved to another point for more group snaps. Frank kept squinting his eyes at Vicky feeling happier than the rest for Vicky's outstanding record. He hugged and kissed Victoria and whispered to her ears that he loved her. Frank left with Victoria and the kids while Freddy drove with Pam. On their way Frank had to tell Vicky that they are going to pass at his house for a minute before they go to the bakery store.

At Sinclair's mansion the garden was decorated with lights and balloons nice music and few of Frank and Freddy's friends were at the house. The sun had set and darkness emerged they had a long drive back and once they got home to Vicky's surprise at the parking there were more than the usual number of cars, they got out and walked few steps before she could hear loud music and see people moving around and that's when she realized it was a surprise party, Vicky went mouth opened and got seriously amazed, she moved closer to the garden and there were few people she happened to know and all smiled back at her, Kayla and the twins were happy being at Frank's place, they ran up and down and disappeared. Pam and Freddy got home earlier than Frank and Vicky they all went closer to Vicky and yelled "Congratulations Vicky!" as she walked closer to them. Frank just stood behind looking at his lady receiving her surprise party gesture. They all got together and the party began. Victoria couldn't be more happier, tears were shading off her eyes, she looked at the kids from far jumping and playing looked at Pam, Freddy and lastly Frank all were happy for her and words couldn't come out of her mouth as she kept smiling. Frank took his lady excused themselves and went upstairs to refresh. On their way up to his room he couldn't help touching Vicky, when they got up he took the gown off her body unzipped her bandage dress and pulled it down snatched off her bra hooks and pulled it off, he grabbed Vicky and dropped her on bed pulled off her panty and got on top of her. Vicky unbuttoned Frank's shirt as they kissed, slowly flung off his shirt and vest, as they kept kissing, she unbuckled Frank's belt, unzipped his trouser and Frank pulled it off his legs, she got her hands at his boxer brief, Frank went for her neck, her left and right nipples, her navel, kissed it and grabbed her legs up as he put his tongue in her cunt, he sucked her gently, licked her slowly, played with her clitoris. Vicky got her cry up and louder as Frank got his head on point, he kept playing in and on her vagina every part of it licked and sucked her as he kept grabbing her ass and thighs, Victoria's cry increased as she kept feeling heaven on earth, before she cried out louder Frank penetrated his erect knob in her, he grabbed her legs up to her head level and got himself comfortable inside Vicky's wet punani. Frank pounded that pink vagina back and forth, she cried and cried in pleasure, Frank kept whispering on her, how proud he was for her and how good he was feeling as he kept pounding Vicky back and forth not for long they both felt to climax, Frank was about to explode and so was Vicky and both got off the same time. It was amazing, they felt like never before, laid on bed for seconds and afterwards cleaned-up as they were about to leave Freddy and Pam walked in to see what was taking them long and behold Vicky changed to a loose above the knee lace dress and she looked amazing, her curved figure protruded out nice and pretty, Frank was in a jogger and a t-shirt both looked casual and cute. They all walked down to their guests, had their evening filled with laughter and happiness. The kids had fun at the pool and on the playground. Later on George joined the party and as usual it began to disturb Freddy seeing Pam and George together. Brenda also arrived later that evening and the party went on. Barbecue was delicious, drinks were plenty and the music was perfect nothing seemed to be off the hook. Vicky wanted Kayla and the twins to go home but Frank ordered them to remain. Fadhil was sent to go pick some changing clothes for the kids from their apartment and the kids had the guestroom down the stairs MaryJo supervised the kids as they took shower and changed to pajamas, had their dinner inside and went for movies in the theatre. Outside the mansion adults had their night going on, people drunk and ate and laughed and had it all. After sometime they began to leave and so did Brenda. Freddy and Brenda's relationship was on and off one. The two had enough of each other yet kept seeing one another. Whereas George and Pam had been on and off from the start, got used to it and life went on. There are times when Freddy would call Pam over his room and make out and return outside like nothing happened. Pam was so happy about it and felt her night totally complete. Frank had the manners to entertain their guests. After a little longer all guests had left except for George. Frank George and Freddy kept their drinking game going, Pam went to the guestroom refreshed and changed to something loose and sexy. The night was lit, Vicky besides Frank and Pam besides George and Freddy was on and off to the kids at the theatre, after sometime kids went to bed, George and Pam left and Frank was left with his ladylove and Freddy, appraising how the day went. Afterwards Freddy left the two outside and went to bed. Frank and Vicky jumped to the pool and unclothed each other and made love. They stayed in the pool for sometime reminiscing from the day they romantically met to where they had reached, each was reminding another of every step of their way they enjoyed the stars above the sky and later went to bed.

Weeks and months passed by, Vicky got busy with her new bakery store and kids kept growing bigger, taller and smarter, Pam and George kept their on and off relation going, Freddy broke-up with Brenda and secretly dated Pam. It got official with Frank and Victoria, the company knew about their affair and so did the public. Vicky maintained a good and pleasant persona and so did Frank. They were loved by the majority, Frank took her to almost every occasion he was invited, introduced Victoria to every of his friends, business stakeholders and so forth. Freddy loved a sister in the family;

he aborted the surveillance operation on Vicky's life and focused on creating a strong family bond with her. Mrs Zoya had included Vicky on their family group chat and their scheduled Skype and video calls. Kayla finally began calling Frank dad and not Uncle and the twin maintained uncle Frank.

Couple of months down the lane Mrs Zoya started initiating plans for the holidays, asked for her team to join her or else she joined them. And they all came to a conclusion over a family movie night at the theatre in Sinclair's mansion that: Mrs Zoya should come and join her family, get to meet new members of the family and new family friends, she was ready and so Wanitha got in place for Mrs Zoya's flight itinerary and in few weeks Mrs Zoya was in the country with her family. She met Kayla the twins and Pam. Frank had a business trip in West Africa and got back two weeks after his mother's arrival. Freddy and Vicky got in charge of handling Mrs Zoya. In the usual weekday Vicky picked Mrs Zoya and went with her at the bakery store for almost the whole day they later met with Pam and sometimes Freddy for lunch if not dinner at home or different restaurants. Mrs Zoya was a friendly woman and fun to be around with, she blended with the girls very well and not once could anyone think she was far older than the rest. She had a firm body and a glowing skin looked matured but not for a sixty plus aged woman. At times she dodged going to the store with Vicky got her body to gym, exposed her skin to morning sunlight, stayed in the pool and felt good throughout the day. At times Freddy would pick his mother for a dinner date just the two of them and have a long beautiful evening. One weekend Mrs Zoya went out for the day with the kids.

Fadhil drove them around; she loved babies and always had been wishing for grandchildren. Frank got back from his business trip happy to see his mother bonding with the new people in his family. He spoke to MaryJo to organize dinner for everyone soon. At different nights Mrs Zoya would sit with her sons talk them out, she also had some time alone with Vicky and posed the same question; if she was going to have babies anytime soon. That was her major cry. The big family had a wonderful dinner organized by MaryJo, Mrs Zoya was pleased and had a blast, the kids kept her laughing throughout the night, Frank and Vicky noticed their mother's love for the kids and at night as they had their bed time game Frank dropped a request to Vicky for them to consider having babies going forward and Victoria couldn't agree more as a matter of fact she was waiting for Frank to introduce the idea and so they decided she will have her contraceptive undone and ready for the making. It was pleasant for Frank. They had their game on and slept.

As the office was about to close for the holidays Mrs Zoya visited the firm and had a drink up with the employees and talked to them on one-on-one and some in a group. It was the courtesy of the firm to throw a party or dinner occasion for Mrs Zoya when she paid a visit.

Kids closed school for the holidays and went on a school trip for a week. It was the first holiday at the bakery store and Vicky unlike the rest was very busy. She had numerous customers each day Pam's law firm also went closed for the holidays and sometimes she went over to the store and helped Victoria. Frank and Freddy were organizing a safari for the whole team for the last two weeks of the holiday to New Year. Once all the arrangements were confirmed they had lunch after coming from church as a family and yes Frank and Freddy went to church at least when their mother was around or during holidays. They presented the idea to the ladies and all seemed to like it and so Vicky had extra task to see through how the store was going to operate on her absence.

Few days later the kids got back from their school trip and had the news regarding safari trip they couldn't wait. Vicky and Frank kept their romance and game stronger than before, everyone was happy for them. When it was actually time the team had a sleep over at the mansion and the next day, at noon airport pick up drove off and collected them and left for their flight. They were going to a safari camp at different reserves and parks in Eastern Africa. Mrs Zoya was excited and so was everyone else. George didn't show up and Pam never expected him on board. Freddy had Pam all to himself, Vicky and Frank were no doubted couple and very responsible for the rest of the team. They flew for more than 14 hours and finally landed to JKNIA and took a private flight that landed them straight to the airstrip of the game reserve, Vicky was on a white Gucci jumpsuit and Frank had Denim trouser and white Polo Givenchy they looked amazing, the kids were excited jumped up and down one to Freddy one to Mrs Zoya while Kayla was stacked by Frank's side. They arrived at the game reserve and had a first class treat; on their arrival the weather was nice. It was almost sunset and they were shown to their grand camp house that seemed to be the spacious, beautiful inside out and best from the rest. It had a private pool outside the lounge, wooden floors and ceilings glass doors and windows beautiful sundown view from the house terrace. The place was rocky greenish and a far view of a mountain peak it was a beautiful place to be breathtaking and refreshing.

Later as they settled, in-house attendants came and introduced themselves there was a woman and a man in uniform they helped the kids settle in their room and the rest got their luggage in their rooms. Mrs Zoya was excited, she took pictures, enjoyed the weather and a great mountain view. Freddy and Pam settled in one room, the kids shared the room but Mrs Zoya had a room to herself and asked Kayla and Jayda to join her and leave the room to big boy Jayden. They stayed at the camp for almost a week had an amazing experience from the game drives, visited the Rhino awareness center, the kids enjoyed birding and some indoor activities such as board games and documentary DVDs, the ladies took a day for safari spa treatment, they visited wildlife rehabilitation center and went to see big cheetah sanctuaries. After their stay at the camphouse, they moved to another riverlodge house that was a neighboring national park which was along a river, they had their site visit and enjoyed to the fullest. Frank and Victoria had their sex game on, from different angles and venues. Pam and Fred slept together throughout their safari. Some day in between their safari they had sundowner & barbecue party for all, other night they threw a pool party while Mrs Zoya had indoor activities with the kids and the bonfire party at the New Year's Eve was the top of them all. They were filled with love and joy, the kids were happy throughout, pictures and videos were taken. Time to head back home the memories created were immeasurable to everyone, they all had fun and couldn't thank Freddy and Frank enough. On the second day of New Year they took their private flight back to the city and the next day boarded a plane back home.

Mrs Zoya had some shopping to do before she headed back to US and so Vicky and Pam took Mrs Zoya to purchase her favorite locally produced cheese from the market. They had last dinner with Mrs Zoya before she left. Vicky, Pam and the kids went back to their apartment after the dinner and left Frank and Freddy with their mother. Mrs Zoya thanked her sons for a wonderful treat and urged them to keep up the good work and the love they had for their people.

It was back-to-business-day kids went to school, Vicky got back to her store, Pam went back to office, Frank and Freddy left to office and Mrs Zoya remained at home packing and getting ready. In the evening Frank and Freddy took their mother to the airport and Mrs Zoya flew back to her country.

Few months had passed the kids jumped to a higher grade-growing up fast, the bakery store progressing well, Vicky had faced some challenges in her business yet kept it going. Freddy and Pam had their secret relation up and strong, Frank went to being more responsible and busiest businessman. His love for Victoria escalated and it was the best thing for everyone around him or her.

It was one month to the twin brothers' birthday Vicky as always wasn't considering anything enormous for their standard but Pam kept insisting that they should throw something huge for the boys. And so they planned for a big yacht party with some of the boys' friends. Vicky and Pam got on top of the plan secretly without letting the boys know. They had to involve one of the Frank's friends whom owned a yacht and they requested to rent it for the weekend. The friend having known the aim was for his friend's party, he gave it with no demand and asked to cover for maintenance involved. On one of their double date night the ladies mentioned to the boys that they were organizing their birthday party and so they shouldn't plan for anything. Frank didn't want Vicky to hustle but again he couldn't make her stop. They had their evening going and as they were leaving from the restaurant Vicky trembled and fell on the floor, they all thought she might have had too much too drink and missed her steps as she walked but that wasn't the case. Frank took her to the car and asked if she was okay. Suddenly Vicky felt dizzy, Frank drove her home. Freddy and Pam were on the passenger seats behind. Vicky wanted to get home at her apartment, the feeling was unusual and thought may be she had less sleep and rest lately. Everyone kept insisting that she may have had a little too much or she missed some rest but technically Vicky knew she had no much than usual. They reached at their condo got inside and she went straight to her room pulled off all her clothes and jumped to shower then changed to something loose for bed. Pam and Freddy were in the kitchen trying to see if they could get something for Vicky to dilute the alcohol in her. Pam sliced some pieces of watermelon and went with a glass of water. Frank and Vicky sat on bed and kept talking. The two got in with the treat on the plate. Vicky was pleased she had some bites, drank some water slowly as they talked. Frank gave her some painkillers as she complained about the headache. After a while Freddy and Pam left the two on bed and went to the living room. Frank's arms went on Vicky's neck and shoulder massaged her gently, and kissed her neck, he kept his arms busy for sometime as he caressed Vicky's boobs went for her thighs and massaged them gently he got on top of Vicky pulled off her silky dress and kept playing with her nipples kissed around her neck. He could feel the fever from Vicky's body, Frank noticed something was not okay with Vicky but kept going. Vicky's body temperature was a bit up than normal, she was indeed hot and Frank couldn't cease kissing and licking and sucking her down to her punani, Vicky felt good and responded with her usual cry, Frank kept his head game gently and slow as he grew bigger underneath his trousers. Vicky felt the pleasure and grabbed Frank's bold head massaged it gently as the cry intensified, she moved her waist left and right as she felt good, his tongue and lips on her cunt, he went to his trouser unzipped himself and dived right in her. She was extremely hot than ever Frank felt the temperature more than before, he loved it and kept copulating Vicky gently as he grabbed her left and right ass. Victoria was incapacitated yet felt well in every move of Frank's knob in her. She came earlier than ever and her body went restless, Frank had to turn Vicky around to spooning, he kept holding and massaging Vicky's boobs and nipples as he kept mating her in and out. After a little while he whispered on her ears that he was about to explode and indeed he did. He rested in her for sometime, Vicky had fallen asleep; Frank realized that - went to the bathroom cleaned up and came out dressed Vicky up. She was half asleep and very responsive. Frank kissed her one more time on her neck, lips and nipples, asked how she was feeling and told her that he will check on her from time to time, he covered her with the duvet switched the lights off closed the door slowly and walked to the living room. Pam lay on Freddy on the couch the TV was on but both passed out. Frank switched the TV off and woke them up.

Frank: "Yoo! Let's move" as he tapped Freddy's shoulder.

They woke up Frank hugged and kissed Pam goodbye also told her to stay closer to their phones as he was going to call from time to time. Freddy hugged his lady and they walked out locked the door and the boys drove off. After some hours Frank called Pam with no reply, he tried Vicky not even her answered, he knew they were fast asleep. He set an alarm to call after three more hours and got Pam on the call and everything was fine.

The next day Frank called his Doctor. The Sinclair had their family doctor whom attended them from time to time, he asked him to set time to meet with Victoria for a thoroughly check up, he also gave him the whole scenario of how Vicky had been the previous day. The doctor scheduled Victoria for evening time later that day. Frank got up earlier enough as he went to work he passed by Vicky's place and found that Pam had left with the kids to school and office. The nana was already in the house for her daily households, he walked in greeted the nana and went straight in Vicky's room, Vicky was still asleep but burning up, Frank pulled the duvet off her body opened the blinds at the window and allowed some light inside the room, he called the doctor and asked if they could meet at home for Vicky was not doing well and they both agreed. Frank called Freddy and told him that he will be running late for Vicky's sake. Frank grabbed Vicky from bed and slowly talked her out that they needed to see a doctor. Vicky was conscious and responsive except for her temperature, she got up slowly went to the washroom, Frank helped her cleansed up and she had to change to a truck suit. Frank refused her from too much clothes as her temperature was up and he chose a cotton top dress for her, very intriguing dress by the way. She took an overnight LV handbag and put some of her essentials got her slippers on, Frank carried the bag and they both walked out. She saw the nana cleaning up, gave her some instructions on what to do and they both left. Frank drove back to his place, MaryJo received them from the entrance Frank walked with Vicky up to his room as he talked MaryJo on what was happening with Vicky. Vicky went straight to bed and got under the duvet, warmth was what she wanted yet burning up. Frank insisted on not covering herself since she was burning-up. MaryJo went to organize some meal for Victoria and Frank sat on the sofa looking straight to Vicky wondering what would be the problem. After less than thirty minutes the doctor got home and MaryJo brought him in. He started examining Vicky asking her some questions as Frank had some phone calls to attend to at his home office. After some checkups the doctor prescribed Vicky some medicines to regulate her temperature and told her that he will get back to her later that day with the results of her tests. He walked out went to see Frank in the office room and told him the same except he added that Victoria might have conceived but didn't tell Vicky yet until the results confirms so. Frank was startled to hear that, for once it didn't occur to his mind that Vicky might had been pregnant, he thought Vicky might had a serious infection on. He was dazed with the news but the doctor insisted to wait for the results later that day. The doctor left and Frank got back to his lady he wanted to share the news but again thought what the doctor had told him to wait for the confirmation from the results. He went over the bed hugged, kissed her deeply just like how he starts his game on. Victoria wasn't in the mood.

Victoria: "I'm tired babe, I can't do it" in her little sweet voice.

Frank understood how Vicky was feeling. And aborted the mission. MaryJo knocked on the door with the soup ready, she got in and placed a huge stainless steel tray on the coffee table and asked how Vicky was doing. Vicky was grateful for MaryJo's generosity and went over the table for her soup. Frank got the energy and sat beside Vicky as she took her soup. He asked her what she wanted for lunch for MaryJo to prepare and Vicky was okay with anything. After she had her soup, Frank begged Vicky to rest and let the pills do the work and not go to the store for the rest of the day. Vicky couldn't agree more as she felt the dizziness on and off. Frank ran a bath for Vicky and left her cleaned up smelling good on his black extra large printed horse Balmain t-shirt. Vicky had to make some phone calls to the store and to Pam and afterwards she fell asleep for three straight hours. Frank got to the office at past midday he called home to find out how Vicky was doing and it turned out she was still asleep. Frank was a bit moody that day despite of the tentative good news. Freddy went to see him and had the news although was not confirmed yet to being the News. He was happy to hear that. They had their busy day going and so did Pam since she almost forgot to pick the kids and was in a meeting hence sent an email to Freddy to assist. Freddy went to pick the kids from school and dropped them home spoke with the maid at Pam's house to ensure everything is settled and left to work. The kids had their schedules up and running once they got home. They had an hour to refresh before attending some home tuition that the teacher came over thrice a week and that day was a tuition day and so they kept their schedule going. Meanwhile Victoria slept for three good hours MaryJo went to check on her but she was fast asleep and so she let her sleep. Frank had been calling several times to check on Vicky but still found her asleep. After sometime Vicky got up all wet and sweaty her temp backed down, she went out for a sunshine, she sat at the balcony called Frank on her mobile, they talked for sometime and Frank begged her to get something to eat. MaryJo served food for Vicky whom chose to sit outside and enjoy the sunset they arranged a table for her at the garden near the pool had her meal and made some calls to the bakery and at home to the kids. Freddy worked beyond business hours, he had reports to run and so he stayed behind. Frank left early passed at Pam's place and went to see how the kids were doing Kayla asked for her mother and Frank told her that she was doing just fine. After sometime Pam got back early and had a discussion with Frank on how Vicky was doing and after sometime Frank hugged and kissed Pam and the kids and he left. Pam stayed in with the kids for the rest of the evening that day.

It was heavily raining outside Frank got stuck on traffic, cars were not moving, he called Vicky and talked with her. Vicky wore Frank's black jogger and a black long sleeve t-shirt jumped to bed and turned the TV on she felt cold as her temp was back to normal. Pam called Vicky and spoke with her for sometime as they were speaking Freddy's call came in and Pam had to hold Vicky and replied Freddy's. She got back to Vicky, they kept talking on the phone for quite sometime until when Frank got in and Vicky had to hang-up. He got loose with his coat and everything the traffic was crazy on his way back. He went to shower, his phone was buzzing and it was the doctor, he missed the call when he got out from shower and got himself a pair of matching jogger and t-shirt just like Vicky's, Frank took his phone and walked out to his office room.

Doctor: "hello Mr Sinclair"

Frank: "yes Doctor, what news do you have for me?" he sat on his giant black leather contemporary office chair

Doctor: "some good news, if I may say" he paused and then continued, "the results show that Ms Victoria is pregnant"

Frank: "wow! That's good news." Smiled and squinted his eyes simultaneously.

Doctor: "indeed, congratulations, she may need some more resting as the body regulates itself and also encourage her to have carbs in her diet as I have noticed she is not a carbs consumer."

Frank: "doctor, say no more. I will keep an eye on her and will keep you posted. Thank you so much"

Doctor: "other than that, I will keep her on my schedule and will proceed with regular check-up until clinics begin. Thank you and have a good evening" he hanged up.

Frank smiled while squinting his eyes put his phone on the desk and for once he imagined being a dad. He went back to the room and Vicky had fallen asleep as she was watching TV. He got underneath the duvet and lay beside her as he kept thinking on how his mother will be delighted hearing the news. He then got up went down to the bar poured some of his brand on a glass with ice on and went back to his room. Meanwhile, Freddy had left office and passed by at Pam's, he & Pam had a quickie at Vicky's house since the kids were all over Pam's place, they also talked about Vicky's situation Freddy realized that Pam had not had the tentative news with regards to Vicky's situation, he wanted so badly to share the rumor but again had to mute, they had their sex like never before and Freddy had to leave.

He got home and went straight up to Frank's room. Frank was on his laptop reading emails as Freddy walked in. Frank had his drink on and Vicky was fast asleep on bed. Freddy went over to the side couch and sat asked on how Vicky was doing and the report from the doctor.

Frank: "she's pregnant" smiled and sipped his drink and flipped off his laptop.

Freddy: "Wow! I'm proud of you" he stood up and hugged his brother he added, "Mother will be excited, have you told her?"

Frank: "haven't even told Vicky yet" he faced Vicky on bed.

Freddy: "she doesn't know?" looked blithesome.

Frank: "yeah I haven't. Had doc's call in the office and came back found her asleep. No wonder she sleeps too much. Imagine she slept three hours straight and now she's like that…"

Freddy: "all for good man, I'm so happy for you guys" he walked out and went to fetch some more drink and came back.

Frank: "I'm going to marry this woman Freddy, let me just settle down, she deserves it. I asked her once didn't have to beg for it and she said yes." Felt overjoyed and in high spirit.

Vicky's phone rang and she woke up, the phone was beside her pillow, she saw Freddy and got shy.

Freddy: "hey mama what's up? Is the alcohol still in you?" he joked.

Vicky: "hey Freddy, this is another bottle I had in the afternoon and not the yesterday one" she joked back and woke up went to the bathroom cleaned up and went to sit next to Frank.

Frank kept smiling and kissing Vicky whom wasn't sure of the reason to Frank's good mood. Vicky went for her phone and it was Pam's messages, she replied as she leaned on Frank. Freddy asked what he could bring her and it turned out she wanted something to eat. Freddy walked down to get something for Vicky and MaryJo was slicing some fruits for her, he waited for them to be ready. Frank kissed Vicky stood up and carried her to bed pulled off the jogger out of her beautiful long legs and pulled off the t-shirt over her head. Vicky had socks on her feet. Her beautiful curved body was laying on bed facing Frank, her round flirtatious boobs and supple nipples, her small curved waist, thick thighs and her coy eyes faced Frank, she didn't know what to do as Frank kept looking at Vicky's eyes and body with his squinted eyes, He bent down and started kissing Vicky from the lips to the neck down to her boobs, Vicky folded her legs around Frank, wrapped him or locked him up by her legs, he kept kissing her, made her feel like a goddess, she felt spectacular as Frank licked and sucked her nipples got down to her navel all the way to her pelvic grabbed her ass firmly licked and sucked her cunt and dipped his tongue in Vicky's vagina all that time Vicky couldn't help crying out of pleasure, she held Frank's bold head and touched his muscular arms and kept moving her curves, they were in their world. Frank pulled off his jogger, boxer and t-shirt threw them down the floor maintained eye contact with his wet horny lady, he held Vicky's legs apart to her head level and gently penetrated his hard phallus on her overly wet hot honeypot as he got in he couldn't help fucking her hard. Vicky loved it yet was very feeble to keep up with the coition. Freddie walked in holding a big glass bowl of fruit salad and his eyes landed on Vicky. Frank couldn't careless. He kept going.

Frank: "let's go on baby, I love you, he knows that" whispered on Vicky's ear as he penetrated in and out of her vulva.

Vicky felt shy for a second Frank kissed her on the lips as he kept making love to her. Freddy went to the couch turned the TV on and he couldn't stop peeking on them mostly Vicky. He was amazed on Vicky's shape, her big round fluffy ass, her glowing skin, her curves, her boobs, he kept spying on her and got really destructed by her cry voice, her tone of pleasure, Freddy not even once laid eyes on his brother, it's as if he had seen him naked before but throughout he had his eyes on Vicky. Frank kept whispering on Vicky's ears tried to ease her and made her feel comfortable to the situation of Freddy being around, he told Vicky that he was very happy he swore to not leave her nor forsake her, he whispered a lot of promises some heard by Freddy some didn't and when it was time for Vicky her cry intensified and spattered water ran out of her, Frank felt charged he went for few rounds before he exploded. He fell on bed beside Vicky and they went silent. Freddie broke the silence by a big round of applause. Frank got up and walked to the bathroom butt naked, Freddie was not even looking at his brother, he picked his bowl of fruit salad went sat next to Vicky covered her with duvet and started feeding her pieces of fruits slowly. Vicky had a coy face, she hardly looked at Freddy and Freddy noticed how uncomfortable Vicky was, he picked Vicky's t-shirt from the floor and helped her wore it and she felt better. Freddie leaned on the bed next to Vicky and fed her the fruits one piece after the other, Frank came out of the bathroom happy like he worn a lottery went over kissed his lady "eat mama" he said and went refill his glass.

Vicky: "I'm feeling so shy right now" in her little sweet voice.

Freddy: "why? You shouldn't be" he added, "Frank is my brother, never done this before but I guess he's overly excited" he gently massaged Vicky's hair as he spoke.

Vicky went silent for a minute as she kept chewing her fruits. "Thank you Freddy," she whispered.

Freddy: "for what?" he asked looking at Vicky from an angle.

Vicky: "for the fruits, for caring, for Pam, for the kids, for everything"

Freddy: "say no more baby girl, eat. Dinner is waiting for you and so is Frank" smiled at her and kept feeding her the fruits.

Frank got back with two glasses one for him and one for Freddy. He got under the duvet facing Vicky. She had no clothe underneath but the t-shirt on. Frank tossed his head under the duvet next to Vicky's pelvis as Freddy was feeding her fruits, Frank kept playing with his lady's wet genitals and she felt very shy. The fruits were over Freddie put the bowl aside and got on hiss phone texting, Frank crawl over on top of Vicky the duvet ran out of them, he got in her one more time and slowly penetrated back and forth, she grabbed Frank's back as the knob got in and out of her wet red punani. Freddy didn't move an inch, he sat right beside Vicky witnessing their sexual intercourse and that time around he had a closer look at Vicky's alluring body parts: her boobs, her nipples, her thighs, her thick beautiful legs. Frank got in and out as he lay on Vicky's chest kissing her passionately, he gently mate her and she pleasantly enjoyed and responded, caressing Frank's bold head and back. After minutes of fornication, she started breathing out loud moving her legs in different motion caressing and holding Frank tight. Frank didn't stop for he knew she was having an orgasm he kept penetrating back and forth at the same pace, Vicky held Frank tight and suddenly released her hands around him. Frank rose up to see how excited his lady was as the waters ran out on her. Her face was red, her legs trembled and she looked exhausted. Frank got hold of his hard erect knob as he immersed it in and out of Vicky's wet punani, he did that repeatedly looking at Vicky until he discharged on her. He got off from her top and held her hand and both walked butt naked into the bathroom. Freddy again gave them a round of applause. They took shower and came out clean and smelling good and fresh. Freddy had left the room; he might have had an erect from what he saw, after a while they all met for dinner at the dining room. Frank supervised what Vicky was eating and made sure she had enough carbs on her plate just like what the doctor said. Vicky called back home and spoke to Kayla and Pam as they were having their usual scheduled movie night and wished them a goodnight. After the dinner they stayed on the balcony for fresh air, Freddy kept replaying the sex scene back in his mind. The three of them had a wonderful time as they had their drinks on, Vicky wanted some wine and Frank had to stop her from taking alcohol for a reason that she was not fine yet. However there was a well prepared mocktail for her and she kept having it throughout the night as the boys had their drinks. At night on bed as they were about to sleep Vicky couldn't help asking Frank about what had happened.

Vicky: "I feel like I was being a slut that time when Freddy was around" in her little sweet voice leaned her head on Frank's shoulder.

Frank: "hell no, I wanted you that way and I liked it and it's just in front of him and none other." He caressed Vicky's right arm and boob.

Vicky: "have you." before she finished the sentence

Frank: "no I have never and don't know why today" he interrupted Vicky in his deep voice and added, "Freddy is my brother and best friend for life. I got much respect for him and so does he and whatever had happened in here not even Pam would know about it despite Frank shagging her. I want you to feel comfortable not that he will lay hands on you nah! But Freddy will always be there for you on my absence no matter what and never will you ever feel a difference"

Vicky: "okay, you sound like I will loose you" in her little voice caressing Frank's chest.

Frank: "no you wont, but I want you to know you will be safe nevertheless. Freddy has got big heart than me. I just hope he gets someone serious and settle down." He spoke in his deep voice as he played around Vicky's luscious body.

They slept like babies that night and early morning Vicky woke up before the rest went to the gym, got back took shower and wore one of her white Versace jumpsuit and Valentino Garavani knitted rockstud ankle boots she looked dazzling Frank had some sound of moving objects and woke up it was late than usual he was impressed with Vicky's outlook and strength quickly he jumped to shower and after some minutes both came out with white smart attires they dropped down and the table was set with breakfast. Frank didn't have much than a glass of orange juice but Vicky sat down and had pretty much everything, she was starving. Frank realized it wont take him much effort to supervising Vicky's food affair, the nature had it all under control and Vicky was eating shamelessly more than usual.

They left each on their cars. Freddy had already left early in the morning, Vicky drove to her store and Frank followed behind and headed to the office. She made a call to Pam spoke in lengthy and couldn't mention the threesome episode she had last night. That was the first thing she tried to keep out of Pam and she felt bad about it but had no choice. That evening Vicky went back at her condo feeling better except for the nausea that kept coming and going. She asked Frank about the test results and Frank had to lie nothing wrong was found.

A week had remained for the boys' birthday party, both Pam and Vicky were busy on the preps, they had invitation cards printed and rsvp addressed to their friend Ian, the ladies tried to find a gift for the boys but didn't get one so they decided to get an artist to hand draw a photo Frank and Freddy took together on the New year's Eve at the bonfire party and the ladies hand signed below the picture and it said:

"We Love You"
V & P

They framed the picture wrapped it well and had courier deliver it with some other presents from the kids at Sinclair's home address early morning of their big day. George had visited his mother out of the city and decided to take the twins with him and so Kayla joined them and before they left they made birthday cards for Uncle Freddy and Frank wishing them a happy birthday.

Vicky kept having night sickness sometimes-daytime dizziness too, she had been complaining wanted to go see another doctor but Frank had been discouraging her. He planned to break the news to Vicky on his birthday and he had everything in place. Mrs Zoya had the news about Vicky she was extremely happy but was told to not tell Vicky yet for there was a whole plan in place for that.

It was Frank & Freddy's 38th birthday a courier van drove by the gate and delivered the gifts as planned. MaryJo had the parcels besides the staircases for the boys to see once they dropped down. The parcels were wrapped in white gift papers and big white ribbon you could notice it from far. When Freddy got down he saw it, took it, opened it and found the picture framed of Frank and him and the note, he loved it, called MaryJo and told him to get it hanged on one of their walls. Later that morning Frank woke up to a very romantic text message from Vicky wishing him more years filled with laughter, Love and blessings he read the text several times with a big smile and squinted eyes and replied to her with the "I love You." He got up went down found Freddy and MaryJo discussing on where to hang the frame, he looked at the picture and was filled with a smile, he loved it. They also found cards from the kids with their handwritten messages. Vicky and Pam drove to the mansion that morning they looked beautiful in their matching full white off shoulder jumpsuits. Frank and Freddy looked miserable wondering what was next and as they wondered Vicky and Pam got there they hugged kissed and wished them a happiest birthday ahead, the boys thanked the ladies for the gift and showed them where they hanged it. Pam briefed them on how the day was going to be and had them prepare for the yacht cruise party. Frank and Freddy couldn't thank them enough they started making phone calls to their friends to confirm on their availability it turned out almost all of their friends were aware of the party and were on board even Shirley confirmed on her availability, the turnout was positive after all no one had ever missed a Sinclair party of any sort because they were known to have thrown the best lit parties in the history. They packed their belongings got to their range and drove to the dock where the yacht was parked. It was one mega yacht with double deck four bedrooms two lounges on both upper and lower deck a huge kitchen spacious and extremely luxurious piece. Frank and Freddy had been in it several times cruised it and so very familiar with it.

The weather was good, Ian had already arrived and saw everything under control, and the birthday boys could not imagine how the ladies pulled out everything so well and exactly of their taste. There was a dj, a bar set and of course barbecue corner and one room was set for the foursome family and the rest three were for other close friends. The foursome room was the one Frank, Freddy and the ladies had to use for changing and resting. When they got there Vicky, Pam and Ian had a briefing and ensured everything was set. Vicky kept having her daytime sickness on and off, she sometimes excused herself went to the room laid on bed recharged and got back to everyone. Frank was happy to seeing his friends even the ones he couldn't expect to see had come through, business partners, longtime friends and even his series of ex were on board, he was so happy likewise Freddy did not think Brenda was going to show up and so was grateful. Ian seemed to be master of ceremony he kept talking over the microphone as music played, Frank started drinking and enjoying and so did everyone else. Freddy was partly enjoying and partly concerned on the welfare of his people, he kept following Vicky wherever she went yet had an eye on Frank and Pam. Shirley and Brenda showed up looking gorgeous, they had time with Frank and the rest of the people, at a certain point of time the yacht had to start moving slowly the party was lit and everyone was enjoying, Vicky took some of barbecue on plate and a glass of mocktail and went to the room. She took a quick shower changed to a mini white flare dress eased herself on bed as she ate her barbecue and sipped her moktail. She then called George and talked with the kids afterwards. She lay on bed turned the TV on and kept munching her barbecue. Pam, Freddy and the rest were outside enjoying and partying. She after couple of minutes fell asleep. Frank excused himself from a group walked around as he peeked trying to find Vicky, he went up to the room and Vicky was deep asleep. He covered his lady with a bedcover sat beside and kissed her on the cheek. He took the box out of his trouser pocket opened it one more time looked at the gem closed it and put it back on his trouser and slowly walked back to the party outside. Thirty minutes later, Freddy went to check on Vicky and he found her asleep not moved an inch. At sunset she got up cleaned up and walked outside to the rest of the people. Frank was happy to seeing his lady all up fresh and strong, he got up went for her and let her seat beside him. Freddy went to get Vicky something to bite and Pam went to the bar for Vicky's favorite mocktail. After she had eaten and felt satisfied. Frank went for the microphone he was very active he asked for everyone's attention and started by thanking everyone for their presence love and support thanked Ian for offering his yacht for the party, he thanked his twin brother, Freddy and Pam for being the best friend to the family, and turned to Vicky and thanked her for countless of reasons, Vicky was shy, very shy before people and as Frank kept showering her with compliments she got more shy and whispered to Frank to stop but Frank didn't listen he kept complimenting his lady as he caressed her left hand, held her closer and kissed her on the head everyone was happy for them. After he had done showering the compliments he went to his knees took the box out of his pocket opened faced Vicky whom could not believe what Frank was about to do.

Frank: "babe, I am beyond grateful for discovering you. You've literally completed my life. Would you please marry me?" said Frank as he squinted his eyes towards Victoria.

Vicky was astonished covered her mouth and her face with her both hands. Freddy and Pam didn't see that coming nor did anyone in that yacht.

Victoria: "Yes baby! Yes!" in her little sweet tone Frank shoved that white diamond gem onto Vicky's finger. Vicky stood up, pulled her man up and they both kissed passionately. Everyone was surprised and clapped happily for them, Pam went closer hugged the couple and she couldn't be more happy, congratulated her friend and asked her if she knew about it and it turned out to be a monumental surprise that had top their surprise. Freddy congratulated them and so did everyone else. The ex Shirley and the rest shamelessly walked towards Vicky and Frank and congratulated them. The party went on, Vicky had half a million dollar worthy of a rock on her finger, everyone was happy for her except for few, she moved around thanking everyone for coming and met Shirley, Brenda and other ladies, it was weird between them but she had to keep it neutral and natural then she went to hang with Pam and described how uncomfortable it was facing Shirley and also wondered who invited her but they couldn't careless.

The sun had set, darkness emerged, some dazzling lights on the yacht went on, dj had put on loud music people were dancing and enjoying, Frank laughing out loud and drinking with his friends, Freddy with his as well, Pam Vicky and Lettoya – Ian's girl friend all at a corner talking and gossiping, Lettoya dated Ian for as long as they could remember and so she knew most of Frank and Ian's squad and the girls they had been seeing. So she was like the storyteller to Vicky and Pam. Her and Shirley never really liked each other-a little of girl's jealousy situation had been going on between them and hence was not Shirley's fun. So they had their girl's chitchat while on drinks, laughed and danced. Vicky was not taking alcohol but was having fun from the ladies. She felt hungry again and went for some barbecue ate as their stories lit among them. Pam started wondering if Vicky was okay because her eating and sleeping situation was abnormal, she thought about it for once and ignored. They had their corner lit with gossips and stories as they danced to music. Frank came over.

Frank: "hello ladies, how are my girls doing?" as he caressed Vicky's back and kissed her on the lips.

Frank seemed to have had a little too much. Pam went for a bottle of water and handed it to him.

Pam: "here, have some the night is still long" as she hands the bottle of water to Frank.

Frank: "thanks Pam, you damn right, but are you guys enjoying? I see mine is biting in silence" he drunk the water and teased Vicky.

Lettoya: "yes we are bruh, thanks" she replied to Frank smiling and looking at him.

Vicky fed Frank with a piece of her barbecue chicken and another and another as they made stories. Pam went for some more of the barbecue and gave Vicky to keep feeding Frank. He seemed to not have eaten a thing but drunk enough. Frank was fed some barbecue by Vicky and felt a lot better he thanked Vicky, kissed her and held her on his chest kissing her hair. They were looking very cute together. Ian joined the circle and so did Freddy, the ladies had their men around and the stories changed to the usual ones - how the party was going, their next gathering party and so forth.

Vicky: "babe haven't you had enough of this? May be you should drink water before you have another one" she whispered on Frank's ear caressing his back.

Frank: "yes baby, worry out. I'm good" he took more water and suspended his glass of brand for sometime.

Vicky: "who invited Shirley?" she whispered on Frank's ear again.

Frank: "not me definitely, not even Freddy or Ian, I'm sure some other friend, are you bothered?" he asked in his deep voice as he kissed Vicky on the lips.

Vicky: "no, was just curious" she said in her little voice looking at Frank's eyes. Pam pulled Frank a side.

Pam: "Do you think Vicky is fine?" looking at Frank's eyes.

Frank: "why? What's wrong?" he knew where Pam was heading.

Pam: "I don't know, she eats too much and every time, that's unusual and she has these break naps, totally unlike her"

Frank: "You are damn right" he pulled Pam far a bit from the rest "she's pregnant"

Pam: "what? Does she know?" looking surprised.

Frank: "not yet, I wanna tell her later today." I wanted to surprise her with the ring and the news all at one." He kept talking in his deep voice "but do me a favor don't tell her yet but will do it today" squinted eyes on Pam.

Pam: "wow! That's news. I'm happy for you guys better tell her. She told me of how tired she had been lately and I thought may be it was the pressure of your party and her store now that the party is over and if she keeps feeling the same she may find out in some other way"

Frank: "I got you, hey Pam thanks. You really are damn good for all of us" he kissed Pam on the cheek and they walked back to the group.

Vicky: "what were you guys talking about?" as she kissed Frank on the lips massaging his bold head.

Frank: "You." He looked at Pam and his hand went on Vicky's back, down to her ass.

Vicky: "what about me?" she smiled as she felt Frank's hand rested on her ass.

Frank: "I love you" he kissed her on the lips and held her hand. Vicky stood up.

Frank: "where to?" he asked in his deep voice.

Vicky bent and whispered on his ear that she was going for a nap and will join them later. Frank was listening to her while looking at Pam whom was also looking at Frank. He stood up and walked with her all the way to the lower deck. They got in their room, Frank unzipped Vicky's dress and pulled it down, he carried her to bed lay her on bed facing her as he kept removing his t-shirt and trouser off and went for his boxer. Frank started kissing Vicky on her lips, neck, he snatched off the bra hooks and pulled it off her shoulder while kissing her, he went to her hips, thighs and pelvic kissed her all the way down to her wet vulva, he held her legs up and high as he gave her a head licked her clit and rolled his tongue in her wet cunt. Vicky had her usual cry that she exerts before as Frank thought of getting in her, she whispered to him "I want you to lay down babes" Frank stopped got off and laid on bed beside her, she got on top of him held tight his hard-on thick lengthy phallus and took it in her mouth, sucked it, licked it all the way to the balls, she did it repeatedly. Frank kept his hands behind his head as he received alluring sensational desirable blow job of all time, he kept his hands back to his head until he couldn't anymore and massaged Vicky's hair and shoulder as she got busy with her tongue mouth and hands on Frank's erotic knob. He whispered to her that he was going to explode and Vicky wanted his in her mouth. Vicky stopped rose up and Frank turned Vicky 180 degrees and got in her, she was extremely hot and wet, he felt good as he penetrated in her, here's what he said in motion to his cock's coition: "baby-I-want you-to know-that-you are-pregnant" as he finished the word pregnant Vicky splashed out.

Vicky: "what?" she cried out loud as she discharged.

Frank turned her around and got in her from behind and told her how he came to find out and wanted to surprise her in a special way. Vicky was happy to hear that.

Vicky: "OMG! I thought so myself and had planned to go for a check up tomorrow." She smiled as Frank exploded in her.

Frank: "yes babe, we did it! Mom's very happy, Freddy and now Pam" he added, "Pam called me a side to alert me, well I had to tell her the truth"

Vicky: "Oh my goodness, you all knew and kept silent now I get it all that sex in front of Freddy was for this" she added, "I still feel bad for not telling Pam what had happened that night"

Frank: "you don't have to feel bad, I'll help you break the ice" he squinted his eyes on her and kissed her. "Hasn't George fucked Pam in front of you?"

Vicky: "well I can't say he hasn't but whenever they start doing it, I walked out. So I have not been around their full moon. Why are you asking?" she paused and looked at his eyes.

Frank: "no was just trying to figure out the closeness of you all" acting smart.

Vicky: "we're close and George is a great guy but wasn't my thing" she said.

Frank and Vicky laid low on bed for sometime, he massaged and caressed Vicky's nipples until she fell asleep. Frank covered Vicky with the sheets, cleaned up, refreshed and came out with a different look - a jogger and a matching hood smelling way good. Pam and the rest in the group were squiffy, they were laughing out loud shouting and having good time. Frank went to the other group of friends were Shirley and other of his ex were mingling, they were joking him that he was the nanny getting baby Vicky on bed and he had to change to fresh clothes. Few of the girls on the group had enough of what they were drinking and got a little handy on Frank. On the other side Frank was having fun with the group, he had a fresh glass of his drink and kept stories on. Freddy was also occupied with his friends and Pam as well. At midnight Pam went to the room refreshed and changed to different outfit, she felt fresh and lay on bed with Vicky and passed out.

The group that Frank was, got more bombed the lashed ladies couldn't keep their hands off Frank and nor did Frank stop them. After a while Frank took the ladies to the corner on the back of the yacht and Rob one of Frank's friend had to do a standby guard. The ladies were leaning under Frank's hood for a kiss one after the other, they had it going as they had some fresh sea breeze, Frank got a little handy on the ladies grabbing and kissing them randomly and the ladies were going for his manhood on the jogger but he couldn't let them.

Meanwhile Vicky got up and found Freddy all up on Pam doing their thing, she got to the washroom peed cleaned up, walked out of the room slowly and climbed on top of the deck, the view was good, people were drunk some were making out, she went and leaned against as she faced the ocean, she stood there and thought about what Frank told her earlier - her pregnancy. She was delighted and smiled as she faced the ocean, she had someone calling Frank's name, she looked around didn't see any and for once as she looked down on the lower deck there was a man on a hood standing behind a lady who bent over facing the ocean and making out. She tried to look to spot the man but could not. Rob was standing a bit far from the two smoking his cigar. Vicky kept enjoying her sea breeze and before she thought of getting down to her man, Frank's name was mentioned a gain, it was a lady's tone, she looked down and there she saw Frank standing still leaned on the yacht and the woman went down on him. She could not believe her naked eyes. Frank was about to getting another blowjob apart from the one he had an hour ago with her. She yelled "Frank" but not quite loud her legs were shaking, her hands on her mouth, her eyes about to explode as she shed tears and for once Frank looked up and saw Vicky standing right above him looking terrified. He was extremely shocked, pushed the lady a side, pulled his jogger up and pushed everyone else. Rob and the ladies had noticed what had happened, Frank went around running, climbing to the upper deck. Some of the people were wondering what had happened. Rob rushed and told Ian what had happened. Ian was busy with his girlfriend he went a side listened to Rob and told Rob to get hold of the girls and not let them out of his sight. Frank went up to the upper deck and Vicky had already gone to her room. Vicky got in the room - Pam and Freddy were on bed making stories after their intercourse. Vicky was upset crying out like a baby

Vicky: "I wanna go home" as she moved around looking for her bag and started packing her things.

Pam: "what's going on?" she looked shocked stood up butt naked and went to Vicky.

Vicky: "I found Frank" she couldn't finish up and busted on tears leaning on Pam.

Freddy walked also butt naked to the bathroom cleaned up and got his trouser and t-shirt on. He already knew what happened.

Pam: "woo! Hold up, it's okay don't cry baby girl, it's alright" as he petty Vicky on the shoulder.

Vicky kept crying like a baby, they sat on bed. Pam was undressed as she kept hugging her friend and calming her down. Vicky cried in pulses nonstop. Freddy dressed up and went over to Vicky, hugged her and told her everything was going to be fine. He kissed Vicky on the forehead and looked at Pam trying to communicate to her to calm Vicky down. Frank got in the room.

Frank: "Vicky" he called and repeated, "Victoria!"

Vicky: "DO NOT TOUCH ME!" she shouted at him.

Freddy went over and asked Frank to step out and leave Vicky alone. Frank insisted that he wanted to stay. Freddy went for Pam's dress and made her put something on for she was naked. Vicky stood grabbed her bag and insisted that she wanted to go home or else she will jump off the yacht and swim to the shore just to get home. Frank stood a side looking at Victoria in a shameless face. Pam didn't say a word to Frank but was talking to Freddy.

Freddy: "okay you all listen up, the party is over, the yacht is heading back, Frank please, she doesn't want to speak to you now, It's best you leave her alone. Vicky – I'm sorry for everything please calm down and will get you home soon. Pam – get everything together don't leave a thing back." As he spoke there was a knock on the door, it was Ian he walked in silently took Frank out and went to talk to him.

Freddy: "now tell me, what happened?" looking extremely unhappy.

Vicky: "I got out left you guys on bed and went up for some air, I was looking at the ocean and heard a voice of a woman calling Frank's name, I looked around and didn't see a thing after some time I heard the same name and when I looked down there was him on his hood behind a lady who bent over him. I didn't know if it was him all I could see was the hood and I kept looking and saw him turning around facing the woman who was about to give him a blow job, he looked up and saw me looking at him" she spoke in pauses as tears ran out of her. Pam stood and listened as she was packing their stuff.

Freddy: "I'm sorry" he hugged Vicky passionately as Vicky kept crying in silence.

Vicky: "why me? I didn't ask for all these if that's the life he wants why bring me in it?" as she shed tears.

Freddy: "I know. Calm down, let's get you home first"

Vicky got up took off the dress she had on and changed to a pair of leggings and matching top. She didn't care about

Freddy and Pam around, she walked naked got her clothes on and was ready for home. She took off the ring and gave it to Freddy. Freddy didn't want to take the ring he insisted that it was best for Vicky to give it back herself. Vicky got the box of the jewel and put the ring back in it and left the box on top of the side drawer of the bed. Meanwhile Ian and Frank had everything sorted the yacht was on its way back to the dock and rumors spread on Frank's cheating and some questioned and others acted like they did not know a thing. Victoria kept talking to Pam as they got themselves together. Freddy went for bottles of water and some bite for Vicky whom was not in the mood for anything. Pam and Vicky stayed in as Freddy went out to get things together.

Freddy: "Ian hope we are heading back?" he looked furious.

Ian: "ooh yes, everything is under control" replied to Freddy.

Frank: "Freddy I need" before he could finish his sentence.

Freddy: "I can't help you, go get your ring it's on the bed side drawer" and he walked away from Frank.

Freddy for once believed in his brother about the settling down move but again he didn't see this coming. He was beyond pissed at Frank. He walked around ensured that everything was settled and everyone was fine.

Freddy: "hey Rob, where's the slut?" looking extremely vexed.

Rob: "calm down Freddy, I got it under control" he pleaded Freddy.

Freddy: "under control? – Just like how you got it in the first place. I want to know who she is and who invited her" looking annoyed at Rob.

Rob: "well she's Shirley's friend probably got here with Shirley – I don't know much man" he replied politely.

Freddy walked away and went to Ian asked if there was anything to settle with regards to payments and apparently Vicky and Pam had already sort that out.

Frank felt embarrassed and alone. Shirley and her crew were nowhere to be seen. Freddy moved to each room knocked and asked for Shirley and finally got her in one of the rooms with the rest of the ladies.

Freddy: "I have never said this to you but I'm officially saying it now: STAY AWAY FROM MY FAMILY" he sounded beyond irate to Shirley and walked away.

Shirley couldn't careless; the ladies in the room were shocked and worried seeing Freddy that furious. Freddy went back to the room where Vicky and Pam was and checked on them. Vicky had calmed down and was on a call with Kayla and the twins. The yacht got to the dock and people were vacating they managed to see everyone out of the yacht, Lettoya got to Vicky and Pam, she gave them a warmth hug and encouraged them to sort out their differences and move on. She was also furious on the one who invited Shirley and the girls to the party. Ian and Frank walked inside the room Vicky's eyes had swollen and turned extremely red, she complained of a headache and Freddy gave her some painkillers. Pam was so devastated at Frank and didn't say a word to him. They all gathered in the room

Ian: "ladies and gentlemen, we are the only ones left in this yacht as of right now and we were the reason for this wonderful party until it broke out, let me thank Vicky for being such a brave and loving woman for Frank and We are very sorry for what had happened let's hope you both will resolve and move forward. Victoria we love you, we need you, please stay strong" as he held Lettoya by his side.

Vicky: "thank you Ian for everything and goodnight" in her little voice she looked at Ian and her eyes were beyond red and swollen.

Ian and Lettoya left and walked out of the yacht.

Freddy: "okay listen up Frank get my car go home, I will drive Pam and Vicky back." He added, "don't forget to take your." he pointed at where the ring was.

Frank: "can I say something?" he begged politely.

Freddy: "no, do not say a word, just do as I have told you. Babes let's go he held Vicky up and let Pam walk out as he came behind them.

Freddy stopped and looked at Frank: "you're lucky you're my brother I would have cursed your mother" he walked out.

They got in the cars just like how Freddy ordered. Frank drove alone back home and Freddy drove the ladies back home. Pam and Freddy were on the front seats while Vicky lay behind crying in silence as they kept heading back home.

They reached safely. Freddy helped them to settle in. Vicky went to shower had water running her body as she cried and cried and cried, she scooched down as she cried, water running on her from her hair down. Pam and Freddy were discussing in low toned voice what was going to happen and Freddy told Pam to watch her friend since she was pregnant which Pam had already knew they agreed to keep an eye on her and Freddy was going to talk to Frank on the next step. Vicky kept crying in the shower, they went to the room to see her and she was still in the shower. Freddy got in and he found Vicky miserable in the shower cubic her eyes lit in tears and swollen more, she hardly opened them wide. Pam got her a towel and took her on bed, she was trembling they dressed her on one of her night dresses and Freddy went to grab some hot milk for her, she took it fast like she was starving and asked for more painkiller and thanked Pam and Freddy for their support and laid down. Freddy massaged Vicky as she fell asleep; he whispered at her that things were going to be fine until she slept. Pam took shower and got herself ready for bed.

Pam: "I don't want you to go" as she walked Freddy to the door.

Freddy: "me either but I have to go meet Frank and put some sense in him" he kissed Pam and grabbed her ass tight as they kept kissing "I will call you every time to check on you guys stay close to your phone." He kissed her goodnight and walked out.

Pam: "ok" sounded horny she locked the door and got to bed.

They slept calm, Freddy kept calling to check on them and he had a lengthy discussion with Frank listened to his crap explanation and lastly they reached to a conclusion that he needed to beg for forgiveness even for a thousand times and for hundred years until Vicky forgives him. Also Freddy kept insisting that Frank should ignore some of his friends since they are not good for him a song he had been singing in Frank's ears for ages.

They slept that morning and agreed to go see the ladies in the afternoon. It was half past twelve in the afternoon, nana never came to work on Sundays; Vicky woke up and went to the restroom, peed and got back to bed. She wasn't feeling very well, she couldn't sleep again she kept thinking on what happened few hours back and started shedding tears, she felt hungry and went to the kitchen made some omelet toasted bread and hot milk. She sat in the living room turned the TV on and took her breakfast. After few hours of starring and wondering how and why she got into the mess, a phone buzzed, and Pam woke up, Vicky went to the room to get the phone and found Pam awake and on the phone it was Freddy he called to check how they were doing. Pam told Freddy that Vicky was up and they were all fine and so he told her that they were coming to see them in an hour. Pam woke up and sat on bed and started talking to Vicky, she was very sorry for what had happened and told Vicky that Freddy and Frank were coming to see them.

Vicky: "I have nothing to say if Freddy is coming for you that's fine but I have nothing to say to Frank I can't even face him Pam. I don't know what to say to him all I want is to move on. I have a family to raise and a growing baby in my womb to care about" she spoke freely and opened to Pam.

Pam: "I totally agree with you but I also want you to listen, if you have nothing to say at least listen to what he has to say and I will assist you from there. Damn! Frank he's such a son of a bitch!" she added, "I never saw this coming" she continued "I haven't said a word to him and will not say until we here what he has to say, I can't even face him myself."

Vicky got to the bathroom took shower cleaned up changed to a matching leggings and short sleeve bodycon top she looked beautiful yet devastated. Pam woke up, cleaned up, and changed to something chic as well. They stayed on bed talked other things that didn't involve Sinclair. They planned their week a head Pam had promised to take her friend for a vacation. Vicky thought of so many things getting her beetle back and returning her car to Frank and the credit card as well. Frank and Freddy got at their place, went straight in to their room, Pam and Vicky were on bed talking.

Freddy: "hello" as he walked in with Frank behind him

Pam: "hey babe" she went for Freddy hugged and kissed.

Vicky: "hey" in her little voice yet looked sad.

Frank went over to Vicky hugged and kissed her on the cheek he was going for the lips but Vicky diverted.

Frank: "hey Pam" in his deep voice.

Pam: "hey" short and clear as she walked out and pulled Freddy and both left the room.

Frank: "Vicky, I'm beyond sorry my love there's nothing I can say that can make things better than to say sorry, I sincerely apologize. I love you a million times yet I wronged you." He sat next to Vicky looking at her swollen red eyes as he spoke. He tried to massage Vicky's back as he talked but Vicky couldn't let him and kept her eyes down.

Frank looked remorseful yet had all the best and sweet words to say to Vicky. Vicky said less as Frank was being apologetic to her.

Pam and Freddy were in the living room making out. The two couldn't stay without seducing and caressing one another. They made out in the kitchen against the kitchen counter as Pam blended juice for everyone. She was hopeless in love with Frank and everyone could see through her. Frank demanded for Vicky's love back, he went towards her lips held her face gently and kissed her passionately Vicky at first was hesitant but Frank kept demanding for Vicky's attention asking her if all was well between them but Vicky didn't reply to the question. He spread his kisses to her neck and she slowly fell for since Frank's kisses were irresistible. Frank slowly laid Vicky on bed made her face him, he got on top of her and kept kissing her as he apologized one more time. Frank undressed Vicky and got on her neck, all the way to her breasts he licked them supple nipples and every time he would stop look at Vicky in the eyes and ask her for forgiveness but Vicky said no word. Frank kept the romance going sucking Vicky's breasts and nipples, his hands were all around his lady's thighs and ass, he looked so determined to take the wrath out of Vicky's chest and so his game got way above the margin. Frank gently kissed Vicky all the way down to her navel, he held Vicky's legs high and went down on her punani, he kissed her, licked her vulva and sucked her clit, she felt pleased and way good and started breathing heavily. Frank kept heading his lady back and forth and at some point he stopped and looked at her eyes asking if all was well but Vicky still said no word, he knew that was not enough and so he got down and kept the suckation and lickation and kissation going as much as he heard Vicky's voice murmuring out of pleasure, Frank then pulled down his pants and boxer and penetrated right in without saying a word. He looked like he was serious on business aiming on getting his lady's response. Frank slowly and gently copulated Vicky's wet punani back and forth as he bent over her; kissed Vicky's lips and neck, he went several rounds before he saw Vicky's legs trembling and her body moving sideways Frank did not stop, he kept the pace up, pounding the lady's punani vigorously and looking at her eyes and after several minutes of Vicky's cry of pleasure, Frank looked her in the eyes and asked for forgiveness one more time, that time she replied, nodding her head and Frank wanted more than a head nod and asked her again and Vicky said yes in her little sweet voice but this time Frank wanted a louder yes than the usual one and so he asked her again looking at her eyes and copulating her non stop and as she screamed yes with a "Yes babe" splashes of water discharged out of her as much as never before, Frank kept sexing Vicky back and forth and as he did so she couldn't stop discharging. Vicky climaxed as she replied to Frank's apology that was the coolest thing ever. Frank felt the pressure of exploding he turned Vicky side way and crossed legs as he penetrated her one more time he felt thrilled that Vicky said Yes, and on his third round he whispered looking to her eyes that it was time and there he came. Silence emerged as they both lay down on bed restless facing the ceiling, she wondered if that was how their life was going to be - clearing wrongs by a wild sex and he wondered if things were cleared anyway or Vicky would not be the same. After a couple of minutes, Vicky woke up heading to the bathroom, Frank pulled her back on top of his chest and held to his face as he spoke;

Frank: "Victoria – I love You, and I'm sorry for ruining our day, I promise to make it up for you my love" he had never sounded as pitiable as that time.

Vicky looked straight into his eyes blinked and raised her sweet voice "it's fine" she got off Frank's chest and went for a clean-up. Frank followed her in the bathroom and both showered together. He managed to console Vicky romantically with running water above their heads he rubbed her back as he kept holding and massaging her erotic body parts, she loved it, always had been incapacitated with Frank's romance they got their shower done and joined Freddy and Pam in the living room.

Pam: "someone's looking fresh" she teased out loud at Vicky.

Freddy: "yeah right and smelling good as well" he backed Pam "I don't want to know much but I'm guessing we are good"

Vicky smiled at Freddy as she went over for a glass of juice.

Pam: "here's for you Frank" as she hands a glass of juice to Frank.

Frank: "Thanks Pam" he still sounded low-keyed not the hyper, charming active Frank. His eyes could tell how shameful he was feeling.

They had their kitchen counter talks Freddy was chairing the talks than the usual master himself. They were starving and decided to go out for dinner and invited Ian and Lettoya over. Freddy drove, Pam at passenger seat while Frank and Vicky sat behind they all looked beautiful. The ladies were on above the knees flare dresses and the men were on smart casual that distinguished them from the rest of other men around. Frank and Freddy are known as the GQs. So it was no surprise to anyone wherever they appeared. They chose a breathtaking terrace restaurant along the ocean it was sun downing and the sea breeze was pleasurable. Ian and Lettoya appeared with smiling faces believing that things got resolved and their best couple was forever together. They had a table for six each man sat next to his lady there was a strong love vibes around them. Frank got easy as time went on, Vicky noticed how down Frank was and so she had to cheer him up and bring him to his best mood. It was no surprise Frank noticed Vicky's effort and so he got back up with no time. They had their evening filled with laughter and joyful stories they planned for a group vacation at one of the beautiful remote islands sometime in the future. The dinner prolonged to late drinks, Frank at last got back to his attitude and laid a short speech of how sorry he felt for what had happened and how sorry he was for his pink from red swollen eyed lady. They kept their night going, the men had their talks as the ladies got kinky and half past midnight they had to leave.

Freddy drove all the way to their mansion as they kept talking. Obviously Vicky and Pam were in for a sleepover at Sinclair's. They parked and all got out the car Frank was back to his mastering attitude he held Vicky's hand and climbed up with her to his room. Pam and Freddy stayed behind at the balcony they had their drinks as they kept touching feeling one another. Besides their drinks, they had their romance at the balcony. Meanwhile Frank and Pam got easy they ran a bath together he put the ring back on her finger and begged her not to take it off no matter what came around. She was all the way sweet and irresistible just like how she used to be. Her eyes were still swollen but reducing gradually, every time he looked on her eyes he was not impressed. They got on bed laid-low and had a romantic bedtime talk.

Three months down the line her first trimester went pretty well. Her belly grew bigger; she got a proper diet plan, workout plan and even office routine plan. Vicky decided to tell Kayla that she was pregnant; Kayla was beyond happy to find out that she was going to be a sister. Frank got closer and more responsible to Kayla. He kept their movie nights, early morning school drop offs and their one-on-one time very active. Kayla grew up loving Frank so much. Mrs Zoya and Vicky kept their bond stronger; they literally communicated every single day. She wanted to be up-to-date on Vicky's condition. A great mother-in-law she was. Freddy and Pam had their good days and bad days just like any other couple but grateful they couldn't show it to anyone. They kept their relationship out of peoples' eyes and concerns but very few within the circle knew the two were having a serious affair.

One night as Vicky had put Kayla to bed and she was about to have her favorite show a phone rang and she was surprised to hear Kayla's dad on the phone whom sounded polite and brief that he called to inform them that his mother / Kayla's grandmother passed on. Vicky was shocked to hear the news and very sorry for Kayla's dad and the phone hanged up. She then spoke to Frank about the sad news Frank was sorry and didn't say more to it. The next day Vicky slept and thought through about the news from Kayla's dad, she wondered the man had never called him before but he did to inform her on the passing of his mother and so Vicky decided to tell Kayla. Fortunate enough Kayla had few flash memories of her grandmother she remembered liking her. Vicky spoke to Frank about it once again and she introduced the need of paying last respect. Frank denied and told her not to go. The funeral was being organized in the city and plans were to transfer it to their hometown for burial. Vicky was unsatisfied with Frank's out-ruling decision and planned to go regardless.

On the day for the last respect, Vicky took Kayla and drove to the church for the funeral mass there were lots of people, she stayed behind and went over to pay their last respect Kayla saw her grandmother lying in the coffin and all she could do was keep silent and looking around. And after the moment they drove off home. In their way back Kayla asked her mother how the grandmother used to be and Vicky all she could say was the nicest things. Of course that was the truth anyway.

As they prepared dinner at their kitchen counter Kayla couldn't stop getting flashes of her granny in the coffin, they kept the story about her granny going for as long as dinner was ready and served. They ate their dinner, prayed and went to bed.

Early morning as she woke up to prepare Kayla for school, Frank was at the living room in his phone silent reading his emails. The nana was not in yet; Vicky went to the kitchen and was shocked to find Frank on the couch on his phone. He didn't look fine he looked fiercely angry.

Vicky: "damn! You scared the shit out of me" she busted out and went over to Frank wanted to lay a kiss on his cheek "how long have you been in hear?" she bent over Frank's bold head and went for his face for a kiss.

Frank: "did you go to the funeral?" sounded above and beyond angry.

Vicky: "hey babe, you don't want to know how we are doing?" playing with Frank's emotion as she touched him.

Frank: "Victoria, did you go to the funeral?" looking straight at her eyes and diverted the kiss "I repeat – did you go to the funeral even after I asked you not to go?"

Vicky: "Frank you didn't ask me not to go you ordered simply because you knew I would have questioned your decision, you should have wanted to know my views on this instead you didn't and I already talked to Kayla that we could go how was I supposed not to." She continued "but we went very brief, we paid our last respect, Kayla saw her granny for the last time and we left, didn't even meet anyone not even Kayla's dad" she paused and went on "I am sorry but we had to do it"

Frank: "ooh! That's great, so I don't have a say now when it comes to Kayla. The bottom line is you went against my order. I told you not to and you did go still. You're disgusting!" he woke up and went over at Kayla's room.

Frank: "hey bunny, how are you this morning?"

Kayla: "hey dad, I'm good, please help" she turned for Frank to zip her up.

Frank: "you ready?" looked pissed yet contained.

Kayla: "almost" as she got her things together and both walked out.

Vicky was in the kitchen preparing lunch box for Kayla. She told Kayla to have her breakfast and went to Pam's to check on the twins and after few minutes she came with the twins all looking ready for school they greeted uncle Frank, Kayla was done with her breakfast she grabbed her lunch box and the kids rushed to the car. Frank was heading out as Vicky held him back Frank turned to Vicky whom then apologized to Frank. But Frank didn't reply and walked out drove off with the kids.

Vicky went over to Pam and told her what had happened, Pam was very sorry for her friend's situation but yet told Vicky honestly; that was what was ought to happen. They got back to their places and all went on with their daily schedules.

On her way to her store she called Frank on his cell phone and there was no reply. She tried one more time and ended up with a voicemail. She knew Frank was mad for what had happened. She didn't have the best of that day she kept wondering what was on Frank's mind and how to unwind him from his anger, later at lunch hours she drove to Frank's office and went all the way up to his office on her way to Frank's office she met with her ex colleagues and greeted everyone she bumped on. Vicky knocked and got all the way in Frank's office. Frank was starring outside through the glass window his phones on his desk and he seemed far away. He turned around and there she was standing opposite him facing each other.

Vicky: "hi babe, can we go out for lunch?" she sounded low but sweet.

Frank: "I am about to have a conference call, I can not." Sounded brief and clear.

Vicky: "well can we get like a late lunch or dinner, I just want to clear the air about yesterday, please forgive me" sounded so apologetic and down.

Frank: "Victoria, I am sorry. I have work to do and things to figure out that is not what I should be doing now nor figuring out, so if you could excuse me, I would highly appreciate" he got back at his desk and got to his Macintosh.

Victoria couldn't stay any longer since Frank did not want him around and so she walked out and left the room. She asked Wanitha if Freddy was around and it turned out Freddy was out of office at that moment. And so she went back at her store tried to pass time and went to fetch the kids got back home prepared dinner and attended kids' assignments and every time she checked on her phone hopping to see a missed call or a text message from Frank but there was none. She began feeling depressed with the situation, she called Frank like ten times and left above ten voicemails apologizing and asking Frank to call her back but none worked. Kayla got to bed and so did the twins she called Pam spoke to her on the phone and Pam advised Vicky to let Frank be until his anger dropped down. Vicky saw no sign of Frank's anger diminishing other than escalating. But the day had passed she didn't hear Frank and on the next day Frank didn't show up for the kids and so Vicky took the kids to school. Pam had the busiest week that month she and other partners in the firm were opening another country office in southern hemisphere and so they had some launching of the firm preparations to do before they flew to that new country office. And so she was less help full for Vicky's situation and Vicky had no reason to blame Pam. She understood how stressful her friend was at that time of the month and tried to cover her gap.

Two days down the line Frank hadn't said a word nor replied or answered Vicky's calls and texts. Vicky tried so very much not to disturb and let him ease but the situation was sickening. She sat at his store and called Freddy she asked him out for lunch and Freddy had no chance for lunch at that time but he asked if they could do dinner or pass by at Vicky's place to see her since they did not get a chance to meet for quite sometime. Vicky got relieved to seeing Freddy responsive to her request and they agreed to meet later that day at her place.

So later that day she attended the kids just like any other day and after they got to bed. She sat on the couch at the living room and got her mug of hot milk and her TV on. Freddy came they had a nice catch-up and afterwards she had to share the situation with Freddy. Freddy was surprised to find out what was going on for he did not notice a thing from the two as of that week, he had been busy with work to have missed watching over his brother's moves as how he used to. So he asked Vicky not to worry and assured her as to things will get back to normal. They had their moment together Freddy asked how she was doing with the growing belly and after sometime Pam got back refreshed and came to see her friend. Freddy and Vicky had their laughter and happy moments and it lit up the room as Pam walked and joined them. They spoke of Frank and Vicky's situation once more time and both encouraged Vicky that things would resolve soon. After a certain while Freddy and Pam left Vicky's place, Freddy escorted Pam back to her condo and they had their game on. Freddy overstayed at Pam's. Vicky went to sleep as soon as the couple left. She didn't have the best sleep nor did she have one since the beginning of the saga. The next day her routine resumed and there was no call, no text, no sign of Frank showing up. She took it more serious yet decided not to say more word to anyone. Mrs Zoya called Vicky for their usual catch-up call and she could notice Vicky not being at her usual best, she asked Vicky if all was well and Vicky agreed but Mrs Zoya noticed the difference in her tone. She then called Frank and couldn't reach him and called Freddy and heard what happened. Mrs Zoya asked Freddy to speak to Frank and resolve the situation for it was not healthy for both Vicky and the baby.

Freddy agreed to what his mother asked and promised to revert once he talked to Freddy. That evening Frank stayed late as the rest were leaving office, Freddy went to his office poured a glass of brand and had the conversation on. He asked Frank what he was going to do regarding Vicky and Frank was less cooperative on the discussion, he seemed to have no plan and no decision except to prolong the silence between the two. Freddy conveyed the message he had from their mother and asked Frank to break the silence.

Frank: "she went behind my back. No one does that Freddy! Even you don't do that except your delusional surveillance treats on my women which I'm always aware of and so they don't count. I told her not to go but she went! It's like she can do anything she wants regardless of my opinion." He continued "I don't know what I'm going to do with her, I just need more time to figure out but as of now I don't want to see her, I will speak to mother soon. Let's talk some other things please." He sounded pissed and didn't let go off anything yet.

Freddy listened tentatively and urged his brother to forgive Vicky for that was their first fight on her and she promised not to repeat and after his wise advice they went talking on other things and left the office.

A week and another had passed, Vicky had not heard from Frank and neither did Frank, Mrs Zoya and Freddy had difficult time filling the gap. Pam was in the southern opening up their new office and so was far away from consoling her friend. Vicky had her usual workout schedules, her diet plan that made her grew strong besides the kids were under her watch which also made her busy to fill the emptiness but at some point of time in the day and night she was lonely, cold and depressed. She missed her man so very much, she missed their cuddles and their game, she had not put eyes on Frank and began to wonder probably he may had grown hair two and half weeks were too much for an in-love yet pregnant lady. She conquered it had her usual phone schedules with Mrs Zoya and since Mrs Zoya heard the news of what was happening there was nothing to hide than discussing it over the phone. Mrs Zoya urged Vicky to keep being strong and hope things would get back to normal. Frank had his bad days and good days both at work and outside work. Freddy knew why and began to keep an eye on his brother knowing every little detail of him where he went and who he met yet tried to cover Frank's gap on Vicky. Freddy passed by at Vicky almost everyday before he went home, some Sundays he got Vicky and the kids out for lunch and to the park. Mrs Zoya was not impressed of Frank's rigid heart of not resolving their situation hence she planned to visit them.

Two days before Mrs Zoya's arrival in the evening Vicky left the kids with Pam whom was back from her trip and she drove to Sinclair's mansion. Frank was not home yet but Freddy was. They sat on the balcony her favorite spot watching the stars in the sky while she had her usual mocktail and Freddy had his drink on. They sat talked and after almost an hour Frank drove by and saw Vicky's car parked and realized she was around. He went straight through the front door, which was on the other side of the balcony hence he couldn't see or bump into neither Vicky nor Freddy. He heard their voice but ignored them and climbed up to his room something he rarely did. After a couple of minutes Vicky realized Frank wasn't going to come down and greet them and so she excused herself from Freddy and decided to go see him in his room. Frank was in the shower, so she got comfortable on the couch and turned on the TV. After few minutes he got out from the shower and acted like he did not see Vicky.

Vicky: "hey babe" in her low sweet tone

Frank: "whats up" busy putting his pajamas on

Vicky: "how are you?"

Frank: "Good thanks"

Vicky: "can we talk? I have missed you, we have missed you" looking so down and contrite.

Frank: "I have nothing to say to you Victoria, You chose to put your feelings for your ex before mine and that's what you get in return so don't deny the outcome of your own action." He sounded very resentful.

Vicky: "I don't deny a thing and I take full responsibility for my action and the consequences out of it. All I'm asking is for you to forgive me and we move on. It's two months already and we are still on the same page why don't you want to forgive?" tears ran down her eyes as she spoke "I gave you space assuming you will find a place in your heart to let go and move on but you're not. What is this?"

Frank: "you thought silence would resolve things? That's what you thought?" he went loud on Vicky.

Vicky: "I said; I thought silence would make you calm down at least a step towards our reconciliation obviously it has not so please tell me what will make things better?" she added wiping her shading eyes "please tell me what to do to make things better again? I am done with this situation. I have been on my own without you for two solid months and it does not bother you, so please today just spill it! Say it!

What do you want! I am tired Frank" her breath was caught by a cry and she stopped talking.

Frank: "I have nothing more to say to you, you can sleep on bed. I will dive into other room" as he walked outside his room.

Vicky: "No! Please Stay, I will leave. You don't have to move elsewhere" she stood up from the couch wiped her tears, walked passed by Frank and whispered "goodnight"

Victoria walked down the stairs through the front door went to her car and drove off. As Vicky was driving off Freddy saw her from the balcony. He was on a call with his mother updating her on what was happening. He hung the phone and went up to meet Frank whom was in the office room on his computer. Freddy demanded explanation why Vicky left unhappy and Frank did not cooperate, Freddy spoke in wrath to his brother he urged him to change, he also mentioned that their mom's coming was due to his delays in resolving their matter, he also reminded him that he was about to become a father and he was not setting any good example out of it, he spoke in length non stop and lastly;

Freddy: "if you don't love Vicky anymore better let her know and stop wasting the poor lady's time and energy. And if you abandon Vicky rest assured I am going to take over and will not let you come in the way any more." He added looking at Frank's eyes "I am going to sleepover at her place tonight." He walked out and slammed the door on his way out.

Frank felt very ashamed and couldn't keep up with what he was doing on the computer anymore. He got off and went to the bar and grabbed some drink. Freddy went to his room refreshed and changed to some good Armani black matching jogger he brushed his hair and tied his ponytail smelled good and drove off on a convertible Mercedez. That moment Frank realized what was going to happen, he stayed put, kept his night going with phone calls and drinks. Vicky got home feeling miserable for what had happened and she decided to not take any more trouble, she jumped to shower where she always released her anger and cried out loud as the waters ran from her head. She got out put some pajamas and jumped to bed. As she laid on bed facing up the ceiling the door knocked and Freddy was standing at the door facing Vicky. She got up and looked at Freddy.

Vicky: "hey you, he didn't…" as she was about to finish her sentences tears ran out.

Freddy: "I know, I am sorry" he walked towards Vicky, sat on bed next to her and hugged her.

Vicky cried deeply and out loud on Freddy's shoulder trying to tell Freddy all what happened at the same time catching her breath. Her belly was protruding fast you could tell she was on her last trimester but yet not. Freddy tried to console and calmed Vicky down until she went silent. He lay her on bed and went to the kitchen grabbed a glass of water and brought for Vicky.

Freddy: "here take some" he made Vicky drink all the water from the glass and she craved for more and he got her some more and she took half the glass.

Afterwards, Freddy took off his t-shirt, jogger and was left with a boxer and sat on bed next to Vicky he held her next to him and got underneath the duvet. He whispered to Vicky "everything was going to be fine. Let's catch some sleep." That was the first time Freddy dived in a sleep with Vitoria although it was not fun at all. Vicky got uncomfortable throughout the night, she couldn't sleep, she kept turning side ways likewise Freddy couldn't sleep either since Vicky was unsettled and not asleep.

Freddy: "what's wrong" he whispered on Vicky's ear from her behind.

Vicky: "I don't know. I just can't sleep" sounded restless and tired in her little tone.

Freddy: "okay let's see if this works" he grabbed Vicky from behind and massaged her sideline from the arm down to her waist to her thighs back and forth.

Vicky felt calm and her breathing pulse was in order Freddy noticed the calmness on Vicky and so he went on massaging her gently he kissed her neck, he massaged her breasts, he massaged her belly all the way down to her growing thick lady part, he kept going massaging Vicky's round bubbly ass and Vicky was way responsive, she loved it and nodded as Freddy's hands ran all over her body. Her belly was big enough not to sleep on and so she only had sideways and the back to sleep on, so she kept getting comfortable as Freddy kept playing, massaging and caressing her body, Freddy's hands went all the way down to Vicky's vulva. Vicky was extremely hot and beyond wet. She had lots of discharge on at that moment. Freddy strummed Vicky's wet clit and tossed his middle finger in her high temperate vagina, he did that back and forth as he kept kissing Vicky's neck and rubbing her hair with his other hand. Vicky felt good and all she could do was move her thighs and legs adjusting to Freddy's move, she felt Freddy's boner enlarging from her behind and Freddy couldn't stop, he turned Vicky on the other side and had her side ways, he got on top of

Vicky kissed her on the lips, cheeks, neck, boobs and nipples as he massaged her entire body. She was hot and Freddy loved the temperature, he massaged Vicky's belly kissed it all over folded and raised Vicky's heavy legs up, he bent to adjust and tossed his head on Vicky's vulva the lady was hot and highly discharging. Freddy loved every moment of it and he kept doing with pleasure. Vicky's hands were on Freddy's hairs and shoulders, she massaged Freddy's scalp as Freddy got busy with her, the scene prolonged to an extent Vicky started releasing her usual cry that it was about time so Freddy dropped his boxer and there he had not less not more than Frank's, they were real twin in everything. It was strong lengthy erect colored prong just like Frank's. He dived it right in her and penetrated all the way. A deep voice of "Wow!" was heard as he got back and forth inside Vicky. He got the copulation going for as long as Vicky cried out of pleasure, she then held Freddy's hands tight and splashed out on him. Freddy looked right into Vicky's eyes kissed her passionately and whispered to her ear "You will be fine, I promise" He intercourse Vicky gently back and forth for she already looked incapacitated until it was about time for him and he whispered and asked her where she wanted it and shamelessly Vicky begged for it inside her and as she just finished saying Freddy discharged a tremendous amount inside Vicky's pink wet punani as he looked right on her sexy alluring eyes. He lay beside Vicky kissed her one more time and made her look through her eyes and kissed her on the lips and whispered "I love You" at Vicky. Freddy covered themselves with the duvet and slept like babies.

The next morning kids were taken by Pam to school when Pam saw a Mercedez parked on Vicky's parking she thought finally Frank & Vicky had settled. She didn't want to disturb them and so she took the kids and drove off. Vicky and Freddy woke up an hour late. Vicky slowly got up went to the kitchen and the nana had arrived and was on her duties. She made breakfast for Freddy she felt energetic that morning. She ran a cup of Espresso for Freddy and took it in the room. Freddy was still on bed as Vicky took the coffee next to his nose and once he had the smell he got up.

Vicky: "hey you." As she kissed Freddy "you're late"

Freddy: "hey babe" he woke up and grabbed the cup of coffee and kissed Vicky on the lips "all for good reasons" he replied and sipped the coffee.

Vicky went to the bathroom she cleaned up while talking to Freddy who had his coffee going and his phone on. She came out smelling good and she tried a couple of two out fits and Freddy chose one for her. After having his coffee, he jumped to shower they kept talking to one another about last night and how they all felt without mentioning Frank in their conversation. They both looked fresh and ready for their day except for Freddy who had to go back home change to office attire and head to work. But before they left they had a wonderful breakfast at the kitchen counter.

Freddy: "I am going home change to some meaningful fit and bounce to work." As he massaged Vicky's back and ass he kept going "Mom is on her way here so probably late night I will go pick her from the airport"

Vicky: "ok she shouldn't have troubled herself this much" as she kept the romance going.

Freddy: "I'm going to see you and you guys later today" he kissed her on the lips and kissed Vicky's belly

Vicky: "Fred" she called looking at him with her very own romantic natural eyes "thank you" in her sweet little tone.

Freddy: "I don't want to know what for but you should know that I love you" he walked back to Vicky and kissed her on the lips passionately and caressed her back. "I will call later stay put" he walked out and drove off.

Vicky grabbed her belongings and shouted at nana that she was off.

On her way to her store she spoke to Pam and told her what had happened. Pam was shocked to find out that things were not ok with her friend yet was delighted that Freddy was there for Vicky. She also supported Vicky not to bother Frank anymore and let him be. But deep inside she made her mind that she will confront Frank and demand a discussion from him. They talked for as long as she was on the road and when she reached at her store they hung up and went on with their errands. Freddy got home changed to his smart office suits and headed to work. That day Frank got to office earlier than usual and kept wondering what went on with Freddy and Vicky last night. At some point he didn't want to believe that they had a game and some point he knew what Freddy meant by a "sleepover" he had the worse night in the history and yet in the office when he found Freddy not in. After almost two hours, half past ten in the morning Freddy got in looking smart and happy. He went straight to Frank's office and asked if he would go pick Mrs Zoya or he should instead and Frank was relieved to seeing his brother yet curious to know what had happened but he didn't have the guts to ask and so he dodged by letting Freddy pick their mother from the airport.

Freddy left Frank's office looking fresh and settled. He got to his office made a call to Pam and told him what had happened and to his surprise Pam was very grateful for the support Freddy had shown to her friend. At first he thought it would make Pam jealous but he realized how friendly the two ladies were and nothing could crash their bond. He had his day going smoothly and very productive made a call to Vicky to find out how he was doing and proceeded with his day. On the other hand Vicky had one most relaxing day for the past three months she worked her ass off, got to the gym later that day passed by the grocery store and went home. She went at Pam's to see Kayla and the twins and made dinner and ate with them at her place. Pam got back late that day and after she freshened up she went over to Vicky the kids were on bed at Pam's house and Vicky and Pam had their night on the couch, she had her red wine while Vicky had hot milk on a mug. They sat talked for long. This time Vicky was not sorry anymore nor unhappy she grew accepting what had happened and started preparing herself for an expansion of single parenting family. Pam felt deeply sorry yet strong for her friend. Freddy called Vicky to find out how she was doing and told her that she will pass by later as he goes to pick Mrs Zoya from the airport. Pam stayed late and once her bottle was off she had to go sleep. Since Freddy was coming she did not want to indulge in to Vicky's treat given her current situation. Vicky closed the doors and jumped to bed. She tried to sleep and all she could remember was last night, how Freddy was all over her body, how stimulated she became, once she reflected on last night's scene, and as before she kept turning side ways trying to catch a sleep which she couldn't. At last after an hour or two of consistence discomfort she fell asleep. And when she turned the other side her baby pillow was no more and Freddy was beside her. She smiled kissed him on the lips and fell asleep. Freddy grabbed Vicky tight and massaged her gently to go back to sleep. They slept for three more hours before she started turning lefts and rights. Vicky woke up slowly she didn't want to wake Freddy and walked to the kitchen grabbed a glass of water and sat on the kitchen counter she sipped her glass and fell in deep thoughts, she then had some more water. Freddy came out to get Vicky back on bed.

Vicky: "I didn't want to wake you up" she hugged Freddy.

Freddy: "are you alright?" he kept hugging Vicky "wake me up anytime baby girl" he kissed Vicky's head and kept hugging her tight. "Shall we go back?" rubbing Vicky's belly.

Vicky: "yes please"

They went back to bed. Vicky was on an extra large cotton top dress below her ass and fur slippers, Freddy had boxer on. They got to bed and Frank began working on massaging Vicky, kissing her, holding her ass and thighs rubbing her belly as he kissed her navel she kept playing with Freddy's hair massaging his scalp and his muscular shoulders and arms as she received the treat. Freddy had let the lights on for he wanted to see every part of Vicky's alluring body. He got on top facing Vicky and he began kissing her lips, cheeks, neck, he got to the boobs and played with the nipples, he slide down and folded Vicky's legs rubbing her belly, kissing her navel, he got to Vicky's thick thighs and ass again. His hands played a round of massage and caressed her. Vicky's skin was flawless and glowing, she had gained weight proportionally and yet looked amazingly sexy her thighs were thick and firm her ass was round in shape, firm yet bubbly no cellulite, no stretchmark, she looked beautiful. Freddy kept exploring Vicky as he got down to her beaver; she had the thicket front bottom, pinkest punani that never ran dry. He got his sight on every little detail on Vicky's luscious body. Her legs were raised higher and he took a closer look at her raunchy gamy clit, he took his hands explored her as he strummed her clit and tossed his finger in. Vicky felt very pleased yet extremely shy, Freddy went on playing on Vicky's lubricious lady part, he kissed her all the way, licked and sucked her cunt and eventually dived right in her. Vicky was beyond stimulated she couldn't say a word not even a sound came out of her, goose bumps grew all over her body and Freddy noticed. He penetrated inside Vicky gently and consistently looking straight to her eyes while she converted from pale blue to pale pink to pale red, her ears, nose, cheeks turned color as much as she received the pleasure, his erotic knob intercourse Vicky left, right and center until she couldn't take it anymore and there she was, just like how she does it a splash of water ran out of her in pulses and Freddy didn't hold any longer kept fornicating her left right and center once more and he discharged unlike Frank who squints before climaxing Freddy bite his lower lip and exhales loud with words like Woow! Yeah! and so forth. He held Vicky warmly round his arms and both fell asleep. A little longer, Freddy woke up went to grab a glass of water came back stood at the door and starred at the sleeping beauty. He looked at Vicky's curved body under the duvet, part of her body from head to her boobs and her back were exposed, Vicky slept deeply Freddy starred at her one more time and switched off the lights and slept.

It was Saturday; there was no school, no office for the day. The neighborhood was silent no engine cars on, no early movements, each stayed in and slept till late. Freddy had the best sleep and so did Vicky, Nana got in as usual and started her household activities ensuring she did not wake the slept ones. At almost quarter to eleven Vicky got up, she cleaned up, put her gym gears, kissed Freddy on his forehead and drove to the gym. She had her bottle of water. She got to the gym went to yoga classes for twenty minutes, got to aerobic classes for twenty minutes and got on the treadmill for fifteen minutes and drove back home. She found Freddy awake in the shower. Freddy had a dazzling eyes and a fresh face, he kissed his lady went to the living room the kids were on TV had a chat with them and promised to take them out the next day that was Sunday.

At the Sinclair's mansion, Mrs Zoya was in the house, she got up early, did her yoga as she talked with Frank in their gym. She asked him to be available for the dinner she was going to organize that day. Frank never denies his mother's words and so he agreed to be available. Although he was reluctant to discuss about his situation with Vicky, Mrs Zoya tried very hard and wisely to make Frank talk but all she could get from her son was a promise that things will be better some day. Something Mrs Zoya was less patient about. Good enough she got Frank to accept the dinner invite and that was one move to getting what she wanted. Freddy got back home and found his mother and brother Frank outside at the poolside.

Freddy: "hello mother" kissed his mom and smiled at Frank.

Mrs Zoya: "hello son, I didn't know you were out"

Frank: "oooh! He looked more than being out mother, just look at how happy and fresh he's smelling, something tells me he didn't sleep in at all" he sounded annoyed.

Mrs Zoya: "what is wrong with that?" she added, "I like when you all look happy" she looked at one after the other.

Freddy: "unless my brother here doesn't want me to be happy mother" he joked as he removed his clothes and jumped to the pool.

Mrs Zoya: "why doesn't he?" she continued "I was talking to your brother earlier that I'm organizing a dinner for everyone Vicky, Pam and the kids are invited. I also want to see Vicky for she and Frank are the primary cause of me being here." She spoke louder for Freddy to hear for he was in the pool.

Freddy said,:- "That's good move, Mom,:- let's hope it works. I will help you inform the ladies, that's fantastic" he smiled back at Frank and kept swimming.

Frank had his black Ray-Ban Aviators on hence difficult for Freddy to see through Frank's eyes but Frank was looking at Freddy with anger wondering what he had been up to lately with his fiancé. They had a wonderful afternoon outside the pool, Mrs Zoya and her sons had to reflect on so many good memories they had and the experiences they had, she really was wise enough to bring back the bond and the touch her sons used to have for their family, they went all the way back from the previous holiday to far back to when their father used to take charge of the family affairs and no ties or bonds were broken. Mrs Zoya reminded them how close their dad and her were and that was how she wanted them to be, she talked in a nice sweet jokeful way they teased one another until all came to rest at one conclusion that it was high time to stand for one another and keep building their empire. After a long stay and talk outside Frank excused himself he told his mother that he had a hair cut to do and so will be back for the dinner, Freddy had stopped swimming for the sun was on point and so he grabbed his phone made a call to the ladies and Mrs Zoya personally spoke to Vicky and welcomed them for dinner that day. The ladies couldn't deny and promised to be there. After that Mrs Zoya had to discuss with MaryJo and organized everything for the dinner. On the other side the ladies went to salon did their hair and nails and got themselves a spa treat as they kept talking about what was actually trending and that was Freddy and Vicky night affair. Frank was less spoken except after they had an invite call for the dinner and so they knew it would all be discussed over the dinner. Pam advised Vicky not to be defensive on anything rather than to be apologetic. Vicky planned not to talk about it unless Mrs Zoya brings it up. They had their day going their way and later they passed by the bakery store, Vicky went trough the sales and managerial tasks and afterwards they headed home. The nana was ready to leave for the day the kids were playing. So they laid low kept their stories going as they looked for something to wear for the dinner. Pam wanted Vicky to come out sexy hot pregnant lady Frank had never laid eyes on, so they decided going through her closet dress after the other looking for something that will shape Vicky's curves and cute belly yet set her free. They picked from black white to pink dresses, few pairs of leggings and sexy tops laid them on bed and Vicky had to try on one after the other. The black dress looked like she was sending a message that was not good, the white dresses looked like she was craving for a wedding, for the leggings and the tops looked like she was going for a date or movie night or ladies night out which did not incorporate Mrs Zoya's dinner invite. They aimed on catching Frank's eye yet looking impressive on Mrs Zoya and so they picked a white Calvin Klein sleeveless above the knee stretching dress that had big round collar falling back and front. Vicky looked magnificent in the dress. Pam tried a few as well from the closet and picked one that was a purple above the knee flare dress with three quarter sleeves she looked beautiful. When it was about time, they got the kids ready for dinner they were excited to go to Sinclair's, Kayla had been told that Frank was out of the country for business and so she kept asking her mother if Frank was back from his trip and Vicky assured her that she would find him. They all got ready the kids were in their smart casual looks and their moms were stunning. They hooped in Vicky's BM, Pam was driving, Vicky on passenger seat and the kids took behind seats and off they went.

Meanwhile at Sinclair's mansion Mrs Zoya and MaryJo had everything on set, dinner was set at the dining room and everything looked perfect. Freddy and Frank were at home waiting for the ladies and the kids. When Pam pulled over the driveway a man opened Vicky's door and the door behind Vicky's side for the kids to drop, it was one of their maids. Vicky and the kids dropped out of the car and Pam went to park the car at the parking shade.

Freddy went to receive them, Vicky was on Calvin Klein white sleeveless back and front round collar above the knees stretching dress and Jimmy Choo metallic mime perforated mirrored leather pumps, her hair was tied up neatly she looked smashing. The kids ran to uncle Freddy hugged and got in excitedly. Vicky stood at the entrance waiting for Pam.

Freddy: "hey baby girl, you are not lost, you on the right door" Freddy teased as he looked at how incredibly beautiful Vicky was.

Vicky: "stop" she begged in her sweet little voice smiling at Freddy "I am waiting for Pam." She explained.

Pam came out of the car and was walking towards the entrance where Vicky was standing.

Pam: "hey thank you for waiting, hey boo she walked over at Freddy kissed and hugged him passionately and Freddy went for Vicky he hugged and kissed her on both cheeks and walked them in. Mrs Zoya had her final touches on the table and came for the ladies.

Freddy: "Mother your guests have arrived" he shouted to his mother who was at the other end of the hall at the dining.

Mrs Zoya: "my beautiful Victoria" she smiled walked with open arms to hug Victoria "how are you my darling? I'm so happy to see you" she hugged kissed and massaged Vicky's belly.

Vicky: "hello mother, I am happy to see you too." Reciprocated the gesture.

Mrs Zoya: "my dear Pam, nice to see you" she did the same with Pam hugs and kisses except no belly touch

Pam: "hellow mama, I am happy to see you too" reciprocated the gesture as well.

They sat in the living room kids were in the TV room just the next room. There were footsteps and Frank was walking down the stairs and went to see the kids.

Kayla: "Dad!" she shouted and ran towards Frank "when did you get back? I missed you"

Frank: "I missed you too bunny, how's school?"

Kayla: "school is fine we haven't done our movie nights since forever" looking disappointed.

Frank: "we will, how are your friends? Hey buddies" he stood up and went close to where Jayda and Jayden where, they greeted uncle Frank and kept watching TV. Kayla was too excited and all she wanted was to stay close to Frank, they walked together to the living room, Freddy was entertaining the ladies.

Frank: "hey Pam" in his deep voice he raised his hand and kissed Pam's fore hand.

Pam: "hey you" she ran out of words.

Frank: "Victoria" in his voice

Victoria: "hey" in her little sweet voice but there was no kissing no hugging a bit of silence and Kayla broke the silence.

Kayla: "so dad, tomorrow what are we going to do? Uncle Freddy promised to take us out can we have our movie night on the usual date?" sat on Frank's lap as she talked to him.

Frank: "yeah absolutely, you go out with uncle Freddy and we have our movies same days same time. Perfect." As he got cozy with Kayla

Mrs Zoya welcomed everyone at the table, Frank was peeking on Vicky every single time, Vicky was shying away, and she did not even want to look at Frank. Freddy was busy observing their moves Pam had no idea what was going on and was at her natural best enjoying the evening. They sat on the table. Mrs Zoya and Frank sat opposite each other at the far ends. On Mrs Zoya's left Vicky sat next and on Mrs Zoya's right Freddy sat next, Pam sat next to Freddy and Jayden sat next to Pam, on Frank's left Kayla sat next and on his right Jayda sat next, there was an empty seat between Vicky and Jayda a very random sitting situation went on. They had their dinner over generic stories Mrs Zoya was very entertaining. Frank was a bit silent he peeked at Vicky every single time. Vicky's belly grew bigger together with some of her body parts but she looked one hot mama and Frank couldn't stop starring at her. After the dinner the kids went to watch TV as the adults got on serious talks. Vicky was the slowest eater of them all she had her meal slowly after they were done with eating and throwing different stories Mrs zoya brought up the topic by explaining why she came back and all she wanted was things to get back to how they used to be. Once she was done with her speech she turned to Vicky and asked her if she was fine with reconciling with Frank and Vicky did not hesitate. She cleared her throat and apologized to Mrs Zoya for the trouble she went through and answered her as to she was ready since last year to resolve the situation, she also turned to Freddy and apologized for everything she had put him through, she did the same to Pam and after that Vicky stood up walked towards Frank and knelt down next to Frank and apologized to him for everything and all the things she put him through and the misunderstandings. Freddy was not pleased seeing Vicky on her knees, he wanted to walk towards Vicky and make her stand but Pam stopped him from interfering Vicky's moment and so he sat down and let Vicky proceed with her apologetic scene. Vicky was too brief yet less blameful she took all the responsibility for the crack down situation as she was on her knees facing Frank, her hands were on Frank's lap tears ran down her cheeks. After a couple of minutes on her knees Frank stood and raised Vicky up and he looked straight in Vicky's eyes and agreed to her apology. He then grabbed her on the back held her tight and explained that he was not impressed of her going behind his back doing what he stopped her from doing in the first place, he was also sorry for not being there for Vicky. Vicky's eyes never stopped shading tears as Frank kept talking, she sat down for her legs were trembling and her breathing increased Freddy went for a glass of water and gave it to Vicky, she sipped some water and started feeling relieved. Freddy was very annoyed seeing his brother letting Vicky go an extra mile. Mrs Zoya was happy to hear that Frank was pleased with Vicky's apology and that they were going to work things out. Pam looked at Frank attentively as he spoke and couldn't figure him out. At the end of the day Frank opened arms for Vicky and Vicky claimed her man Victoriously. They got off the table and went to the balcony Vicky wanted some fresh air she never thought she would burst into emotions like how she did. Freddy followed her they sat at the balcony Freddy handed tissues to Vicky to wipe her eyes and offered her a glass of water. Pam and Frank were left behind and for once she had to blast Frank comfortably.

Pam: "I didn't want to back my friend nor interfere her apology but you have disappointed me so very much. I don't know how you are going to fill the gap that you have created,

I have tried to understand you but one thing that does not add up is that you have punished her for three consecutive months and yet you claim to be the one offended. Frank, you're a damn lucky man" she looked serious and annoyed but at a very low tone that no one else heard her talking except for Frank.

Frank: "Pam, I understand how you feel. I am sure I will find a way to make it up to your friend and to everyone else. I just want you to trust in me once more" he held Pam's hand as he spoke to her.

Pam: "I wish I could Frank." She by passed and tapped him on the shoulder.

Mrs Zoya went and sat next to Vicky and Freddy at the balcony, she was happy and relieved that things were resolved, she kept asking how Vicky was feeling at that moment and gave her some advice on how to keep up with her healthy pregnancy. Frank and Pam joined the rest at the balcony, everyone seemed grateful, Frank stood behind Vicky massaging and caressing Vicky's shoulders and neck. Freddy got hold of Pam tight, Mrs Zoya was pleased to see everyone back to love mode. They discussed on Vicky's arrangement to US for delivery and the kids going to a boarding school. At last Frank got back to being the master planner, he told his mother to go ahead with the Doctor's appointment when she went back to US and Freddy to prepare fly with Vicky to US since Frank was to join Vicky on the last due month and so Freddy was going to be with Vicky for the next two months before Frank takes over. Pam was pleased to see things got back to how they were and both brothers taking responsibilities for the arrival of their bundle of joy. She promised to assist Vicky on managing her store in her absence.

Frank: "Freddy, you're to escort and accompany Vicky for some two or even lesser months on my behalf and not marry her, please, I insist" he squinted his eyes to Freddy as he kept caressing Vicky's shoulders. And all laughed out loud.

It was time for Mrs Zoya to go sleep, Vicky walked with Mrs Zoya to her room, and she helped her take her night pills and went to bed. Frank and the kids got deep in a serious discussion about transferring to boarding and the kids seemed excited for the plan except for Kayla who was anxious to stay close with her mother until the arrival of the newly ones. Frank had to explain to her that her mother was going to deliver in USA and therefore they both will join her on few days before the arrival of the babies and so she understood. After a long conversation of questions and answers from the kids they all got on the same ground and got back to their video games. Freddy and Pam got romantically closer at the balcony kissing and whispering to one another. Frank climbed to his mother's room and Vicky had sat on bed next to Mrs Zoya listening to her attentively. Frank walked in slowly as the door was open and stood by the door and looked at both of his beautiful women having a one-on-one he smiled at them and kept listening and looking at them without the women noticing that Frank was at the door. After a while he cleared his throat to let them know he was around. He walked next to Vicky and kept massaging her shoulders and neck he then kissed his mother goodnight and grabbed his woman, they switched off the lights and slowly shut the door and walked to their room. It was obvious Frank had missed Victoria. Two months down the lane there had been no sex no flirting no touching, he really seemed he could not wait to unwrap Vicky's garments and get in her. He walked with her on the long corridor to his room as he kept grabbing her ass, her waist and kissing her on the cheek and lips. They got in the room and he held her hand and walked with her outside the terrace of his room, he stood behind her and both were facing out, the wind was blowing on their direction the sheer curtain at the big French door of their room terrace was waving due to the wind. Frank stood behind Vicky, he got really closer to her neck whispered on her ear that he was sorry a million times and he missed her so very much. Vicky was just silent trying to catch her wind breeze, Frank got hold of Vicky's body kissing her neck, unzipped her dress, pulled it down as he kept kissing her, he snatched out the hooks of her bra, Vicky's breasts had grown bigger and tender, her heart pulses are seen on her neck, he kept kissing and massaging his woman's breasts, she was hot probably hotter than the last time he intercourse her, Frank's hands and lips were busy on Vicky's body, he held her curved waist, he massaged her protruded belly which had grown out than the last time he saw her, Frank was like exploring his woman for the first time in three months and the difference was huge, he kept looking at her feeling every part of her body caressing and touching her passionately. Vicky felt really good, she felt rebooted they both had their romance at the terrace by the wind and the stars and Frank took his time feeling his woman, he got his hands to her nipples and around her tender breasts and down to her belly to her grown thick vulva, his finger lingered on her clitoris which was beyond lubricious at that moment, he insert his finger in her wet punani and all he could feel was pressure towards his finger and extreme hotness. Frank had not felt this before it was probably due to the pregnancy development, he loved it so very much, and he kept strumming Vicky's clit and vulva and diving his finger in and out of Vicky's punani. Vicky was responsive; she bent extended her ass trying to catch Frank's arms but could not since Frank's hands were busy. Frank carried her woman laid her on bed and he took another closer look at her, Vicky had grown heavier, her skin was more glowing, her curves were still put and body firm. Frank raised and held Vicky's legs up and took a closer look at Vicky's wet lady-part whereby her vulva grew thicker and pinker. Frank explored in by his tongue and lips sucked, licked and kissed Vicky deeply and passionately. Frank had a certain persona on his sex game, he used to take control of his woman's body, he knew what to do, how to do and when to do. Vicky was hopeless in love with that. She used to go low and very submissive as Frank took control and that was what happened that moment. He licked and sucked Vicky's cunt, he penetrated his finger till the end of the path and strummed her clitoris as he looked at Vicky's face. Vicky cried out of pleasure, she surely loved and missed Frank. Frank kept the move for more than twice as he slowly undressed himself until he was left with his boxer, he whispered to Vicky "I want to fuck you baby" and he got his 9inch erect shaft in Vicky's hot wet punani. Vicky cried out loud as Frank penetrated in her. Frank copulated his woman for as many rounds as Vicky could bear and once Vicky started screaming loud, Frank ordered her not to climax and turned her side ways, he crossed Vicky's legs and got in her once more, he intercourse Vicky and in less than a minute she couldn't hold it anymore and Frank let her ease, she splashed out than ever before as she cried out loud looking incapacitated, Frank kept going one two three rounds and discharged along with his woman. He bent over and kissed her on the lips, he kissed and created a hickey on her neck. They lay down on bed in silence for couple of minutes and afterwards Frank claimed his woman by his side, covered her on duvet and wrapped his hands around her and they fell asleep. Back downstairs kids were put to bed and Pam and Freddy got their romance to the next level in their room.

Few weeks later Frank and George had sorted the kids from day schooling to boarding schooling. Vicky had a thorough hand over to Pam with regards to the store. Mrs Zoya had organized the family Doctor to attend Vicky upon her arrival. Vicky and Freddy flew to US. Frank remained behind running the enterprise and preparing for a long out of office. A month before, Frank and Kayla joined the rest of the crew in US for the arrival of their babies.

Vicky had grown thicker, tender and beautiful. She had a good care from her doctors, Mrs Zoya and the rest. She grew stronger and ready for her babies. When it was about time that was around two in the morning she felt to pee and as she was walking to the restroom her water broke Frank, Freddy and Mrs Zoya took her to the hospital. She was taken straight to delivery room, Frank stood right beside his woman massaging her shoulders and neck as Vicky faced gradual contractions and crying out of pain. Freddy was recording every moment, he did not want to miss any detailed adventure, Mrs Zoya was also around comforting Vicky. The doctors had Vicky ready for pushing and so she began pushing out incredible human lives. Vicky had three to four rounds of push until one's head was seen, Frank kept encouraging Vicky gently massaging her shoulders as she kept pushing the babies out.

At exactly four o'clock in the morning the angels came out crying healthy and beautifully the girl came first and after a second the boy followed. They were all happy and excited. Vicky felt restless yet contented having her babies around her arms. Frank and Vicky were very excited seeing their beautiful offspring; Mrs Zoya was shading tears of joy as she looked at a combo of blessings in the room. It was the happiest moment for everyone. Frank kept starring at the babies and at Vicky; Freddy kept wiping sweat from Vicky's forehead as he kept his camera on. The doctors took the babies from Vicky's hands and had to nurse Vicky and finally were admitted in a private maternal room. Frank and Freddy were beyond excited, they for once did not know what to do next but Mrs Zoya had everything under control. Frank called Pam and shared the bundle of excitement and as Pam heard the news she couldn't wait to visit them in US. Frank was busy on the phone spreading the news Freddy was busy bonding with the babies, he carried one after the other starring at them taking a closer look at the tiny humans. Mrs Zoya and the doctors were settling the documents for Vicky and the babies. Frank got home changed and picked Kayla passed by the florist bought some bundle of bouquet and bunches of white, pale pink and pale blue balloons and went to the hospital. Kayla was excited to see her beautiful siblings. Freddy kept the camera going capturing every moment. Vicky had her beautiful twins, two days after they got discharged back home. In Mrs Zoya's mansion it was a festival all day everyday, they never stopped celebrating hosting guests who came to see the babies and congratulated them, they named their babies Faryl and Farryl. Pam flew a week later the whole crew was in US Mrs Zoya couldn't wish for anything more. Everyday was a celebration. Kayla was the happiest of them all. She couldn't stop starring at her beautiful sister and brother. Faryl and Farryl were beautiful twins and sometimes difficult to differentiate except for Vicky who knew them well. Vicky had her post-maternity recovery nice and slow by the help of nutritionists and midwifery whom had their regular duties on her. After two weeks Vicky began having her morning and evening body building workouts. Frank organized a fitness guard whom kept coming at their place and assisted Vicky in shaping up and retaining her alluring curves. She was surrounded with plenty of support staff and never felt overwhelmed. Mrs Zoya had time to host her guests as they came to see the babies and yet supervised support staff team. Freddy and Pam had their intimate time together as they kept the celebration spirit going. Frank and Kayla had bonding sessions as they celebrated the expansion of new team members and allowing Vicky to recover. Two weeks later, Pam had to return back and a month later Freddy and Kayla also returned back. Frank flew back and forth to attend some business. Mrs Zoya and Vicky had their time alone at some instance when Frank was away.

Two months down the lane Frank, Vicky and the babies returned back and settled at the mansion. Vicky had trimmed to her original shape and size and looked way prettier than before. Faryl and Farryl grew healthier and beautiful they resembled Frank and Freddy. Kayla had to move in with her mother at Sinclair's residence and they subleased their condo to one of Pam's friends. Vicky resumed her work at the store. Once a while they escaped to the river house and had their intimate nights without the intrusion of the kids or even Freddy & Pam. Frank and Vicky knew how to keep up with their sex game regardless the transformation.

A year later on a family vacation at Disney Land they celebrated their twins' birthday and Frank re-announced his need to marry Vicky. Both were in for a small unique wedding nothing extraordinary although Freddy and Pam insisted for something that resembled them. Six months later in Turks and Caicos Vicky walked down the isle and tied knot to Frank. Beautiful wedding and honeymoon treat for few of their closest friends, family and business partners. After a long beautiful romantic ceremony, Frank and Vicky left the party went to their suite refreshed and changed to sexy appealing garments.

"Babe walk with me" Frank pleaded as he extended his hand towards his woman.

Vicky wore a sheer black see through chiffon short nightdress and a matching bikini.

"Where to babe?" Vicky walked towards Frank.

They walked out their suite passed on the other direction away from where the party was ending. You could tell how Frank was excited he kept kissing Vicky and holding her tight as they walked. They went far from their residence farthest along the beach and as they kept walking they approached a romantic setting on the sand - candles and lots of petals, a bucket of chilled champagne bottles, glasses on tray, there were even a mat, folded sheet and pillows. It was romantically beautiful. Vicky had no idea of the sand-sexy arrangement. They stopped when they approached their spot Vicky smiled throughout looking at Frank's eyes kissing him passionately. They sat on the mat on the sand. Frank popped up a bottle of champagne, poured some on glasses and gave a glass to Vicky.

"To the beginning of our dream baby, may the dream never end" Frank said the words looking straight to Vicky's eyes, one hand holding his glass and another slowly caressing Vicky's lower lip as he toasted.

"To our dream babe" Vicky looked sexy on her sweet voice.

They drank to that. Vicky laid her glass on ground and took Frank's glass off his hand, laid it on the ground as well and slowly she pushed Frank down as she got on top of him. She sat on Frank's lap and bent over towards Frank's face and kept kissing her man like never before. At that moment Frank's hands were behind his head eventually he took his hands off, grabbed his woman's thicky round sexy ass massaged her gently as he received his multiples kisses around his neck, his bold head, his lips and all over his upper part. Vicky accelerated her move; she set off Frank's jogger went for the phallus dipped it in and out of her mouth as she sucked it all. Frank was enjoying to the fullest. You could tell from the groaning sounds he was making. Frank turned Vicky over he eased out his jogger and reciprocated the kisses in a very romantic way as he shoved off the bikini from Vicky's body. He folded Vicky's both legs, held the knees close to the chest and widened her as he inserted his ready-made phallus in Vicky's wet pink punani. She never stopped putting out her usual cry as she enjoyed every moment. They copulated left, right and center, changed as much angles as it pleased them. Eventually they climaxed. They slept on the mat on the sand, the wind was blowing gently Frank covered themselves with the folded sheet and Vicky laid on Frank's chest and Frank's arms around Vicky, both taking heavy breaths.

Freddy and Pam kept their relation going. Kayla grew to one big beautiful brave sister of the twins. Mrs Zoya aged happily and favorably flying back and forth visiting her grandchildren. Frank and Vicky grew solid in love and affected everyone around them, in their eighth anniversary, Freddy proposed to four weeks pregnant Pam, a very emotional move, since everyone had lost hope on their relationship. Jayda and Jayden were way grown up. After the delivery of another pair of Sinclair breed - Preston and Peyton, a wedding was ought to occur once the brand new pair of Sinclair managed to walk by themselves to celebrate their parents.

And one snowy night when they were all together in one huge lounge fire lighted, moonlight penetrating across sheer curtains brightened up the room, She looked around and all she could see was happy faces, love, and success. She leaned against Frank's shoulder receiving the warmest cuddles and kisses laughing and cheering as they played charade, Pam and Freddy on the opposite couch, Mrs Zoya sat between Peyton and Faryl, Kayla and Jayda on the floor while Jayden, Preston and Farryl at their corner. And all she could think of was,:- the dream was still on.

To Be Continued…

Printed in the United States
By Bookmasters